Men Like Ours

A Novel

Bindu Bansinath

BLOOMSBURY PUBLISHING
NEW YORK · LONDON · OXFORD · NEW DELHI · SYDNEY

BLOOMSBURY PUBLISHING
Bloomsbury Publishing Inc.
1359 Broadway, New York, NY 10018, USA
50 Bedford Square, London, WC1B 3DP, UK
Bloomsbury Publishing Ireland Limited,
29 Earlsfort Terrace, Dublin 2, D02 AY28, Ireland

BLOOMSBURY, BLOOMSBURY PUBLISHING and the Diana logo are
trademarks of Bloomsbury Publishing Plc

First published in the United States 2026

Copyright © Bindu Bansinath, 2026

All rights reserved. No part of this publication may be: i) reproduced or transmitted in
any form, electronic or mechanical, including photocopying, recording, or by means of
any information storage or retrieval system without prior permission in writing from the
publishers; or ii) used or reproduced in any way for the training, development, or operation
of artificial intelligence (AI) technologies, including generative AI technologies. The rights
holders expressly reserve this publication from the text and data mining exception as per
Article 4(3) of the Digital Single Market Directive (EU) 2019/790.

This is a work of fiction. Names, characters, businesses, places, events, locales, and incidents are
either the products of the author's imagination or used in a fictitious manner. Any resemblance to
actual persons, living or dead, or actual events is purely coincidental.

Bloomsbury Publishing Plc does not have any control over, or responsibility for, any
third-party websites referred to or in this book. All internet addresses given in this book were
correct at the time of going to press. The author and publisher regret any inconvenience
caused if addresses have changed or sites have ceased to exist, but can accept
no responsibility for any such changes.

ISBN: HB: 978-1-63973-522-8; EBOOK: 978-1-63973-523-5

Library of Congress Cataloging-in-Publication Data is available

2 4 6 8 10 9 7 5 3 1

Typesetting by Six Red Marbles India
Printed in the United States by Lakeside Book Company

To find out more about our authors and books visit www.bloomsbury.com
and sign up for our newsletters.

Bloomsbury books may be purchased for business or promotional use. For information
on bulk purchases please contact Macmillan Corporate and Premium Sales Department
at specialmarkets@macmillan.com.
For product safety–related questions contact productsafety@bloomsbury.com.

Men Like Ours

For my family and our penchant for drama

This city is heartless, what can I do?

—ANAND BAKSHI (SONGWRITER), "CHOLI KE PEECHE," *KHAL NAYAK*

INDEX OF CHARACTERS

THE SHARMAS
Anita, a snob
Ashok, her husband
Leila, their daughter, a tart

THE DIXITS
Karina, a housewife
Rajesh, her husband
Riya, their daughter

THE PILLAIS
Mr. Matthew Pillai, who is dead on the interstate
Louise Gordon, his white wife

THE GILLS
Devika Gill, convenience store operator
Her unnamed husband, a gas station operator
Manu, their adolescent son

THE KAUSHALS
Jyoti Kaushal, township tailor
Tejas Kaushal, her husband and the local podiatrist

THE RAOS
Hema Rao, Dunkin' Donuts franchisee

Parth Rao, her deadbeat husband
Hattie and Baloo, her dear Dobermans

THE SHETTYS
Vritika Shetty, who teaches classical dance in her basement
Her bungling lover

THE NAIKS
Aparna Naik, the Cash & Carry checkout girl
Her old father

ETC., ETC.:
Nasreen Farouk, who runs Kwality Meats
Usha Gohel, a lazy-eyed banker, and her teenage son, Arvind, also lazy-eyed
Shayma Matthews, the learning center instructor
Sonia, another podiatrist
Two officers, one average-looking, one ugly

PROLOGUE

MEN LIKE OURS are diabetic. After fifty they have hypertension forever. For years they scrapbook last wills and testaments that leave us at the mercy of their brothers. Men like ours plan their funerals in between routine dental cleanings; they demand from us modest-to-lavish last rites. Men like ours assume we will outlive them. At night they roam hot eager hands under our flannels and picture our bodies without their bodies, wrinkling into reverent widowhoods.

But it's we who don't survive our men. We die of complications during minor surgeries, from cancers of the thyroid and breast, from ulcers we leave bleeding for too long. Our funerals are unfussy. For the convenience of our guests, they are held in American churches instead of Hindu temples.

Men like ours recline into wooden pews and pretend to follow along in hymn books. When our caskets go down for burial, they encourage guests to use their imagination, to picture our bodies burning in their proper places.

Throughout our passing, men like ours are shocked but do not suffer. In our absence they learn to cook small things. Neighbors come by with trays of corn casserole, and in their company, men like ours do what they never do alone, and kneel before our portraits in the prayer cabinets, blown-up images from our wedding photos, with our men (mustachioed, unsmiling) cropped out. The flowers in the garlands hung around our frames are brittle and wilted. Men like ours don't replace them.

Men like ours go on, returning to the corner shops where we once worked beside them, brewing dollar-coffee deals and stacking snack cakes resembling tiny pink bombs. Men like ours are poor at sales math, at taking inventory of what is theirs. From where we hover above, we like to watch them blunder. We wonder how they ever made it out here, those years before our marriages, when they lived in these suburbs as bachelors.

We were smart girls of shit means. We arrived at the homes of men like ours in the late eighties and nineties. Men like ours were last resorts, garden-variety men; if our small dowries hadn't undermined us, they would have stayed bachelors forever. We came to them from faraway cities and forgot the shapes and bustle of our hometowns. The specifics of our histories didn't matter here. The degrees that we earned elsewhere fell to the wayside. We had labored over calculus, and in America, wasted our mouths on the cocks of men like ours. We needed to know only how to set their tea, how to boil ourselves down into plain white rice. As proof of our marriages, men like ours gave us necklaces of onyx and gold, ugly accessories that clashed with our sarees, so we shoved them into the recesses of our drawers, anywhere that was away.

We had children with men like ours, all of whom are scattered and grown. They return home to collect our necklaces and press the beads against their own necks: heirlooms or memento mori? We wish we could tell them to pawn the gold. Our children replace the wilted flowers in front of our portraits and scold our men for letting the petals die, and for other things, like pinching our earlobes when we left the stovetop running, for dishing out our salaries to us in envelopes, like we too were their children living on allowances. Then the silent punishments, the cinematic beatdowns.

All that scolding drives men like ours into mercy, into missing. At night they mourn us and finish into cupped hands. They clean themselves and think back to our deaths, how they were instantaneous, the sparklers at the end of a firework. Men like ours fall into fitful sleep. They dream of us dying in different configurations, meaning sometimes we die as unremarkably as we really did. But sometimes we die by imaginary means: erroneous turns men like ours make on the turnpike while we doze off in the passenger seats; by the steady force of their bodies dipping inside ours, our flannels uplifted, the air cloying with camphor and sweat. Men like ours have unremarkable imaginations.

As they dream of us, we too dream of men like ours, we too miss men like ours, who throw away the dried garlands around our shrines, who cook small meals that taste of nothing, who stop receiving visits from mourning children, trays of food from their commiserating neighbors. We dream of helping them calculate sales and inventory, as we did in life. We are dreaming of birthmark-shaped bruises, of the nonsense soreness between our legs, of the elaborate funerals that we planned for them but will never attend, of the pyre as it grows hotter, of the tea we used to set down from them in the afternoons, scalding, three tablespoons of sugar mixed in, because hypertension would go on forever, but without us, who would help their diabetes along?

THAT SUNDAY IN QUESTION

The Women of Willow Road

NONE OF THE WOMEN down Willow Road remembered if they'd seen Mr. Matthew Pillai that Sunday in question. Only how hot it had been—hard-pressed by the two township officers who came knocking on their doors, that was the lone detail they offered. Certain women lamented over how they'd had to open all the windows in their identical vermilion-shuttered colonial homes, a blanket invitation to common pests and neighborhood filth. Others complained their ears still rang from how hard their children wailed for AC, a plea the women denied them in the interest of saving on utility bills.

"I told my son, Manu, have I not just opened all these windows for you, boy?" said Devika Gill, forty-six, as she counted out the pink Hostess cakes at Mr. Gill's gas station convenience store. "But no one appreciates. And they won't, until I'm dead."

The women hummed in assent. They'd all nursed kindred thoughts Sunday morning, peering out their open doorways at front lawns flush with dandelions and crabgrass. Meanwhile their husbands set out folding chairs near the back porch windows. There they sat, happily alone, foreheads pressed against the gridded wire of insect mesh, feeling for a breeze.

The women were unmoved by the discomfort of their husbands. Tempered by minor and major discomforts, they took pride in enduring what their husbands could not. They knew what their husbands did not: about heat and how to keep things alive. Do not leave small children locked inside hot sedans for longer than an hour, this was one kind of knowledge. When preparing tea for houseguests ("aka freeloaders," Devika Gill said) don't use milk that's been sitting on the countertop for more than two hours maximum. Here was another kind.

These were self-evident rules, and the women followed them piously. Behind the swing of their big hips lay paper trails of obeisance. But even the most self-evident rules grew inconvenient, and in these cases the women knew how to make exemptions for themselves. Like using the bad milk anyway ("Why should I give one fuck about your bad gut?" said Jyoti Kaushal, forty-two, local tailor and *Dateline* enthusiast). Like cracking a car window open for a too-hot child, for an extra hour of child-free shopping at Marshall's.

Like a child overheating, the body of Mr. Matthew Pillai had been discovered at eight o'clock that broiling Sunday evening, slumped over the steering wheel of his black BMW. The car had idled off a backroad in north Jersey. Or so said those two officers called to the scene, one average-looking and one ugly, who documented the finer details with an iPhone camera, as one might document the position of plants for a still life.

∼

IT UNNERVED THE WOMEN to recount the mundanity of their Sundays before such an official audience. (More unnerving was having no audience: *No one bloody banged on my door*, an anonymous woman complained to Jyoti, via WhatsApp). How embarrassing to cop to your own inconsequence. Dying was such a momentous thing to do, and while Matthew, their dear friend, their cousin-brother, had been off doing it, the women had occupied themselves with such frivolities as cleaning and heat.

"If only I had known what dark was to come," said Jyoti, who had spent the day engaged in an on-and-off squabble with her husband, Tejas, the township podiatrist and an International Krishna Consciousness enthusiast. Tejas had asked Jyoti to accompany him to a local bhajan. Alone he couldn't hold a note, but the sound of his voice in the harmony of a group moved him to tears. Jyoti declined the invitation. She had five blouses to alter and two murder-suicide series to binge on television. *You're wasting daylight on depravity*, Tejas accused. *I am depraved, so is anyone who wants to hear you sing*, Jyoti replied. The argument grew feverish; Tejas picked up his folding chair and flung it, legs first, across the driveway, onto Hema Rao's lawn.

Hema Rao, fifty, owned the Dunkin' Donuts franchise on Route 1. She'd taken Sunday off to fight a minor viral lung infection and was lounging outside with her twin Dobermans, Hattie and Baloo, when the chair struck. Hema scratched their heads as they stretched, sphinxlike, on either side of her lawn chair, black-and-tan rumps glittering in the sunlight.

Baloo startled at the chair but continued licking his balls, unperturbed by the foreign object. Hattie, reactive to mailmen and squirrels, growled and bounded across the street toward Tejas. Tejas shrieked. The women knew he'd feared dogs since a snaggle-toothed stray gnawed his shin as a child. The podiatrist pissed his shorts, darted back inside, and latched the door behind him.

Hema Rao
Your husband called animal control. On my one bloody sick day. I have to pay a fine. Next time I pray he pisses AND shits himself ✓✓

Jyoti Kaushal
Keep your prayers and leash that bitch you raise ✓✓

Hema Rao
Typical Bengali Tejas is. ✓✓

Jyoti Kaushal
he is tamilian ✓✓

Hema Rao
Oh-ho. Worse! ✓✓

Jyoti Kaushal
Woman, ur Tamil too. ✓✓

(Disapproval was nothing out of the norm. The women disapproved of everyone: whites and browns, one another, themselves. *Gujarati women put so much coconut oil in their hair, they could fry eggs. Malayali sounds like the line of an EKG, firing up and down. Bengali women are such horrible drivers*, they complained, when the Bengali women among them were not listening. *Marathi women have such loud voices. A whisper is a scream. A scream, an earthquake.* A little hate reserved for everyone.)

The rest of Sunday passed quietly. The women watched afternoon serials on Zee TV. Hema brought Hattie and Baloo back outside to enjoy the sunset and this time tied their leashes to the neon dumbbell she used to tone her triceps. Vritika

Shetty, fifty-two, who ran classical dance classes out of the comfort of her unfinished basement, took a postcoital walk with her bungling lover. Manu, Devika Gill's shrimp of a thirteen-year-old son, sat on the stoop with his cohort of schoolboys. Dressed in pink-and-orange turbans, the boys shared a bag of peach rings and sprinkled sugar over the editorials of an adult magazine. Manu had nicked both from his parents' convenience store. For brownie points, he told the boys the rings were edibles. Now Manu chewed a ring and wiped the sweat from his forehead uncertainly. He didn't know if he was ready for the nudity the magazine offered. Full frontal was for the older boys, block-headed and broad-shouldered, who sometimes smoked hashish over photo spreads of women spreading themselves wide apart.

"I don't feel anything yet," complained Arvind Gohel, fourteen, with an unfortunate lazy eye. "How many milligrams?"

Manu pried a gummy from his braces. "I told you, ten. I feel it in my feet already, it just hasn't hit you yet."

Arvind nodded. "Yeah. I think it's in my tailbone now."

Across the stoop, Leila Sharma, freshly sixteen and already a tart, bent over to pet Hema's Dobermans. The boys clocked her short gingham dress, the purplish eczema patches that wound up her shins.

"Baloo, Hattie, hello hello," Leila said. Baloo curved his spine against her knees. The pink-and-brown frills of his mouth hung open, as if in a smile. Leila stretched her palm out for Hattie to sniff and stroked the dog behind her pointed ears. Hattie flashed her long yellow teeth and curled up on the floor, as far from Leila as possible.

Hema swung the front door open and untied the leashes from the dumbbell.

"They're late for the vet," she said, between coughs, and dragged the dogs inside. It was a lie, but Leila always bothered the animals.

Dogs gone, Leila switched her hips up the Gills' driveway to the stoop where the boys sat. Foundation two shades lighter than her skin dripped down her cheeks, in the shape of tear tracks. She tucked her hair behind her ears, revealing a pair of diamond earrings.

"There's weed in those?"

"Were you eavesdropping?" Arvind replied.

Leila shrugged. "Your voices are so high, they carry. And those look like Wawa peach rings."

"She's lying," Manu said. "As usual."

"I'm not a liar."

"Mom says you are. And that you embellish the truth, for dramatic flair."

Leila held her palm open. "Give me one, I'll test if they're real."

"No."

"It's my sixteenth birthday today, be fucking chivalrous."

Feeling the boys' eyes on him, Manu offered her the open bag. "Fine. But you won't know for an hour. Maybe five. Depends on your metabolism."

"Give me two, mine is slow."

Arvind interrupted: "There's only a few left, Manu. Don't waste them."

Arvind leaned back against the concrete steps and surveyed the diamonds on Leila's ears. Peach sugar stuck to the fuzz of his upper lip.

"Swap us the earrings and you can have them all."

"No way. These are real diamonds."

"Real, are you stupid? Look at the clarity, it's shit."

"I'm not stupid. I got a perfect PSAT score."

Leila untucked her hair and turned to leave, then tripped on her untied shoelace. She fell on her palms and knees. The short dress rode above her waist. Manu's stomach curdled at the dried bloodstains on her underwear. The women in the sugar-covered editorials were ruined for him.

"Are you good?"

Leila nodded at Manu and stood slowly. She dusted the asphalt from her scraped skin, fixed her skirt, then snatched the gummies from his hands and ran.

Devika Gill pushed the mesh door open. She offered the boys a bag of crispy green peas.

"What's this bloody noise?"

"Leila's selling *weed*, Amma," Manu said, in the singsong voice he reserved for his mother. By then Leila had already sprinted halfway down the block, the bag of peach rings in hand.

~

AROUND FIVE, a handful of Hindu women drove to the township mandir for aarti. ("We're not *all* Hindus, thanks very much," one woman clarified.) For a place of worship the temple was plain, with a long hallway of overlapping purple carpet and idols carved crudely from blush-colored marble. Karina Dixit, a housewife of fifty-six, wept before Durga perched on her marble tiger. *Have a little mercy on a mother*, she prayed. *Mercy on a good mother like me.*

An iron bell hung above the hallway entrance. Worshippers were to ring it when entering or exiting the space to announce their presence before god. It wasn't a heavy bell, but the women were very short, and even when they jumped, they could not reach it.

Back home that night, dues paid to god, the women slathered their faces with turmeric cream and went to bed, bitter-smelling, sorry for themselves on that night as every night.

"To think, we spent the day fussing over dogs and daughters, and that whole time, dear Matthew, dying," said Anita Sharma, the thirty-eight-year-old with the thief of a daughter, as she knelt before a marble idol. Grief dripped down her cheeks. She wiped it away, along with a little peach ring dust, with her chiffon dupatta. "I cannot imagine."

MONDAY

Nothing's Wrong with Small!

HEMA heard from the officers first. The officers drove to her house early Monday, seventeen hours after they discovered Matthew's corpse on the highway. Hema had spent the morning working back-to-back shifts at Dunkin'. Her husband, Parth, a deadbeat of disrepute, manned the register and drive-thru, high as a kite. Hema nuked egg rounds in the industrial microwave and slammed egg-and-cheeses on the countertop, still heated from her weekend dog spat with Tejas Kaushal. During the usual midmorning lull in service, Hema opened WhatsApp and searched for Matthew's contact. *Bhai, Tejas is a coward. Prays to Krishna, then beats his wife and throws chairs at dogs. Such a big temper and most likely a small penis. No wonder Jyoti doesn't want to touch him. Why should my animals suffer too? Can you say something to him? He answers to you.*

Ninety-two minutes passed. No reply. Hema worried she'd offended Matthew. *Nothing's wrong with small!* she typed, then left her phone in her car for the rest of her shift, next to the golden Ganesh idol on the dashboard, where she could not be tempted to check it.

Around one Hema clocked out and drove home to Willow Road. She played a round of tug-of-war with the dogs and went to the upstairs bathroom. Hema undressed, stepped into her mildewed shower, and slathered her left armpit with a glob of pink Nair.

The doorbell rang. Hema slathered her right armpit. Probably it was Jehovah's Witnesses offering her yet another chance at salvation or a child selling candy to fund a useless planetarium field trip, as if their lack of funds was her problem.

A third ring. Hema pushed aside the money plant on the shower windowsill and saw the police car parked in her driveway.

"Shit."

Hema toweled off and threw on a terrycloth robe. Chemical pink globs splattered over the cherrywood staircase as she ran downstairs. Sixteen years in the States had taught her that American cops existed for two reasons:

1. To champion white people
2. To terrorize Black people

Being neither, Hema folded herself (neatly) into a liminal space. No one bothered reaching inside. Most neighborhood women hid there too. When several of their houses were robbed by a throng of Nutley teenagers (so incompetent that one, an asthmatic, left her inhaler behind at Devika Gill's and sheepishly returned for it), nobody reported anything. Who wanted to risk her parent's visa, her own tenuous H-1B?

Hema bolted Hattie and Baloo into their crates. The last time she'd dealt with officers was at the Independence Day fair last summer in the park. Hema remembered it well. She'd bought a pistachio kulfi pop from a cart vendor when two fathers, one short, one tall, broke into an argument outside a children's bounce house.

I'll break-a your face, said the tall one, in a fake Italian accent.

I'm going to the police, the short one replied. His little daughter looked on impassively in a knit hat shaped like a frog. The short father flagged down a nearby security officer. *Sir*, he implored and pointed at his opponent, *he said he is going to break my face!*

The security officer listened to both men belaboring the conflict. It was to the little daughter that he finally spoke. "I like your hat."

Hema licked her kulfi and savored the nuts and the drama. The officer, clean-shaven and bald as an Easter egg, merely grinned, told both parties to *please calm down*, and sauntered off to a kebab stall. Hema was incensed on behalf of both fathers. At least they should have hit each other. So when their backs were turned and they walked off in different directions, Hema threw her kulfi at the tall one. *Sir, it was him!* she cried, pointing at the short father, his little daughter.

~

THESE OFFICERS weren't grinning.

"*He-ma Rao?*" the average-looking one said, his leather foot already past the threshold of her front door.

"Well, that's not how you pronounce it, but yes, this is she."

The ugly officer slid a license out of his breast pocket. It bore a photograph of a man, shaggy-haired and broad, with watery light-brown eyes. Did Hema recognize him?

PILLAI
MATTHEW
DOB: old

HT: 5 -09   WT: 200 plus lbs

"Of course I recognize him." Hema's mouth dried. Residual Nair burned her armpits. "He's like my brother." She fanned herself. "Something's wrong?"

In a manner: Mr. Pillai had been discovered dead on the interstate in his black BMW, sitting in a puddle of his own urine and surrounded by insulin syringes. An empty canister of heart medicine was discovered wedged in his crotch. The officers looked for Matthew's next of kin, but he appeared to have no papers, no green card, no record of belonging to anybody, only the women's names and addresses stored in his car GPS under frequently visited locations, Hema's Dunkin' included.

"Impossible." Hema pressed a hand to her cheek. The skin was hot and wet. "Impossible." Hadn't she texted Matthew a few hours back? Had he not pulled up into the Dunkin' drive-thru a week ago, craving a decaf with four Splendas? *How are the dogs, Hema? Baloo, Hattie?* The only one who ever asked her. There had to be some error. Perhaps these officers were mistaking Matthew for some other dead man. Probably all brown men looked the same to them. The room spun. The dogs whined. Hema considered asking the officers for a photo of the scene—it was a crime scene, apparently; even if it was a crime against oneself—so that she might confirm the events with her own eyes.

"I have to see the nasty to believe."

The officers declined. They thanked Hema and left. She retired to the medicine cabinet, swallowed her last antibiotic, and wept.

I Have to See a Horror to Believe It

HEMA SHARED THE news in the women's neighborhood WhatsApp group chat, to multiple anguished-face emojis. There were women like her, who wanted photos because they needed to see a horror to believe it. And there were women like Jyoti Kaushal, who wanted them for emotional closure.

"*Dateline* always has photos," Jyoti said, cradling a baby bump. "Also reenactments."

Tejas, bereft from the news, blew his nose at the kitchen table and tossed the dirtied napkin on his placemat. "The universe is punishing me."

Jyoti blew her nose harder. Even before Matthew's death she'd been grieving. ("And has not shut up about it," said Devika.) Last spring Jyoti's youngest brother had died unexpectedly. Out of seven siblings, she and this brother were closest in age. Their mother raised them as one lump sum. Brother and sister shared textbooks and a room and opposed each other in pachisi and chess. If Jyoti's brother sensed imminent loss in the middle of a game, he loosened his drawstring and pissed on the board, so that certain squares reeked of ammonia forever. The siblings sometimes climbed trees to a richer neighbor's rooftop. Jyoti would stash a kitchen knife in her undershirt. At the top she'd set the blade on the ground for her brother to take, superstitious they'd fight if they exchanged the weapon directly. Her brother would slash two tender coconuts off the neighbor's palm tree.

"We drank them then and there, I thought we'd get flogged," Jyoti said. Her brother harbored no such fear. One, he tiptoed the perimeter of the roof, surveying the city from a new vantage point, the harsh white of the shop lights and the light smog. *It's still shit from here*, he decided. Jyoti watched him. She and this brother leached off the same womb. As infants they drank the same disgusting clots of Nestlé milk powder. Still, a dissonance: Jyoti's brother climbed high. She had not been raised to look anywhere but down.

Then adulthood, marriage, immigration, the whole cliche. The telephone ringing; news of the terrible accident. Her brother, a day laborer, had been working construction at a luxury high-rise when he fell. Jyoti's siblings attended the funeral and watched the brother's soul evaporate in black puffs.

"Me, I could not travel abroad in time, I didn't see the body, I had no closure. I looked for him everywhere, everywhere."

Jyoti cried into Tejas's shoulder. He offered her his dirty napkin.

Months after the missed funeral, Jyoti thought she saw her brother at a Kmart in Hamilton. She was shopping for intimates when he appeared, dark-haired and broad-backed with a slow and delicate gait. Jyoti called out his name. The man didn't turn. She followed him wordlessly, palms damp, her red shopping cart between them as they wound past clearance coats and training bras. In the linen aisle she tapped the man's shoulder. *Bhai?*

"It was Matthew who turned to me and said, *I'm sorry, sister,*" Jyoti said, dabbing her inner eyes with the soiled napkin. "This whole time here nobody has called me by that name. I didn't know I'd lose him, too."

∼

JYOTI DROVE TO THE local precinct to request crime scene photographs, to no avail. After that the women dropped the issue of photos altogether, afraid they might offend the officers, who didn't consider them capable of such sick curiosities.

"As for me, I still would have asked, if only these other women hadn't stopped me," said Nasreen Farouk, seventy-seven, maître d'hôtel of Kwality Meats. Half of Kwality operated as a shopfront selling butchered meat and halal marshmallows. The other half was a canteen-style dining hall furbished with fat green carpet nobody ever cleaned ("*I am the cleaning-people, the cooking-people, the butcher-people, what more people do you want?*" Nasreen commented under negative Yelp reviews). The business was cash only. Nasreen stored her savings inside her bedroom closet.

"Two years ago, someone broke in and stole it all. The police said, *Open a bank account, pay taxes next time.* Assholes. But Matthew, bless him, gave me a personal loan. From then on, he was like a son to me. Or at least a very distant nephew."

The sight of dead bodies didn't bother Nasreen. She told the women how she'd grown up in a town plagued by religious riots. Men fought with so much mania that eventually there was no town left, only foothills of soft black soot. Nasreen wept in her mother's skirt. *Amma, where will we go, what will we do?* Her mother tossed her a week's worth of bloody underwear and said, *The washing.*

Apart from these dispatches, the details of which no one could confirm, Nasreen didn't speak much about her past. Trauma grew jammy inside her, like stone fruit. It dripped out of her unbidden and always sounded out of place. Then again, some memories had no proper place. After Nasreen heard about Matthew, she closed both sides of Kwality out of respect and dined alone at the IHOP on Route 1. A waitress drizzled a ribbon of syrup across her stack of senior-citizen-priced pancakes.

"Let me tell you, I cannot tell you how many bodies I have seen." Nasreen told her, cutting into the fluffy rounds of dough. "Paraded like floats, they were."

"Um, ha-ha." The waitress glanced at the wall clock.

Nasreen swallowed. "I mean, can you believe these officers? Do you think I'm afraid of a little-little blood?"

~

POOR MATTHEW'S BODY. Without pictures the women imagined the scene inside out: Matthew alone, a brooding hulk trapped in a coffin of engine and metal while the other drivers overtook him, sunroofs open, dragging lazy hands through a soft-boiled breeze. Shotgun passengers ate rest stop fries and stank up the car with the fug of grease and fat. The last bits of daylight receded behind a line of orange clouds.

To imagine a horror didn't soften it. That only made its edges sharper. The women debated who this horror had hurt more:

"It gives me chills to think about," Hema Rao shuddered. "My dogs weep."

"My heart is aching so much, I take two Tylenol a day," Jyoti Kaushal said.

"I am aching so *so* much, but I don't take even *one* Tylenol," Devika Gill said. "See what all I endure."

Pain was a moot point. In the four years the women had known Matthew, he'd become a brother to each of them. Though only a visitor, he'd become as permanent a fixture to Willow Road as Devika Gill's trashy Home Goods foyer lamp.

("Hold on, hold on, hold—who said trashy?" Devika said. "Such nasty women. Who cares what they think?")

Twenty minutes later the women spied the hood of Devika's foyer lamp poking out from her recycling bin.

TUESDAY

As It Is, No One Cares About You

AUTHORITIES TRACED Matthew's final hours through his Mastercard purchases. At a mall in upstate New York, where he lived, he'd run up a $304.42 tab at a Macy's bed-and-bath section. He filled up on gas and drove to Willow Road. His final transaction took place at six forty-three P.M., at a rest station back en route to New York. One large Diet Coke and a Big Mac. He'd eaten both the meat patty circles and left the buns untouched in the glove compartment. ("When you realize you are nothing more than an animal in the end, even then you don't care for animals," said Jyoti, a meat-free woman.)

More interesting to the women than the rest stop meal was Matthew's penultimate transaction, $2.50 in cash for a box of Nanak laddus, uniformly orange and encrusted with freezer burn, at the Cash & Carry where the women conducted their weekly shop. Men rarely came in. Markets bruised their egos. Everywhere you looked, you watched the women knowing: How to tell if a coconut is rotten or good by rapping the bark with your knuckles and listening for the water pressure inside. How to extract acne cleanser from the aloe leaves. Whose cousin-brother's-sister was up to no good. How to spot a daughter in heat. How to stop a daughter in heat.

"When I moved here, in 1982, the only thing in this dinky township was Pathmark, Pathmark, Pathmark," Nasreen Farouk said. "My first months in this country, I made saag paneer with creamed spinach. From a can. What's sadder than that?"

"Oh, a lot of things, I think," Hema Rao yawned. "Maybe think of a better sob story."

"Less generic," added Devika Gill. "As it is, no one cares about you or how you got here. Or what you ate."

The women hummed in assent.

"*Acha, acha,*" Nasreen relented.

The Ladies of the Cash & Carry

APARNA NAIK, the twenty-six-year-old Cash & Carry checkout girl, rang Matthew up for the laddus, making her the last woman to see him alive.

"It feels surreal," Aparna told the officers who dropped by her register midmorning. "He was a diabetic. I told him, these are bad for you, man. He smiled and gave me a twenty. I pocketed the change. Don't know if he noticed. He seemed distracted. Sickly. Then again, who notices me?" She smoothed her wavy hair down. "Also, will this interview be on television?"

Because Aparna was beautiful no one paid attention to her depressing comments. Men reached past her sadness to the hourglass waist no number of fast-food nuggets could crack. Aparna didn't care about her figure or her good looks. She lorded them over no one—where had they ever gotten her but to the bottom?—and routinely gave the other women discounts on (expired) Ponds Beauty Creams, which came in the Pinkish Fair Glow and Fair Beauty varieties.

"Why anyone wants either is beyond me," Aparna said, picking the Dorito dust from her fingernails.

An elderly grandmother got in line behind the officers. She tapped her foot and slammed an overripe squash onto the conveyor belt. It sputtered a stream of yellow pulp.

"These fucking suits," the squash woman said, in Hindi. "Are they bothering you?"

"It's fine, Auntie," Aparna winked.

The women loved Aparna because she was motherless. Mrs. Naik died when she was a toddler, a hush-hush suicide by drowning. *Death by septic shock*, the online obituary read.

Aparna kept a Polaroid of Mrs. Naik taped to her cash register. "She's twenty-six in the picture, what I am now." In the photo Mrs. Naik wore high-waisted jeans and a frumpy turtleneck, toddler Aparna hoisted on her hip. On death anniversaries, Aparna lit incense in front of the image along with her mother's favorite foods, though she didn't know what they were, and her father didn't remember.

The women held Mrs. Naik in disregard. As far as they were concerned, she didn't deserve respects or a posthumous plate of her favorite meals. To indulge in her own misery she'd left a young child behind. ("Coward. She could have just drunk, no? What else is a little liquor for?" the grandmother said.) Nevertheless, the women always came around to pay their respects with aluminum platters of food. The steam stung at the corner of Aparna's eyes. Tears never fell.

"How can I love someone I didn't know?" Aparna said. "But she's mine, see, I must."

The ugly officer stared at Aparna's plump lips. "Lovely photograph."

Aparna smiled. Everyone said this about the picture. It was only Anita's girl, Leila, who noticed what Aparna studied so well: how Mrs. Naik's dark eyes bore quietly past the corners of the frame, slanted and pleading. *Gosh she looks so bummed*, Leila said, smacking a wad of watermelon gum. Aparna had wanted to say something (Thank you) but Anita pinched her daughter's earlobe and dragged her and the beetroots out. *Have some respect for a dead woman*, Anita snapped.

Those moments sank Aparna knee-deep in longing. No one pinched her ear or dragged her out of any place. The women offered to put her profile up on a matrimonial website. Nasreen even offered to pay for a double-diamond-extra-platinum membership, so Aparna could scroll through an unlimited number of bachelors. Aparna declined, content to stay in the company of her father, with whom she lived in a townhouse five miles south of Willow Road, in a development of cream-colored townhouses with slats of mint-green roofing, pressed tightly together as matchboxes.

"If he screams, someone will hear," Aparna said.

Mr. Naik worked as a driver for a ride-share company. Despite his dwindling eyesight he delivered takeout to stoners during the day and at night holed up on the waxy sofa to watch his favorite black-and-white films. His beloved actors were now dead or ancient. Aparna watched with her father, acutely aware of his looming expiration date. So easily he could slip in the shower and die on the mosaic tiles, the showerhead scalding him, or crash his car on the way from picking up a stranger's Jersey Mike's order. Aparna rehearsed the calamities in her mind in preparation for the day one struck. Outside on wicker chairs, she begged her father to retire. He said no, insisted on his utility, and then they smoked blunts together. Occasionally Matthew joined. *Take it easy, man*, Matthew used to tell him. *You have cataracts; if money dips low, I'll help.*

"He kept Papa company," Aparna said. "And me too. Matthew lost a mother. He knew lonesome."

The ugly officer scratched into his legal pad. *He knew lonesome.* Also: *cashier— fuckable one.* Could he have Aparna's full name, for the case report?

"I'd rather go anonymous." She laughed throatily. "Or fine. Use my name. Who am I, that anyone should care?"

Again, nobody noticed Aparna's sadness. Only her cleavage. She leaned across the register, so the officers could smell the sourness pooling in her armpits.

"If you're here, buy something," she said.

THE OFFICERS LEFT with some aloe vera gel for acne. The women flocked to Aparna's register.

"Well?" said Karina Dixit.

"I saw one of their notepads, the case notes came down to this." From memory Aparna scribbled a few words on the back of a receipt:

- *Milk, eggs, bread*
- *[an illustration of a middle finger]*
- *Matthew—lover?*
- *Heat*
- *"Ludews" diabetes*

"My god, a whole box of laddus? You never told us," said Usha Gohel, forty-seven, a lazy-eyed, many-moled banker and mother to fourteen-year-old Arvind Gohel, who had inherited her looks. "He came over for dinner a few months back. I spent hours making kheer and barfi. He went on and on about how he couldn't eat it, because he hadn't taken his insulin," Usha said. "What a waste."

Devika Gill hummed in assent. Last Girl Scout season she'd bought trefoils for Manu, his favorites, and offered a few for Matthew to have with coffee. "He told me in passing once, that they were his favorites too," she said. "When I offered him one he said, *Are you trying to kill me, woman?* He ate through both sleeves. For hours I worried I'd have to call the hospital."

"My god, no self-control," said Usha.

"Sugar will do that to a man," said Nasreen Farouk. "Too much of a good thing. No hips to store it in."

"Fatalistic, he was," said Karina Dixit.

The women clicked their tongues and hummed in assent. What went so wrong in that head of his, sugaring himself to death?

"Of course, he had been suicidal," Aparna said. "Press any man over fifty, and he too will admit to despondency."

"For a man to come up from nothing, and pull something like this," said Nasreen Farouk. "And excuse me for saying this. But is it not also selfish, indulgent? Good thing his mother is dead, I'm sorry to say."

"*I'm* depressed, but here I am living," said Aparna, twirling a ratty lock of hair between her fingers. "Case closed."

"Unless," said Usha. She looked around the packed aisles and lowered her reedy voice to a whisper. "Unless they weren't for him. What all did he didn't buy for the Sharmas, no? And still the girl stole candy from Arvind the other day, like a beggar. Anita did nothing, of course. Did I tell you I saw Anita crying in temple the other day, mourning for him?"

Karina Dixit shook her head. "Fake tears. When does she go to temple? That family is full of bad actors."

"Imagine Matthew never got mixed up in their shit," said Devika. "Imagine we never did."

Just then the women heard the clattering of impractical heels, saw the blur of a powder-blue dress, the coiffed back of Anita Sharma's curls as she stormed out of the market with a milk gallon.

"My god," Aparna said. "Did she pay for that?"

The Unhappy Kind

BEFORE PROCEEDING WITH further details, the women wanted to note that there were two kinds of Willow Road families:

a. THE UNHAPPY KIND (E.G., THE SHARMAS). Three bodies cramped in one bed. Cooking and cleaning followed by digesting and fighting. A sadness that crawled inside the drywall so long ago that no one remembers the origin—arrangements, intruders, astrological imbalances in the universe, chemical imbalances in the brain. From the basement and the attic, melancholy secretes the same bad-meat stench. Tight on money, always stretching dollars till the dollars tore in two.

b. THE HAPPY KIND (THE DIXITS). Few families admitted to experiencing happiness, preferring instead the dignity of suffering. So what the happy kind meant, the women had yet to determine. Money was one indisputable marker. Finished basements, another. Paisley print sofas. Brocade. Big parties at the Rasoi, open bar included.

THE UNHAPPY KIND, CIRCA '90s

The Sharmas

ANITA SHARMA, a snob, moved to Willow Road in the early nineties. The Sharmas were among the first brown families to move to a then majority white neighborhood. The women had high hopes for them, having been ignored by the American couple who previously inhabited House 24. That couple used to offer the women strained smiles during walks, but the more outnumbered they became, the fewer smiles they offered. Construction workers installed a cedar salt fence around the couple's backyard. Squash blossoms grew in their private garden. Laborers pruned the weeds. The night before the couple moved to a quiet shoreside town, they stuffed their squash with ricotta and threw a backyard party, where they served it in a butter sauce and poured guests glasses of cloudy white wine. None of the women received an invitation. Country music played from a boom box. The couple smoked and kissed on the steps.

"Closed mouth," said Karina Dixit. "But nevertheless obscene."

So the women were happy when the Sharmas arrived in a U-Haul truck that humid August afternoon, the air thick with pollen and allergy. From their windows, the women watched a slight man hop out of the driver's seat. He was Ashok Sharma, forty-six, quiet-mannered, with multiple chemistry degrees. As proof of his erudition, he wore heavy dress pants no matter the season. A bald spot spread over the back of his otherwise thick and curly scalp and resembled the eye of a storm. He frowned at the house.

"It's worse than the pictures," he announced.

Anita, then twenty-two and severely pregnant, waddled out of the passenger seat. She slid a cheap-looking pair of heart-shaped sunglasses up her widow's peak, handed Ashok a disposable camera, and hurried up the front steps.

"Take a photo of me, man." She posed straight-on, hiding her belly from the frame.

Ashok snapped the Polaroid. His thumb covered the lens.

"She had a baby face, but a banshee voice," Devika Gill remembered. "The photo developed without her in it, and I could hear her screaming from across the street, like a teenager."

"I am a different kind of person, a good, very empathetic kind of person, you know, and so I worried for her," said Karina Dixit. "I would take my daughter, Riya, outside for walks. I'd see Anita walking too, and told her, *What a massive bump you have on such a sickly body. Come over for dinner, you need to widen up, how will you pass a child with hips so small?* And she told me, so proudly, that she was forty-two kilograms and wanted to be nothing more. Indeed there was nothing more to her. Empty girl."

∼

THE SHARMAS soon established themselves as the block's noisiest neighbors. When Anita and Ashok argued, their voices echoed around the block, raspy and green and tempered with ennui.

"Ashok didn't want to live in a suburb. But it made Anita happy to have a place of her own," said Jyoti Kaushal. "She wanted to get as far from her old life as possible, from every place before."

"Mutually, they hated this place," said Devika Gill. "Acted as if they were the only ones."

TUESDAY

The Dixits

AFTER THE ANITA sighting at the market, Karina Dixit excused herself from the gossip circle around Aparna's register and drove home in a state of agitation, flipping off a student driver making a left turn. The nerve of that woman to show her face. First in temple, as if god wanted to see her. Now the market.

Back at her house, Karina saved her THANK YOU FOR SHOPPING bags in the pantry and pilfered through the stack of magazines and newspapers she and Rajesh kept on the mandir. It was where they kept the news clippings about Riya. It had been months since her daughter stopped responding to calls on that Florida spring break trip, months since authorities declared her missing. The first few weeks, Riya's name made local headlines. Then nothing. Karina went to temple every day to pray for her. She'd written to eight local papers and two celebrity gossip blogs with her daughter's photographs to revive the coverage. Editors stopped answering. She leafed through the stack, set it aside, then flipped through the coupons. There, between the detergent and toilet paper deals, was the math prep textbook advertisement with Leila Sharma on it. The girl sat at a desk in a pair of bold black frames, poring over fake notes, the single acting gig she'd booked. Meanwhile Riya, authorities said, must be in the water now, buried under debris, her face bloated with algae, eaten by small fish.

Karina threw the advertisement in the trash. She felt a migraine coming on and drew the pink blinds of the living room window shut. Better to take it easy. Last night, she'd fallen into another one of her bad-spirited spells, smashing glass and ceramic until the neighborhood's infants and elderly awoke.

The spells began when Riya first vanished. Matthew had pressed her to see someone. He knew specialists, he said. Karina never took him up on it. What would a pill help with her circumstances, what would a pill change about the facts? Then he'd sent Tejas Kaushal to her house with an antidepressant prescription.

Karina never picked it up. She preferred the catharsis of her spells. She turned hospitable the mornings after them, the rage of the previous twenty-four hours exorcised out of her. She swiped drugstore concealer under her eyes and knocked on the women's doors, as if nobody had heard her undoing herself the night before. Whether out of common courtesy or routine hush-hushing, the women pretended they hadn't.

("I wish she just took the drugs," Jyoti Kaushal whispered.)

Karina asked the women if she could borrow the very dishware or ingredients she'd smashed the night before. Her forearms often dripped with blood from glass wounds.

The women relayed dutiful sympathies. *Didi, sister, are you okay? Have you heard anything about the recovery effort?*

Karina enjoyed their concern. *I'm fine,* she said. *I've come to borrow a Dutch oven. I'm all out of cumin. All out of sugar. Pesticides. I'm all out of—you are all too good to me. Like a sister.* Devika Gill supplied her with fenugreek. Hema Rao provided yogurt.

～

TUESDAY AFTERNOON, Karina pinned up her saree with a clothespin and made her way to the Sharmas' house, fired up for a fight. Anita answered in the same blue dress she'd worn at the Cash & Carry.

"I'm out of milk," Karina said. "Did I not see you at the store with a new gallon?"

"Fine." Anita clicked her tongue in annoyance and disappeared into the kitchen.

Down the foyer hallway, Karina saw Leila opening a plastic container of laddus.

"Hi, Auntie," Leila said. She walked to the front door and offered Karina a sweet. "How are you?"

"Terrible, as usual," Karina replied. She chewed a laddu. "You know, I saw your old math advertisement in the coupon book today. Famous. What's next, a commercial?"

"Hardly, I regret that whole pursuit."

Anita returned with the milk gallon. "Here. Leila drank a glass this morning, but you can take the rest."

Karina screwed off the cap. She took a swig. "This is the new one, or your old one?"

"New one, of course."

"It tastes off."

"It's skim."

"You keep it," Karina said. She handed the gallon back to Leila and excused herself, the start of a bad spell creeping back inside her.

WEDNESDAY

What the Knife Would Do

The officers left the women the tip line number and the next morning Karina dialed it. The sweets had to be the same ones Matthew bought. She'd tasted the freezer burn herself. So she asked the officers to meet her in person, at her house. The night before, she stayed up reading Patch articles about the last three deaths the officers had investigated:

1. Last October, a middle school teacher on her cell phone swerved past a buck running along Sandy Hill Road. The buck survived, antlers intact. The teacher, three months pregnant, drove headfirst into a tree and was slowly incinerated by electrical wire.

2. Not long after, a divorcée in East Brunswick pushed her son out a window and jumped after him. *Baby and I are good, we're better than good*, read a Post-it note the officers found on a mildewed fridge.

3. Most recently a teenager stabbed his girlfriend in the middle of a Target parking lot. Witnesses said the couple had been arguing. No one could tell what the argument was about. *You fucking child!* witnesses reported the girl screaming as she stomped her feet on the parking lot divider. The boy later told officers she'd slammed her double chocolate chip Frappuccino onto his Nissan. He hated tantrums, he said. The girl allegedly demanded the car keys. The boy wondered: What story would the girl spin about him if he were to toss her the keys and let her go? He should have let her go, he told himself to let her go, but before the message made it from his neurons to his fingertips, he pulled an army knife out of his pocket and plunged the blade between her shoulder blades. The boy was sixteen, freckled, with strawberry-blond hair. In court he pleaded insanity. He

told the jury he was sorry, that he was haunted by the dinner crackle of vertebrae. He hadn't meant to hurt her. He only wondered what the knife would do.

～

BUT WHEN THE officers parked their disgusting cop car in Karina's driveway, with its dormant blue-red lights, as if she was some common criminal, she regretted calling. Nevertheless she greeted them and walked them down her corridor, to her blush-cushioned kitchen chairs. She reheated the morning's coffee (a little chicory, lots of cream) and set three mugs on the table.

"So." Karina fished a film of milk skin from her mug and flicked it away. "You have questions for me?"

"Actually, you called us," the ugly officer said.

Karina grew hesitant. Maybe the market gossip was just market gossip, the sweets a coincidence. So she cut him off and rambled—about straining fresh yogurt, about the CASH-4-JUNK-CARS scam signs on township elm trees, about a news segment she'd seen on college girls selling their eggs to pay off loans, the doctors putting the eggs on the black market. Sick of her voice, the officers zoned out and stared at the yellow walls.

Karina took pride in her interior decorating skills. Taped to one wall was a reprint of an Amrita Sher-Gil mural.

"*Bride's Toilet*. You know it?"

The officers didn't. In the mural five women sit in stages of undress. Cross-legged attendants in green blouses surround the eponymous bride in the center frame. One attendant sweeps the bride's hair from her shoulder, revealing a single breast. Behind the attendants sit background spectators, rendered in shadowy brushstrokes. Hair shorn close to the scalp, they sit in fetal position and watch. Karina loved these spectators. How their spines arch into parentheses around the women viewers are meant to look at.

"So sad it is," said Karina. She loved *Bride's Toilet* for private, abject reasons. The rest of the house she'd populated with beautiful things: pink hydrangeas on the windowsill; the PETE'S-SAKE-NOT-YOU-AGAIN doormat, which she'd ordered after seeing one on Usha Gohel's front porch.

"Uh-huh," the ugly officer replied, his eyes fixed on the attendants. The average officer doodled in his legal pad.

Karina frowned. That they had noticed *Bride's Toilet* and none of her more beautiful things made her throat constrict. She complained of a sudden earache and kindly offered to escort both officers outside, thanks for coming, *goodbye*.

"Ma'am," the average officer said, "next time, please don't call the tip line without a tip."

"The laddus," Karina said. "The ones Matthew bought. The Sharmas next door have the whole box."

The ugly officer jotted down a note. Karina watched the men recede into the landscaping, up and over the high stalks of onion grass. She waved and slammed the door, but it was weather-stripped, and the sound didn't reach the dramatic heights she hoped for.

Devika Gill
Did someone call the suits ✓✓

                                                      Karina Dixit
                                Me. Should Anita not get her karma ✓✓

Jyoti Kaushal
Didi has she not already received it ✓✓

ANITA IN THE NAMELESS TOWN, CIRCA '80s

Did She Really Have It So Difficult?

"Listen, Anita told her bloody life story all the time. Thought she deserved good karma for the strife," Karina Dixit said. "Did she really have it so difficult?"

"We all came from little means. She came from shit means," said Devika Gill. "Worst dowry of the lot."

"Shut up," said Karina. "Mine was worse."

"I thought you had a cook abroad," said Jyoti. "And drivers."

In the nameless town where Anita grew up, she attended engineering college as a day scholar, one of only two women in her class, and top of it. Her father collected ticket stubs at a local train station. Her mother, a housewife, spent decades trying and failing to launch small businesses out of their home. First came pickle making, then soaps and cosmetics. Anita's mother made clay pots and instructed buyers to run a damp index finger around the edge to extract red lipstick. The color faded after fifteen minutes of wear.

Anita and her father and mother lived together in a one-story house. Half the concrete was painted blue, the other half blush pink, like a deranged gender reveal. The aesthetic separation gave the illusion of two rooms. On the blue side of the house Anita's mother watched soap opera programs on a tiny television and coughed. On the pink side, Anita's father smoked the fumes that irritated his wife's lungs.

Anita had four younger siblings, first twin girls and then one boy, all of whom died of assorted and altogether preventable tragedies. (The wrong dose of a cold medicine. Anesthesia malpractice.) The death of the boy flung Anita's father into a depression from which he never fully emerged. After work he drank a solid measure of brandy and napped in his cot, sleeping soundly through his wife's coughing and wheezing and the suicidal geckos that fell from the ceiling into Anita's coffee cup. He never minded his daughter's shrieks or the shrill barks of the neighbor's Pomeranian, who scratched and whined at the door until gleefully Anita let him inside and set her father's rejected rice bowl in front of him.

"Papa doesn't eat anyway, he just drinks," Anita told her mother, who hated the dog. It tracked dirt inside and showed up with dried waste around its anus, which Anita gently toweled clean.

Anita's mother wrinkled her nose at the Pomeranian. "Can't its real owners clean the shit? And a drink gives Papa peace, everyone needs one peace minimum."

Anita scratched the dog's ears. "Papa smokes, that's another peace. Think how ugly his face will become."

"My brother is a smoker. Is his face so terrible?"

"It is."

"What a shame, he looks just like me."

This brother, Anita's least favorite uncle, owned a garment shop down the road. Business was good. The uncle loaned money to his sister and to strangers who let him hold on to their gold chains as collateral. The uncle collected the chains in a bowl next to the sink where he shaved.

Four times a week, Anita picked up shifts at the garment shop after school. It was her job to unroll fabric samples for rich patrons who argued her raw silks were counterfeit, and for poor patrons who were content with cheap georgette. *You'll look lovely in this color, and this color*, Anita lied, to everybody.

Her uncle was a skinny businessman with thick, blue-framed spectacles and a large mole on his lower left cheek. He hated socialism, gourds, and women with long hair. He tolerated Anita because she was beloved by his customers. Women were more comfortable talking about sizes and colors and blouse cuts with her. More men came to the shop during her shifts. Shy boys with fresh mustaches. Fat creeps with thick wallets.

Patrons tipped Anita handsomely. If she named a high price, they accepted without haggling. Her uncle encouraged her to flirt with patrons. *You have the charm, the unteachable charm*, he told her. His encouragement prickled Anita, who knew he'd never make the same demand of his own two daughters, her unattractive cousins, who used to play with the jewelry in his loan-shark bowl, whom the uncle scolded when they made eyes at the man working the ice-cream stall. Anita's uncle took pride in the fact that he'd married his daughters off early, at nineteen and seventeen, to men who provided for them. One daughter lived in Pune with her policeman husband. The other married a lawyer and moved to another state but never disclosed her location. *They don't call me, and that means I have done good,* he bragged. *I've given them enough; they need no more. Simple, modest girls.*

The fates of her cousins seemed nightmarish to Anita. Before starting her engineering program she dreamed of delivering infants and got accepted to study medicine out of state. She used to boast about the accomplishment to favorite shop patrons, like the violet-lipped auntie who complained she experienced prolapse even after a surgeon removed the offending uterus. *I'll treat you for free,* Anita promised.

But the uncle put his foot down. Even a dud could facilitate a birth, he said, a bodily function as natural as defecation. Moreover it was improper for Anita to attend to an overnight college without supervision. And she was a pretty girl, a skilled flirt. He'd seen it with his own eyes, at the shop. If she were not so poor, she'd be a hot-ticket item. With too much freedom she'd do nasty things.

"Imagine," he told Anita's mother. "She may not even marry, after."

To test her nastiness out, the uncle dug secret fingers under Anita's skirt while she counted bills at the register. Anita tensed. She continued counting.

~

AT THE DAY COLLEGE she ended up at instead, Anita sat in the back of the lecture halls in slim jeans and oversized sweaters. She grew her hair out in waves that reached past her hip and took glory in its length. She woke up early to steam it with an iron and wore it loose on her moped, letting it knot as she zoomed past vegetable stalls.

College boys circled Anita like ants around a crumb. Because her father could not be bothered, the uncle took it upon himself to worry about her marriage prospects.

"Her dowry couldn't buy shoes in America," he told Anita's mother during afternoon tea. The three sat cross-legged on ottomans in his flat. Static hissed on the radio he never tuned. A soap opera blared on the television, an adaptation, the uncle explained, of a Mexican telenovela that had been adapted from a Peruvian telenovela, a nesting doll of melodramas.

"Are you offering to open your wallet, then?" Anita asked.

The uncle flicked a mole on his nose and dropped three sugar cubes into his cup.

"Now is the time to start looking for a groom," he said, addressing only his sister. "People in the shop call her a tease."

Anita's mother was a squat woman with furry eyebrows and deep jowls, relics of a joy she'd been too exhausted to maintain. A formerly shit student, she hadn't made it past the ninth grade. She didn't protest when her brother assumed control of the meager inheritance they'd both been left, trusting him to dispense it to her in increments alongside the loans. Her dependence embarrassed Anita, who believed her mother lacked discipline and too easily gave in to small gratifications. (Anita's mother defended herself: "*Am I supposed to sit and wait for a big one?*") Anita's mother liked nights at the cinema and overspent on meals with friends. She'd fallen in love with Anita's father purely for his good looks and overlooked his laziness and frivolous addictions.

Now her mother nodded somberly as the uncle spoke. She plopped a cube of sugar into Anita's cup.

Anita fished it out and flung it onto the carpet. "Don't fatten me. Uncle, if I get married, who makes the big tips?"

"Both my daughters married quickly."

"Neither went to school, you don't hear from one at all."

"Didi, did we ever speak to our uncles like this?"

"Never," Anita's mother said, looking down at her folded hands.

Anita set her teacup down and excused herself to the bathroom. She hovered at the door and eavesdropped as the uncle drawled. *She'll become a problem; I'm telling you. The boys will smear her name into a mattress but never marry her. See how she won't take any sugar in her tea? Obsessed with the mirror, with her own face. She thinks she'd deliver babies for others. Meanwhile someone should tell her to put on more kilograms. No hips to pass the kids.*

Maria

"I'M FINDING YOU a boy," Anita's mother announced, as the two sat outside on the love swing and peeled pistachios. Down the street, the neighbors with the Pomeranian bickered. Somebody's grandmother retreated outside to soap her feet in a blue plastic basin. The Pomeranian ran to Anita's love swing and barked at her toes.

Anita's mother shooed him: *Dirty dog.*

Anita lifted the animal to her lap. She pressed his soft mane to her cheeks.

"I said, a boy," Anita's mother repeated.

"Don't joke, Amma."

"I'm serious."

"Nobody takes you seriously."

The Pomeranian squirmed his fluffy legs. He licked Anita's nose.

"If I leave, who'll take care of this boy? The neighbors don't even notice he's gone."

"That dog, thoo! I'm finding you a human boy."

"There's boys at school."

"Good ones or gutter ones?"

Anita scratched the Pomeranian's ears. Some boys were nice to look at, and on occasion Anita thought about their chiseled, mustachioed faces at night. She'd feel a warmth in her cheeks and between her legs, but the fantasies didn't go far. She never knew how they were meant to end. Those boys paid her attention in class, but then there were only two girls to pay attention to, and Anita knew she was the more fortunate-looking of the pair. The other girl, a Christian named Maria, came from a wealthy family and dressed in quietly expensive silks, but she had a mediocre face, wore a bob, and told crass jokes. For months the girls sat beside each other without exchanging a pleasantry. Anita could feel Maria side-eyeing her raggedy notebooks, the fronts and backs of the thin paper sheets covered in marks, the ballpoint pens with so little ink left.

"Anita, how will you read your notes?" Maria asked one day, as the girls unpacked for the lecture.

Anita shook her pen. "We can't all be blessed with a rich father."

The next day, Anita discovered a felt pouch on her desk with twelve new pens inside.

A blessing from your rich daddy, a note read.

TO BECOME friends, Anita and Maria carefully avoided the chasm between their upbringings. Maria never mentioned the luxury trips to Dubai and London and Ceylon. Anita kept mum about her work in the garment shop. She listened attentively to Maria's travel stories and never mentioned that she'd never boarded a plane, or that the farthest journey she'd taken was a bus trip as a girl. Her uncle had wanted to tour three temples down south. Anita tagged along with him, his two daughters, and a slew of distant cousins. The uncle's wife, a nurse, also joined, moon-faced in plunging blouses. On the bus she sat beside Anita, whose own mother was then pregnant and bedridden with the brother who wouldn't make it past childhood. After all that effort to gestate, he insulted his mother with death.

The aunt's lilac perfume made Anita motion sick. Unaware she was the root of the problem, the aunt tended Anita's sickness. She offered Anita cream crackers and lime sodas. Anita drank two. She waited for a rest stop. Each looked filthier than the next. *Keep this up and you'll go in an open field*, the aunt said. Anita shook her head, offended. An hour later she relieved herself in a wet green thicket. The aunt kept watch. *Shame, shame, puppy shame, all the boys know your name*, the aunt teased Anita for her nudity. Later, when the aunt cheated on her uncle with a doctor and the two divorced, Anita was happy. She'd never have to see the woman again.

Maria would never understand that bus. The girls focused on common ground. Both had attended Catholic precollege and bonded over trash-talking the nuns who'd smacked their wrists with rulers. They tried to recall the psalms they'd been made to recite, most of which they'd forgotten, except for 109, a psalm of revenge. When boys slipped them dirty notes, the girls wrote the psalm back to them, with minor adjustments:

Let his posterity (READ: cock) be cut off; and in the generation following let their name be blotted out.

Midday, Anita and Maria congregated at the filter coffee stand and walked arm in arm with Styrofoam cups.

Anita dragged a stirrer through her coffee. "Did you see Arjun wrote us back?" she said. "Asking one or both of us to the cinema."

"One or both, how flattering. Will you go?"

"My uncle would explode. Mole by mole."

"You know the notes are meant for you," Maria said, laughing. "So go with him."

"I'll tell him my dowry is a fountain pen."

Maria downed her coffee and walked ahead. "I'm tired of sorry arrangements, domestic-dowry-doom."

"My family wants to arrange me."

"So say no. There are better things to do than live unhappily with a man. I told my mother, I don't want to be like you, with your instant-noodle marriage. I'll work. I'll wait. My father said he'll get me an office at his firm, so long as I don't run it into the ground. If only I had brains like you, doe-eyes."

"If only." Anita trashed her cup in a nearby bin and strode ahead of Maria, her mood soured. So Maria could say no and people would listen to her. Maria made bad marks but would go on to have an office, whereas Anita had not been allowed to study out of state.

Breathless, Maria caught up and looped her arm back through Anita's. Anita smelled her sweat and bergamot perfume.

After class the girls rode home on their respective mopeds. As usual Anita drove in the wrong direction. She never wanted Maria to see her house, with its illusion of two rooms.

"I don't know why you're hiding," Maria said. "It's not like I care."

"Of course you don't." Anita stopped her bike in the dirt and dug her heels in the ground. She kicked up an earthworm, gelatinous and long, and sliced it in half with her sandal. "You've never had to."

～

TWO WEEKS before final exams, someone stole Anita's moped from the university lot. Anita sobbed into the neighbor's Pomeranian, wetting his immaculate red fur. She would have to work so many shifts to make up the money for another; there would be no time to study. Better to walk home, she decided. But one morning a man on the opposite side of the street stared at her, hungry and expectant. Men often watched her. She didn't mind when they were good-looking. This one was particularly offensive, a fiftysomething with a limp in his left leg and eyes in different directions.

"The ego on him," she complained to Maria, the next day in class. "Look at me. What would I want to do with someone like him?"

"Get a new bike."

"I can't."

"Borrow my old one."

Anita refused handouts. She switched up her walking route, speeding up or ducking into shops when the man reappeared, or trailed packs of aunties, protected from view by their age and jowls.

A figure with bobbed hair pulled up on a moped.

"Auntie," Maria called. Her stalled engine hummed. "Hop on."

"No need," Anita said.

"It's just a ride. Take it."

Anita climbed onto the back of the moped. The seats were real leather. She perched herself close to the edge. It would be indecent to ride with her legs apart. Not wanting to hold her companion's body, she gripped the underside of the seat.

"You'll fall off," Maria said.

"I'm very coordinated."

The engine revved. Anita lurched backward. She grabbed the back of Maria's blouse, closer than she had ever been to another person.

The girls sped off into the smog. Two blocks from her uncle's shop, Anita hopped off for her shift. That was the last ride she would take from Maria. She wouldn't rely on the fickle kindness of friendship. Without blood ties, care could be revoked easily and without consequence.

The shop was flanked with an afternoon rush of patrons. The auntie with uterine issues had snagged the threads on her cheap fabric border and needed an exchange. Anita was pushing past her to the counter when she felt blood pool on her underwear.

She hurried to the dirty teal stall in the backroom. There was no blood. Clear gelatin had leaked onto her liner in its place, not unlike the worm she'd killed on the street. She dipped a finger into it and held it uncertainly to her lips. It tasted of the place it came from, and which Anita avoided, that void of salt and heat.

~

NOBODY QUESTIONED the closeness of the two girls in class, huddled over the same notebooks, joined at the hip during breaks. The babbling professor admired their dedication and studiousness, the modesty of their sweaters and oversized jeans. He told them he had friends in high places, a robust alumnus network, colleagues at global firms with a need for dedicated girls. The prospects excited Anita. And yet it annoyed her that Maria, already destined for an office, Maria who nonchalantly failed a major exam, should hear them too.

So Anita soiled the fantasy them both. "I don't want to leave the country," she told Maria, over sandwiches and Cokes at the off-campus pub. "Only sellouts think foreign is better."

Maria laughed. "Sure, homebody."

They squared the check. Maria drove Anita home on the moped but dropped her a few blocks away from the house, aware, for some reason, that they had to keep the friendship a secret to keep it at all.

Anita walked the remaining distance home and pushed the front door open. Across the street the Pomeranian barked and ran over. He licked her face and chewed at her book satchel. Anita kneaded the knots from his tiny back.

Anita's mother didn't question her whereabouts. She was too busy or else too stupid to be suspicious, Anita reasoned, sewing peasant sleeves on shop blouses or pickling lime skins for another business venture. She handed Anita a bag of the fruit.

"Peel these."

"Tomorrow's the last exam, Mummy. I don't have time."

"I too went to school, Anita. You're not the only bloody bitch who's worked hard."

"School, not college." Anita clicked her pen open and set her books down on the table, next to a pile of green lime skins. "I've helped you for years. Who did the cooking when you went to the movies with friends? Do I ever go to the cinema?"

"Yes, yes. You've sacrificed the most, you win. Careful, or your ego will grow an ego."

"The professor says there's openings in some firms abroad. He writes recommendations for top students. And I'm the top."

Anita's mother frowned. "Probably he wants something else from you, men only help themselves."

"And so what if he does? Better than staying here."

"Aiyoh! If he does, you'll give him something?"

"I'm tired of your platitudes about men."

"From where you have got these ideas? I was once a big shot too. Still I've ended up here, with prolapse—"

"The doctor said that was indigestion."

"In any case! Still I ended up here, in this small-small place. Probably when your children remember me, they won't know my name. They'll call me *Anita's mother.*"

Anita swiped a pickle from the jar and laughed. Red oil dripped from her index fingernail. "I don't want children." It was true. Anita knew it from watching her siblings. Another a mouth to feed, an anchor looped around the ankle, the looming possibility of pointless tragedy. "How can I fit someplace small, with an ego so big?"

Her mother smiled. "Yes. I hope you get a house with room for both your egos. You and your daughter's."

THE NEXT DAY Anita and Maria went to the cinema to celebrate the end of their final exams. *Salaam Bombay!* screened. Maria loved Mira Nair. The women split a fizzy drink from the refreshment stand and spiked it with a generous measure from Maria's brandy flask. Anita sipped gingerly. Pure liquor she avoided, afraid to touch the brink her father loved to reach.

Maria downed her drink. The rich could hold it, Anita knew; they spent long, festive evenings pontificating over meaningless ideas with endless pours and nightcaps. Nobody wavered in speech or step.

Maria offered her the flask. "Try it."

"It smells like acid."

Maria took another swig. She tapped Anita's shoulder and beckoned for her ear, as if to tell a secret. Anita leaned forward. Maria brushed her lips against hers. Anita tasted bitterness and smoke and bergamot.

"See?" Maria said. "Does it taste so bad?"

Anita hooked a finger in the other girl's collar and drew her close.

WEDNESDAY

If a Thing Wants to Die, Let It Die

By Wednesday afternoon the township heat wave had subsided a few degrees. Humidity rose into the ninetieth percentile. Supersaturation, the weather people warned. *The Matthew fog*, the women called it.

Pure heat was manageable. But wetness stilled time. It upended the careful atmosphere of bodies. The older cohort of women—brides who'd arrived in the seventies, in mustard-yellow sarees—swore they'd never witnessed such a bad American summer before. Market fruit rotted. Jyoti Kaushal got hospitalized for dehydration and low amniotic fluid. Blades of grass assumed the texture and hue of tiny stalks of wheat.

Anita managed a particularly tawny lawn. Next door the Dixits ran their sprinklers eight hours a day.

The Kaushals lived on the other side. Home from the hospital, Jyoti dried her sheets on an outdoor rack.

Anita waved and lit a cigarette. "Jyoti, who gets a sprinkler system?" she said, cocking her chin in the direction of the Dixits'. "Did you hear that Karina told the officers we had Matthew's bloody laddus? They called me, I had to dig up my receipts from the trash, show that I bought them myself. As if I need a handout."

Jyoti hummed in assent. "The sprinklers are a waste."

"Mhm. If a thing wants to die, I let it die."

～

ONE BY ONE the officers collected the women's testimonies, which came together slowly, part gossip and part fact, inconsistent as a stream of old frying oil. The women loved testifying. Like the stories they told their children and captive hairdressers, their testimonies digressed into speeches about the ingratitude of husbands and gray hairs so stubborn they defied box color. (The women used Garnier Sensation 3.0, in Reflective Auburn Black, Natural Black, and, during summers like this one, whatever attracted less heat—Golden Medium Brown).

How long had the women known Matthew? *(Three years.)*

With whom had he been closest? *(With whom was he not?)*

Most questions the women swerved in favor of other grievances. Last week, for instance, Aparna got a ticket driving down Henderson Road.

"And that too I was only five, maybe ten miles over the speeding limit," Aparna said, tut-tutting as she rang up a muddy bushel of mint leaves and stuffed them, wilted side down, into a THANK YOU FOR SHOPPING bag. "Maybe twenty-five."

Weeks prior, across from Allen's Auto Body Shop, a driver gossiping on her cell phone made an illegal right turn and totaled Devika Gill's Civic. The airbag burst open and pummeled Devika in the chest.

The offending driver was a woman in her early twenties, with ginger hair and a sleeve of twisted vine tattoos. She sustained a slight dent to her bumper, minor chipping in the glossy blue paint. Devika watched, her lip split, as three Good Samaritans rescued the woman's chubby toddler out of a car seat.

"We waited for help to arrive, she didn't say a word to me the entire time," said Devika. "But she cried and cried when police and EMTs came. Told them it wasn't her fault, the audacity. We all went to the emergency room. The baby was fine, the woman too. Meanwhile my bones were broken. To the doctors this woman cried, *My child could have lost me.* I have a child. No one asked about him. Thirteen years old, already growing mustache hairs. They look horrible, like black alfalfa sprouts. I keep telling him, Manu, I'll wax you. He refuses." Devika pantomimed yanking depilatory wax off her upper lip. "Boys are like babies, no good with pain. He could have lost me that day, too. From a mother I would become nothing. I would become air. I'd never get to see him become a man. Who cared about that? I know how these things go, whose side gets taken."

∼

BEYOND APARNA'S TICKET and Devika's car accident, there were communal issues the women of Willow Road wanted addressed. The municipality sent fine notices to them because the institutional maple trees in their front lawns had overgrown. The notices included photos of each of the accused women's sidewalks; evidently, branches that extended more than fourteen inches past the inner bounds of the sidewalk were hazards. If the officers could do nothing for Aparna or Devika, couldn't they at least do something about the stinking fines? On top of everything the women dealt with, despite the taxes they paid to this mediocre township, should they now be expected to be cutting down branches too? And who were the bloody voyeurs taking photos of their sidewalks anyway? Had the municipality nothing better to do? Who except Sunday proselytizers had ever pursued them like this?

I, Too, Have Lived a Terrible Life

THE TOWNSHIP CORONER conducted Matthew's autopsy early Wednesday morning, wielding her knife and scalpel with the enthusiasm of a high school biology student dissecting a fetal pig. *Male, 55, Type-1 Diabetic, Apparently Super Depressive, Likely Suicide* read the paper report that accompanied the body bag. The coroner sliced through Matthew's Hermès pants, now dried with urine and waste, his Oxford shirt, and the Bunyan beneath. Secretly she pocketed the fine gold chain around his neck.

High presence of ketones in the blood, the coroner wrote in the official autopsy report. *Seems unlikely he was taking his insulin. Also, possible presence of antibiotics. Stomach contents: laddus, meat patties, Diet Coke, yellow cake.*

~

THE BODY WAS CREMATED and sent to a stuffy funeral home in Edison. Next door a paan shop operated. NO BETEL-LEAF SPIT ON SIDEWALK read a handwritten sign hanging out front. Red saliva stained the pavement.

Several women chewed paan and offered to claim the Matthew ashes.

"I know the address of his family's tea estate back home, a new family lives there now," said Jyoti Kaushal. "Who knows if they'll have the decency to do right by the dead. Let me take them, we'll spread them. Bad news to let a soul sit on a shelf too long. Probably it'll be reborn someplace terrible, like Florida."

But no, only family could claim the ashes, the funeral director said on a scratchy phone message. Did Matthew have no other family?

Aparna Naik called the officer tip line and invited them to her townhouse in the hope that they could intimidate the funeral home into relinquishing the remains.

"We're good as family," Aparna told the officers, who stood on her front porch. The stench of cooked rice wafted through the mesh door. "Everyone else is either abroad or dead."

Well then. If that was all Aparna had to offer. Goodbye.

"Goodbye now," Aparna said. Upstairs her father snored. The sound carried outside.

The officers walked down the front steps. *Useless,* the average one whispered to his partner.

"He had a wife," Aparna called after them. "Matthew did."

~

"THAT FUCKING APARNA," said Nasreen Farouk, sitting alone in the canteen side of Kwality Meats. "So needy for attention. I'm making a matrimonial profile for her, who cares if she knows?"

News of Aparna's loose lips had traveled fast, in part because Aparna spread it herself in the group WhatsApp.

Aparna Naik
Told them about Matthew's wife ✓✓

Nasreen Farouk
get married and get lost ✓✓

Nasreen blotted the sweat from under her breasts with a napkin. The good fan had broken down that morning and now stood, dusty and inert, in front of the wall with a Choking Victim poster and a prayer scroll with graceful lettering scrawled across the length of faded linen. A wall clock told the wrong time.

Wincing, Nasreen slid off her stool and hobbled to the buffet. With a marker from her brassiere she crossed out the existing price on a tray of minced lamb puffs (TWO FOR ONE $) and wrote in a new one (ONE FOR TWO $$). Nasreen took a puff for herself. The lukewarm breading dripped with animal fat. She wiped her hands on her satin blouse, staining it.

The door chime sounded. Anita Sharma stepped inside the canteen in kitten heels and linen slacks, her bob styled in crisp finger waves, Leila behind her in tight dark-wash shorts. Anita removed her sunglasses and squinted at the menu.

"You know what we have," Nasreen said. "You have lived here for years, superstar."

Anita set her purse on the display case. "One rack of lamb, please, and nothing old again."

"Please. I never give old."

Nasreen slid the rack onto a cutting board and sharpened her cleaver. Twin cop cars flitted past the strip mall window.

"Fuck this, I'm tired of seeing police," Nasreen said. Animal blood splattered onto the scale. "When I was a girl, after the rioters burned down my town, police pillaged the good things that were left. Mummy and I took the train into a different city. We passed ditches and canals. Bodies flooded the water. You could have bobbed for them like apples. My mother covered my eyes with her scarf. It was sheer. I could still see."

"Yes, sure, sure," Anita nodded. "My life was also difficult."

"That's so terrible, I'm sorry," Leila interrupted, her eyes on Nasreen.

Anita huffed. "*I* too have lived a terrible life, Leila. You cannot imagine what all I've been through."

"Sure I can." Leila popped her gum and slid a pair of headphones on. *Born to Make You Happy* played. "You never talk about anything else."

"Stop, how you lie," Anita said. But she flushed as she handed Nasreen a wad of bills and reached for her parcel of meat. Once she had been interested in arts and people and politics, once she had read and finished novels. Now her mind was limited to the traumas of her own insular and terrible life.

"I need to count the change, hold this," Anita said, and handed her daughter the lamb.

Leila held it. The parcel felt fragile and warm with blood.

"No way I'm eating this," Leila said. "Clearly it had a terrible life too."

"These younger girls, they don't know when to keep their mouths shut," Nasreen slammed a hunk of goat hard against the weighing scale. Droplets of blood splashed her forehead. "Disrespecting mothers. Revealing wives."

～

THE WIFE, LOUISE GORDON, WAS WHITE. She and Matthew met on the rail in Glasgow. He was a college student who had just started going by Matthew; Manoj was his given name. On a train ride to London he came across Louise sitting alone in a near-empty compartment, he'd told the women. He said, *May I?* Delighted, she responded, *Oh yes, yes, please.*

"It was some hypergamy nonsense, in my opinion," said Devika Gill. "Yes, genuinely people can fall in love, I am not saying it's impossible. But with Matthew it was different. The woman could be the dowdiest white woman in the world, and still he'd roll over."

After twenty years together, Matthew and Louise opened their marriage. It was an arrangement the women found shameful ("For me, it validated the truth, that she never loved him," said Devika Gill) and one Matthew boasted about.

"Louise was the one who suggested it. But he asked me, was I jealous that Tejas wasn't as progressive, as devoid of ego?" Jyoti said, shuddering.

Despite the shared sexual freedom he afforded Louise, Matthew believed she remained loyal to him alone. That she craved the fantasy of other men but could never cross the corporeal line. The couple lived alone at a large New York property upstate. It had cornices and a sauna. The women had never been invited, but they carefully observed the property on Google Earth and dragged their cursors along aerial views of the rolling green hills.

∼

APART FROM GOOGLE EARTH, marital openness, and whiteness, Louise remained a mystery to the women. The countless times Matthew drove to Willow Road and popped into their houses for dinner, he never brought her along.

"Always an excuse. *Louise is sorry, she's busier than you housewives can imagine, she's a pharma executive*," Devika said.

"I thought, for sure she is ashamed of him," Jyoti said.

Louise's whiteness colored the women's dislike for her, if only because Matthew fawned over her for it, as if she was the adult version of the baby in the nursery rhyme they'd learned as schoolgirls: *Chubby cheeks, dimple chin, rosy lips, teeth within, eyes are blue, lovely too!*

Once, and several times thereafter, the women searched for Louise on Facebook. Either to confirm or dispel the hype Matthew built up around her beauty, but mainly to dispel it.

"She went by her maiden name, Gordon, instead of Pillai. Her privacy settings were tight," Aparna said.

Most of Louise's photos and activity were hidden. Recent visible posts included a listicle of "22 Life-Changing Spiritual Podcasts to Recommend to Your Inner Circle," a photograph of a fresh manicure, and Louise with her arm around an orange-clad guru at a New Jersey ashram. Nowhere did photos of Matthew appear. There were, however, several of Louise riding horses, a passion that evidently consumed all her free time.

"If I ever asked him where she was, he'd shrug and say, *Out riding*," said Usha Gohel.

The women zoomed in on Louise's most recent profile photo and took inventory of Louise's slate-gray eyes and slippery brown hair that grayed beneath her riding helmet.

"She was nothing much," Vritika Shetty concluded. "My lover is much better-looking."

"Plain as grains of rice," Vritika's lover agreed. "He was talking out of his ass."

Matthew and his wife had no children, though the women knew he badly wanted to be a father. He spoiled their children in lieu of his own. He took their bowl-cut-haired sons to good barbers. Over the holidays he presented their frumpy daughters with gift cards to the trendy clothing stores where the women forbade them to shop. *No thank you*, the girls said, and dutifully slid the plastic cards back across the kitchen table. This was a lesson inscribed in the women's bones, by some mother or aunt or great-aunt, rote as an alphabet. *Take nothing from no one.*

The women redeemed the cards for cash. They pitied Matthew's childlessness and enjoyed their child-free hours. He thanked them for their pity and trust. *So many people can get the wrong idea*, he said. *What a shame*, the women thought, *that a man with so much wealth should have no kids of his own to spoil.*

"He used to tell me how beautiful his own children would have been," said Aparna. "He said the kids would get his wife's rosewater cheeks, her whole-milk complexion. I'd tease him, *What, from you?* He just laughed."

The women didn't completely pity Matthew. After all, his lack of progeny was a choice, not a tragedy. These two things the women considered mutually exclusive: you could have tragedy, or you could have choice. ("Tragic choices" were a luxury they reserved for themselves.) Neither Matthew nor his wife had been impotent. The women knew because they asked all kinds of questions they weren't supposed to, e.g.:

- *How much do you have invested in that stock?*
- *Tell me how she can be loose if also she is hideous?*
- *Her salary?*
- *Your salary?*
- *Benefits?*
- *Are you infertile? No? So, she is?*

- Go abroad for the operation. Saves money. My sister/cousin/aunt did it that way. Doctors here don't bother with old wombs.

Matthew claimed Louise suffered intense migraines that prevented them from conceiving. *To get pregnant, she'd have to get off her meds*, he'd explained. *I couldn't see her in pain like that, for nine months.*

Having endured a whole breadth of pain themselves (sweet, pungent, bitter, sour, umami), the women determined this excuse was bullshit.

"Tell me who wants to bear children?" said Shayma Matthews, thirty-four, a township learning center instructor, as she bent over to unbuckle her daughter's jelly shoes at a trampoline park birthday party.

The women hummed in assent.

"Who wants to balloon and blow up?" said Devika. "Selfish creature, she is."

"She *is*."

Sometimes, as the women switched lanes on the turnpike, as they strained milk through cheesecloth for yogurt, as they watched the green microwave seconds tick down on the frozen food they heated for their undiscerning children, they allowed themselves to imagine Matthew's intimate moments with his wife. They used to do it for ridicule and fun. Now they scanned their respective imaginations for some sign of a monster. But the scenes the women imagined were pathetic and prosaic as ever: Matthew suckling from his wife's chest with the hunger of a newborn; Matthew licking the toe jam clean from her feet, worship paraded as love.

The women changed out of their chiffon dresses and into cotton ones. They sat on the chairs their husbands left in front of the back porch windows and prayed for a gust of cool air to soften the stickiness that had been accruing inside them, a somber, secret goop. Then the children, those bowl-cut boys, the frumpy daughters, cried out again for AC (Mummy, *please!*) and snapped the women out of their reveries, which had anyway been so fruitless, so boring. But that was the tedious thing about dangerous men, the women thought, as each cracked her window wider. At first, they were just ordinary.

ANITA MEETS ASHOK, CIRCA '90s

An Old, Stupid Fuck Like You

AFTER THE EXAMS Maria's family flew her to Mumbai to interview at one of the engineering firms the professor recommended. The day before she left, she and Anita had lunch at the pub.

"Good luck," Anita said, the words lackluster as soon as they left her mouth.

Maria reached for Anita's hand. "Why do you sound like you're lying?"

"What's the lie? Don't touch me in here."

With the rejected hand Maria swirled a straw around her soda. "What's wrong, have I done something?"

"Nothing."

Maria eyed Anita's cold sandwich triangles. "You haven't eaten anything."

"I just don't understand, why do the best opportunities go to those with full plates?"

"You mean me, my interview?"

"Did I say your name?"

"No." Maria narrowed her eyes. "Are you so helpless, such a victim?"

Anita didn't respond.

Maria dropped a few bills on the table. "I should be going."

"Good luck again."

∼

MARIA CALLED FROM Mumbai. Anita didn't pick up. The more she didn't answer the more frequent the calls became. Anita registered Maria's nervousness with pleasure. How easily people allowed you to punish them.

The days leading up to graduation moved with languor. One afternoon, after class let out, Anita took an afternoon trip to the market and bought herself a gossamer blue scarf. She walked back home with it tied around her neck and discovered her mother stone-faced on the love swing. The Pomeranian barked behind the neighbor's window, doleful behind glass.

"Hi, Amma."

"You told me you never go to the cinema."

"I never do."

"My brother saw a film the other day. Mira Nair. In the audience he saw two girls splitting a drink."

Anita's stomach dropped. "Your brother talks bullshit."

"You think you can do whatever you want. That girl is unnatural, but money clears up all her problems. You can't afford the same mistakes."

"What mistakes?"

Anita's mother folded her hands over her chest and exhaled loudly. She'd been moved by a similarly hysterical performance in the uncle's soaps and had been waiting to replicate the drama in real life.

"Who will marry you with this reputation? You'll be fruit that fell from a high tree. Do you want that? To be floor fruit?"

"I can't be floor fruit, I'm top of my class."

"I don't care if you're the top, if you have no bike. Don't take her rides. Don't see her anymore. Man, woman, dog. Take nothing from no one."

∼

FORBIDDING MARIA only made Anita want to see her, as if the lunch spat never happened. When Maria returned from Mumbai, Anita returned her calls.

"Doe-eyes!" Maria said. "I'm so happy to hear from you."

Anita invited Maria to come by her house in the evening. Anita waited outside, sweeping dust in a terry cloth robe. The two women stole away behind jasmine shrub. Maria's kisses were wet and disorganized, like she was leaking from the mouth. Anita hated the sensation, the way Maria smiled at her afterward, a foolish tenderness on her face, an amateur who thought herself exceptional.

"I won't take the job if you don't want me to," Maria said.

Anita wiped her mouth. "It's your life, I won't be part of it."

Secret keeping thrilled Anita. Alone in the garment shop bathroom she finished the pleasure their two bodies could only start, then washed her hands with a squirt of orange soap, dizzy and ashamed. She imagined punishing Maria for the aberrant hunger she inspired. Anita would flirt with the college boys in front of her or invite her over again and watch from the window as Maria waited in the cool twilight.

After a string of secret evenings Anita decided, one night, not to call Maria. She swept the perimeter of the house and retired to the love swing, smoked a beedi, and massaged the Pomeranian.

The dog ran home for dinner. Anita was putting out her ash when she heard footsteps in the walkway.

"I didn't tell you to come," she said, but when she looked up it was the uncle, cheeks red and bloated. He yanked Anita's broom from its resting place against the swing and chased her around the house with the bristles, the way he snuffed out rodents from the shop.

Behind the house Anita tripped over a stone. Her uncle helped her up and smacked her hard across the face.

"Whore," he said. "Ruining our name. No man will pick you."

"We don't even have the same name to spoil. Already you sold your girls off. I wonder why they don't speak to you, pervert."

A vein in the uncle's temple pulsed. He grabbed Anita's long hair and struck her once, twice, thrice, until bluish blood leaked from her nostrils and her ears rang. Anita cried for her mother, but probably she was inside, pickling the skins of fruits, pretending not to hear.

When it was over the uncle handed Anita a handkerchief from his pocket. Anita pressed the one clean corner to her cheek. The uncle inspected the damage on her face, so close his nose touched hers. Anita clocked the wrinkles on his forehead, the large pores on his cheeks, the sweat that slid his glasses too far down the crooked bridge of his nose. He was looking up at her, she realized. She had never noticed before how many inches she had on him.

Anita spat on his glasses and shoved him backward. He fell on his wide ass and emitted a little shriek and little gas.

"Who wouldn't pick me?" Anita said. "I'm educated. I'm beautiful. Not an old, stupid fuck like you."

~

AFTER THE BEATING Anita never spoke to Maria again. No one was worth the sanctity of her face, which took two full weeks to heal. In that time Anita applied for work at firms in her city and two nearby. After she recovered she resumed shifts at the garment shop as she waited for responses. A new customer had started coming around, a lanky man with tired dark hollows around his eyes who wore the same taupe trousers each visit. Anita could never persuade him to buy new clothing. Presented with samples of fabric, he put his hand over his face. *Don't trouble yourself,* he insisted.

The fifth visit, the man came clean: He had a nephew in the States who needed a bride, a long-term bachelor and chemist in New York. The man had been watching Anita. He'd asked the uncle about her. What a pretty girl she seemed, the man said, and college-educated too. *You're twenty-one?* He asked Anita. The nephew, he explained, was older, in his forties, so comfortable in solitude he'd forgotten to marry.

"I'm not looking," Anita said. "Older men are like fruit flies, they die so quickly on you."

The man laughed. "Sure, sure," he said, and took his leave.

Anita didn't dwell on the interaction. Two mornings later, as she spread tomato jam onto toast, her mother told her a formal proposal had arrived from the nephew, as good an offer as Anita could get. Anita with her shit dowry, Anita so loud and rude. The man, Ashok Sharma, seemed decent. He was reserved on the telephone when he spoke to Anita's mother, quiet when she exclaimed how excited she was to be done with a child, to offload it into new hands. Anita could live in New York with him.

"No." For a moment Anita wished she could call Maria and laugh about it, this man who ordered a bride without trying her on for size.

"You wanted a city to work in."

"He's old."

"He can be an old man, a loser man, a garden-variety man. I don't care what kind of man he is. He is an American man."

"I'll kill myself."

"Fine. Find yourself a drunkard, dig through the gutter."

"Tell them I said no."

"Of course. You'll kill yourself if I don't."

Anita finished her toast and went to the garment shop and treated herself to potato cutlets and lime soda at the pub after her shift. She ate outside, in the warm glow of the afternoon. Afterward she found her mother outside on the love swing, crying into a little napkin.

"Is Papa dead?"

"No, my god, Anita, touch wood."

It was the proposal. Her mother had accepted it on Anita's behalf.

On the blue side of the house it was Anita's turn to cry. On the pink side she raged. She smashed angel trinkets and a brandy bottle and sliced her foot on a glass shard. Afterward her body felt spent, as if it had run many miles. She sank into bed with her bloody foot. Her mother swept the glass.

In the morning Anita heard scratching at the front door and opened it. The Pomeranian trotted inside, wagging its tail. Such a handsome creature; such curious black eyes. He followed Anita back to her bed, his untrimmed black nails tip-tapping on the floorboards, sat at her feet and licked her wound.

"At least he cares about me," Anita said, cradling him against her chest.

"He cares about blood," Anita's mother replied.

"If I'm gone, who will watch him?"

"His own people."

"They're idiots," Anita said. "Letting him so freely into other people's houses, into this house. I hate this house."

Anita's mother picked a shard of glass from the ball of her left foot. "Good thing it is. In America, you will have a house bigger than this one to hate."

∼

ANITA'S UNCLE BOOKED a one-way economy ticket to New York.

"My wedding present. Be a good wife, not like my last one," he told Anita at the airport. "Don't open your door in New York. Assassins will shoot."

"I'm not important enough to kill."

The uncle belly laughed. "Oh, no, dear, not because you're important. Because you're easy, because they can."

The gate attendants boarded the first few groups. Anita's mother blew her nose into her shirtsleeve and opened her arms. "Come, come, Beti."

"I'll miss my plane."

"Please." Her mother stretched her arms wider. Varicose veins striped her biceps. "Who knows when I'll see you?"

"Yes, who knows."

Her mother's arms fell. The sight of her resignation set off a low ache in Anita's stomach. She would have liked to hold her mother, to soothe her, but then she was the one rerouting Anita's life.

"I'll miss my plane," Anita repeated, and like that she waved and boarded without taking the hug or inhaling her mother's hair, its familiar scent of sebum and jasmine. One last time before who knows.

Cramped in her seat, Anita pressed her nails into her skin until her skin turned white. At least she would take off soon. But there was a fuel issue, the pilot explained on the loudspeaker. For forty excruciating minutes the plane dawdled on the tarmac. Anita considered getting off and returning to her departure gate. It was too late. Passengers who left could not reboard. Anita slept and woke three hours later in the sky. A flight attendant handed her a tray of nuked greens and mushy rice with a corner compartment of lime pickles. Anita dipped her fork into the pickles first. She licked the tines. Her eyes watered. Why hadn't she peeled the lime skins when her mother asked? Why hadn't she accepted that hug? Anita pressed her face against the window and cried. So quickly she'd become cruel.

THURSDAY

Bonnie & Clyde Gordon

The officers tracked down Louise Gordon. She hadn't been living at the address she shared with Matthew in upstate New York, the one the women procured off Google Earth. Nobody did. Neighbors of the Pillai-Gordons said the property was abandoned. They'd last seen Matthew a year ago. After his disappearance they saw little of Louise. Now and then she gardened tomatoes in the back in her wide-brimmed sun hat. Then she drove away with two packed suitcases in her trunk. A long vacation, the neighbors assumed. She'd left behind Bonnie and Clyde, the gray-and-orange tabby duo she and Matthew shared, and she never returned.

"Skinny, desperate things," said the anonymous neighbor who took them in.

Louise had returned to her family's home in Glasgow and remained there, according to the officers, who reached her via international call. The women wondered how they delivered news of her husband's demise. Gentle? Gruff? Peppered with apology? How little? Too much?

In any case, Louise's only reaction, the officers said, was a prolonged silence and a declaration that she and Matthew were separated now. At least informally. They hadn't been properly together for two years. *Irreconcilable differences.* Shame he passed when he did; she'd been waiting on him for the odds and ends of divorce paperwork and suspected he'd been holding out on purpose. He left her his net worth, whittled down to a measly forty thousand dollars, and the New York estate. She accepted the money, sold the property, but, *No thanks,* she whispered, regarding the ashes; don't ship them to her. *That Jersey woman* could keep them.

~

ON WILLOW ROAD, news of the divorce spread like butter.

"Man, I had no clue, and I don't know what Jersey woman she was talking about," said Aparna Naik, as the officers followed up with her in the Cash & Carry parking lot. She tapped her foot impatiently. All shift long she'd been looking forward to the tiny blunt stored in the back pocket of her jeans. "I would have told you the last time you bothered me."

While the average officer was distracted—a girl on a dating app unmatched him after he mentioned his pigtail-schoolgirl fetish—Aparna sidled her phone out of her pocket and opened WhatsApp. Her blunt plummeted to the parking lot handicap symbol.

Aparna Naik
Did anyone know Matthew and his wife split? ✓✓

Jyoti Kaushal
NO ... ✓✓

Devika Gill
He was talking like they were still married?? ✓✓

Jyoti Kaushal
Why would anyone lie about that? The effort alone ✓✓

Aparna Naik
Maybe he was ashamed ✓✓

Devika Gill
Matthew, ashamed? ✓✓

"My break's ending," Aparna said.

The average officer scribbled into his pad:

Timeline—divorce—woman—Matthew sexually involved with woman?

"Ugh, please cross that out," Aparna said. With her sneaker she nudged the fallen blunt closer to her, careful not to crush it. "This isn't your soap opera. No one opened their legs for that poor man."

Tears, Watch!

Leila
Are you on campus right now? I can come to town. ✓✓

Adrian
Sorry, studying for finals. ✓✓

Leila
I'll be quick. Twenty minutes? ✓✓

Adrian
I said I was busy ✓✓

Leila
Ok then. my uncle just died. needed some company but nvm ✓✓

Adrian
I'm sorry about your uncle, but you already told me five times that he died. Wasn't he sick? ✓✓

Leila
Yeah but I'm still sad about it. I'm in mourning. ✓✓
Can I come over? ✓✓

Adrian
Girlfriend's over. Can't talk. Maybe you should be with family now ✓✓

Leila
fine. I'll talk to other guys. ✓✓

Adrian
Ok ✓✓
Thought you were in mourning? ✓✓

Leila pocketed her phone and logged on to the family computer. She doomscrolled Tumblr for an hour. Through the window blinds she could make out the glittering summer sky, but Anita had warned her when she left for work that morning to stay indoors and not open the door for anyone. There were officers circling about, and if Karina came around again, she could shove a skim milk gallon up her ass.

Leila scrolled past a Siberian husky singing into a microphone. An orange cat walked on its back legs like a circus animal. It resembled one of Matthew's cats. He used to keep pictures in his wallet.

To think of the cats without him depressed Leila. She opened Facebook. Anita had forgotten to log out of her profile. Leila read her mother's latest two searches: *Louise Gordon who is that bitch*; *Maria Kumar engineer.* Anita had also left two tabs of local news open.

Family Still Looking for Missing Rutgers Freshman Riya Dixit After Two-Month Search; A Mother's Passionate Plea [WATCH]

Immigrant Man, 55, Dead on Interstate

Leila opened a private browser for a porn break. She tried to think of Adrian as she flipped through the titles. Nothing labeled "tender" was ever any good. "Passionate" bored her. She settled for a casting couch video under "rough." TINY TEEN SLUT GETS RAILED—TEARS—WATCH.

The supposed teen in the video looked approximately thirty-five, of average size, with thinning hair and hot pink shorts several sizes too small. Behind the camera, a man asked her a series of questions. How bad was she (terrible, she attested), how long had she wanted to be in the business (forever; doubtful), and what excited her the most (to be struck.) On cue, the man appeared in frame and slapped her fifteen times across the face. Leila imagined the man was striking her, or that she was striking somebody. Both prospects shamed her, as did her viewership; it signaled depravity on her part, a subconscious collusion with the casting couch man, the exploitative producer of the video. Just short of pleasure she stopped streaming and read the comments section. *Love to slap a bitch, but this is excessive, my dude*, one read. Another quoted Corinthians.

ANITA IN QUEENS, CIRCA '90s

Don't You Feel So Sorry for Me?

ANITA LOVED TO TELL Leila this story: She was twenty-one, thin, and beautiful when she was cast away to marry a man in his forties. "Don't you feel so sorry for me, Leila? I was top of my class, trapped by a shit system."

Anita and Ashok lived in a Queens studio, above a busy pawnshop where immigrants sold ancestral gold. The space was smaller and more underwhelming than Anita had anticipated. A hard blue mattress consumed most of the floor. Running the antique white stove made the whole studio reek of gas. Air bubbles dotted the sticky teak table and linoleum floor. In the bathroom, the previous tenant had connected an illegal portable washing machine to the shower.

"It's so loud," Anita complained. "It sounds like murder when it runs."

"It's a luxury to have one," Ashok replied, calmly. Insults about the studio didn't bother him; he wasn't attached enough to it to care. He was comfortable with a spare life; he knew how to spend little and subsist off instant noodles and hard-boiled eggs. The addition of a wife into his life hardly changed his routine. He left for the lab early in the morning, hair and face freshly oiled, and came home late at night, tired and withered. Anita joined him as he watched *Wheel of Fortune*, where strangers won island vacations for their knowledge of stupid idioms.

"Pat Sajak is like a gnome," Ashok remarked.

Anita enjoyed his spare commentary and missed it in the daytime, when she was alone. The studio window faced the back of another building and an alleyway piled with black trash bags.

Anita kept house. She ran laundry in the bathtub. She ironed and steamed Ashok's wrinkled shirts, occasionally singeing holes into them. She read the Yellow Pages cover to cover, then napped. She dreamed of the Pomeranian at this apartment door, his bark like a bird chirping. She cried after waking. She watched the news. So many segments on a Midwestern criminal who ate parts of his victims. The doorknob turned in the evenings; Anita grabbed a butter knife from the utensil drawer and clutched it, anxious and inexplicably aroused to stab the attacker she hoped had come for her. It was only ever just Ashok.

Anita ate little other than bowls of bran flakes. Progressively the bowls got smaller. One Sunday, as if to address her self-starvation, Ashok slid her an envelope of money over the table. There was a grocery store a few doors down. Anita could buy whatever made her happy.

"Groceries do not make me happy, thrilling as they may be for you," Anita said.

Ashok slipped the money back into his breast pocket. "I'll go with you." Before Anita could object he was throwing on his mothball-smelling winter coat and oiling his hair, so the strands fell neatly to the right.

Anita followed him down five flights of narrow stairs. Ashok pushed open the frosted glass of the building vestibule and let her outside.

"I don't know what they told you about me, how exactly they disappointed you," he said. "Maybe they said I was rich. Or young."

"I knew you were old."

"At least they didn't say rich."

Anita laughed. She and Ashok walked a short distance. Shapeless gray clouds blurred together with the steam of idle engines and food stalls.

Ashok opened the shop door. A bell chimed overhead. He picked up a red shopping basket from a stack. They filled it with eggplants, Bourbon biscuits, limes, and a packet of urad daal. At the register, Ashok took the envelope from his breast pocket. He tossed the cashier a twenty-dollar bill, whispering aloud as he clumsily counted the change. His slow math embarrassed Anita, as did his labored breathing while he carried the bags upstairs.

"You didn't need to do it alone, I would have helped," Anita said.

Ashok unlatched the door. "So long as my arms work, I'll use them."

He pushed past her to the fridge. Anita thought she smelled bergamot on his shirt.

~

ON SUNDAY MORNINGS, Anita's mother called and left messages on the landline. Anita let the rings accumulate, then listened to them in private after Ashok left to do the food shopping:

Dear Anita, are you cooking well? Good that I taught you the things you called useless. / Dear Anita, did you get your work visa? / Dear Anita, you are a bright girl at the top of your class. Get a job, make your money. Leave him if you want to. / You have two legs, use them.

One by one Anita erased the messages. She dialed her mother's number, but at the second ring her residual anger won out and she hung up. The longer they went without speaking the harder it became to imagine a conversation. Anita worried having one would make her too homesick to carry on here.

Anita hid the messages from Ashok. Watching him reading his newspapers, listening to him insult Pat Sajak, she could not picture leaving him, as her mother advised, though she suspected he would be unaffected by her departure, calmly reverting to a solitary life of noodles and eggs. The audacity of her mother to suggest it. Her mother who could never launch a business and now urged her to get a job.

As if reading her mind, Anita's mother left more voicemails. *Don't act so helpless, Anita. / You have options. You are not some castaway, some victim like you like to think, with nowhere to go.*

Anita shut off the machine. Where would she go?

~

WINTER FELL. Anita had more nightmares about assassins. She stuffed tea towels under the door so not even the courier's local papers could slip through. Who cared? The news was miserable or graphic; why be informed, Anita would rather keep her mind fresh and clean. She traded out crime segments on the local news for talk shows about obscene familial peril. *Jerry Springer. Maury.* How did a family remain a family after hitting each other on reality television?

At noon a fitness special aired on a free channel. Elderly folk sat in chairs and wielded tiny dumbbells. Anita followed along and substituted bottles of oil for weights. She cooked dinner for Ashok, lied that she'd eaten before he came home, and went to bed early.

Slowly Anita adapted to the claustrophobia of city living. It soothed her to think of her life layered between the building's cabbies and grad students, the old woman in 4C who played Celia Cruz on loudspeakers, the Bangladeshi divorcée downstairs with her many raucous sons.

Midwinter, that divorcée knocked on Anita's door and invited her on a walk.

"It's freezing," Anita said.

"You're depressed," the woman replied. "You never come outside. Get your coat. The cold is like a facial."

So Anita slipped on Ashok's jacket, embarrassed by the woman's simple kindness. To be watched with concern by a stranger, to be so plainly observed when her own husband made no such effort. Anita zipped up the jacket. She wouldn't have thought to keep the same careful eye on anyone.

That night Anita lay awake beside Ashok on the blue mattress. Downstairs, the divorcée's boys played Mario Kart. A character yahooed. *Here we go.*

Ashok turned onto his side. "It's late for games. Someone should tell them."

"I like the sound."

Ashok turned onto the other side.

"Their mother came around today. She asked me to go walking. I went. She said I never leave the house. Spying on me, she must be."

Ashok feigned sleep.

More Nintendo, followed by shrill laughter. Ashok snored.

Anita turned on the lamp. "You're already sleeping?"

"Okay, I'll be awake, only."

Anita thumbed the pilled quilt. "Why should everyone be happy but me?"

"Their mother is divorced. Are they happy, how can you know? It could be the cold, your sadness."

Anita fell back into the pillow. So he'd noticed. "It could be."

Tentatively Anita snaked her fingers around Ashok's wrist, more delicate than hers and covered in faint silver down. She moved her hand to his chest. The pace of his breathing didn't change. Anita wanted to change it. She burrowed her face into his neck, inhaling the faint sourness of his underarms, present even after his evening shower. A waste of water, he apologized, but he had to rinse out the smell of the lab. The gray hairs on his chest glistened in the dark. Her tears, Anita realized, and kissed his palm.

Ashok turned to his side. "Don't do what you don't want."

"Don't you want to?"

Within minutes he was snoring again.

~

ANITA TRIED LOVING him. She pretended she was a film actress in the pictures her mother loved and played a dutiful, soft-spoken wife. She looked forward to the weekends when Ashok was off from work and never complained when he spent the calling card minutes to ring his mother and sister for hours on end, dreadful women though they were. She cooked for his friends and their wives, bloody freeloaders who took the leftovers home in Tupperware and never thanked her.

Sunday morning, Anita carried the landline to the bathroom and played her mother's voicemails: *Dear Anita. I am so sorry to say it. The Pomeranian next door is dead. I found him under the love swing, where you used to sit. I thought he was asleep. / Dear Anita. Have you found work? Have you left your husband? / I spoke to the neighbor. The dog was sick, its fate was sealed / Your father misses you. He does not talk, but these things I can tell.*

Anita tried to call back. The line went flat; no minutes left. She felt a slow twisting in her chest. That little dog, waiting for her at the love swing. What loyalty. Trotted outside his own house to die in her lap, only to die abandoned. His small black lips, softer than the leather they resembled. Anita wished she could have died with him.

Anita called for water.

On the television, a Hindi music video countdown played Madhuri Dixit dancing in *Khal Nayak*.

Ashok lowered the volume and ran the tap. He opened the bathroom door with a steel cup. "Why are you crying?"

Anita didn't know him well enough to explain her little dog. "I'm dizzy, I haven't eaten," she lied. "There's a lunch buffet across the street. Can we go?"

"It's a vegetarian day," Ashok said. "That place is all meat, it would be a waste of money. There's plenty here."

"It's thirteen dollars each, that's nothing. I checked the Yellow Pages."

"Some people make less in two hours of work."

"I want to make an international call. I need minutes."

"Sure."

Anita watched as he rinsed out her cup. What would she say to her mother, who had never liked the dog? She had no job to report. "Never mind, the minutes are expensive."

FRIDAY

The Men of Willow Road

THE MEN OF WILLOW ROAD decided to throw a memorial for Matthew. Normally they organized nothing. On birthdays, funerals, baby showers, and tax days, they waited for enough time to elapse until the women succumbed and took over.

It was a belated effort with no body or ashes. The Edison funeral home had already airmailed them to Matthew's distant family in Kochi. A vengeful maidservant flushed a few grams down the toilet and drained the remainder down a stretch of holy river.

"The memorial is a performance, my husband's leading the planning," said Jyoti Kaushal. "He's a performer, sings so loud at bhajans."

"Is this the seventies?" Hema Rao waved a Hare Krishna pamphlet in the air. "Tell him to stop leaving these bloody things in my mailbox."

In addition to spearheading the service and managing a lucrative podiatry practice, Tejas was a feverish recruiter for his local International Society for Krishna Consciousness chapter. He slipped pamphlets inside the neighborhood mailboxes and was undeterred by the sight of them piled up in the women's recycling bins. The pamphlets advertised community bhajans in Atlantic City and Las Vegas. As part of his reverence for life, Tejas ate neither meat nor tubers and only (in)frequently beat his wife.

"He cares too much what other people think," said Sonia Ram, thirty-one, a fellow podiatrist at Tejas's practice. "Like that Mr. Pillai," Sonia said. She tapped an orange acrylic nail to the front page of the local newspaper: A SUICIDE, A SECRET DIVORCE, AND UPDATE: ASHES SHIPPED ABROAD.

TEJAS TOOK FRIDAY off and spent the morning on the phone, arguing with a local florist about the prices of calla lilies and carnations.

"It's this evening, I need them today," he told the florist.

"You do no housework," Jyoti accused, as she inspected the inseam of Nasreen's jeans. She took a fresh needle and a stale biscuit out of a Royal Dansk tin. "Yet you have time for this."

"He was like your own brother. If I was the one to die, what would he not do for me?"

Jyoti rolled a beedi. A winged queen ant crept across her turquoise lighter. If Tejas were to die, he had left her lavish funeral instructions to carry out, and instructions for a robust catering menu.

"I'm going to temple, I need to book the hall," Tejas said.

The door shut behind him. Jyoti devoured the bag of dried chickpeas coated in garlic shells that she hid in the back of the pantry; Tejas prohibited onions and garlic. She watched *Dateline*. An episode in the front door creaked. Jyoti heard Tejas rubbing his shoes on the doormat. "What's that smell?"

"Your body odor, sir," Jyoti replied.

"I stopped at Wawa. Those officers were there," Tejas said. "My god, can a man not kill himself in peace and dignity? Don't talk to them."

"I never talk," Jyoti said, and returned to her sewing. She felt a prickle across her neck, the winged ant reemerging. Jyoti crushed its thorax with her thumb. Yellow larvae squirted out.

JYOTI DROVE TO WAWA. "All the husbands can't stand you," she told the officers, who were leaving with coffees and customized hoagies. "They think of you as two walkie-talkied suits, trespassing through their properties, pissing on their shrubs."

"I'm under a microscope," spat Parth Rao, Hema's deadbeat husband, eavesdropping with a smoothie in hand. "This whole week, Hema has not shut up about your blasted visit."

Further men claimed they had woken up with sleep paralysis that week, motionless under the alleged weight of eyeballs. Eyes pressed down on them when they opened medical bills, when they knelt before the home mandirs—wooden Ikea fixtures stocked with tiny silver deities that only men could touch. After prayers the women scrubbed the deities' faces away. To the men it was a tragedy of scouring pads. To the women, it was a natural result of the same belligerent, on-your-hands-and-knees cleaning that could erase anything.

~

SPEAKING OF BELLIGERENCE: How could wives bear witness? What could they have seen, with their cartoonish sloe eyes, that the men had not seen better? Why was no one questioning them? The men pondered these questions as they brushed their teeth at night, in the pink bathrooms shared with witness-wives. Square mirrors hung above the sinks. The women squatted onto chamois toilets, sang soft schoolgirlish *fucks*, yanked the sanitary napkins off their underwear. Exhaust fans hummed, cutting through the stench of Listerine and rot.

"My *god*, old man, stop watching me," said Karina Dixit to her husband, Rajesh. She hiked up her underwear and flushed the toilet with her left foot.

"I said stop *watching*," she snapped. "Brush your stinking teeth."

ANITA IN QUEENS, CIRCA '90s

Death by QVC

Five months into her new life in Queens, and Anita had lost thirteen pounds. Her hair broke when she brushed it with Ashok's fine-tooth comb. She took the scissors he used to trim his nose hairs and sliced her long mane shoulder-length. Her bobbed reflection stared at her in the mirror, haggard and gaunt.

At dinner Anita watched Ashok chew lentils and rice with his mouth open. Her portion congealed in the center of her plate. Red pickle oil bled into her rice.

"Anita, please eat."

"I had a life before you, you know. I was the top of my class. Men appreciated me. Handsome men."

"Okay, so you've said."

"Women too."

"Okay."

"I'm depressed. Don't you notice how small I've become?"

Ashok glanced at her untouched food. "Yes. You've been wasting food."

"So frugal you are. Lentils again. Real men spend."

Ashok blew his nose into his dinner napkin. "Kill me off," he suggested. "What else do you want?"

"I want to work. I want to hang myself."

"Then work. I've never said not to. I'll help you do the paperwork."

"You mail-ordered a younger girl. You say it wasn't your choice, but you didn't say no. Lucky man, you are. But you don't appreciate."

Emboldened by his silence, Anita pressed on, happy to set the hat of her rage on a man as gentle as Ashok, who carried it inanimately as an actual coat rack. "I cried when my mother said I'd marry you. At least you'd have a house, she said. I thought a middle-aged man would be established. I come here, and it's smaller than the place I left."

She yanked at her mangalsutra. "I'm suffocating. This country is death by QVC."

"I didn't bring you to suffocate. I didn't bring you at all. You came on your own. It was your choice."

"I said no. My choice isn't mine."

"Listen to yourself. Are you not an adult?"

"Heartless man, you are."

Ashok studied his rice. His chair squeaked on the linoleum floor. Anita stared at her plate as he walked behind her seat. She felt his fingers, tacky from the rice, on the nape of her neck. For one thrilling second Anita thought he'd choke her, the veneer of the gentleman cracked. She waited for the vertiginous dark. Instead he hooked a finger under her chain and tugged. Gold and black beads splattered across the ground.

As quickly as Ashok made the mess, he swept it away. He gathered the beads in a drawer and set his dish in the sink, then ate the leftovers from Anita's. He washed both plates.

"Leave when you'd like," he said. "You'll get your papers, start somewhere new. Isn't that what your mother calls and tells you to do?"

~

BEFORE THE ARRANGEMENT, Ashok loved the woman in the apartment below. The divorcée with the Mario Kart sons who walked with Anita on frigid afternoons and kept an eye on her sadness. He'd wanted to marry her, but his family disapproved; the divorcée wasn't part of their community. They accused her of being opportunistic and cruel, conning a single and unfettered man into raising a deadbeat's mess. As penance for spoiling the match they promised to find Ashok a young bride. Ashok told them he didn't care what she looked like.

The divorcée revealed it all to Anita on their fifth walk. By then Anita looked forward to the outings. The divorcée made a meager salary as a court stenographer, but she was a spendthrift and stopped to buy snacks off the street. Pillowy bao buns with curried mustard greens inside. Egg yolk custards. Soft vanilla ice cream enrobed in hard red shells.

That walk she bought a cone for Anita, who refused.

"You're wasting away," the divorcée said.

They sat on a bench. The red coating tasted of plastic.

"I wanted to tell you something," the divorcée said. "Old history, of course."

The story nauseated Anita, though she didn't understand why.

"He didn't care what you looked like, then got so lucky," the divorcée said, laughing.

Anita thanked the woman for the ice cream and ran back to the studio, kicking away the tea towels sealing the threshold of the studio door. She slid her suitcase out of the bedroom closet. On top of her unpacked summer clothes sat the envelope with the lone photograph developed from the wedding. Anita slid it out. She and Ashok stood in profile, hands entwined and eyes averted, Ashok in his ivory turban and cartoonish eyeglasses, Anita unsmiling, her dour expression at odds with the bright rouge on her cheekbones, her gaze fixed on a private spot of carpet. Her uncle threw rice in the background.

That night Ashok reclined in his undershirt and flipped through a lab report.

"You wanted another woman," Anita accused. "I went walking with her today, she confirmed."

He turned a page. "Okay. Why be sentimental? You made it clear you have a history too."

Anita rummaged for the pack of cigarettes. The one item her father packed for her, along with a lighter. She lit one.

Ashok pinched his nose. "I didn't know you smoked."

"You know nothing about me."

"Okay. You know nothing about me either. You never ask."

Anita watched a roach crawl out of a ceiling crack. "Sorry, men are not very interesting."

Ashok didn't reply. Maybe he was right. Anita had become sentimental. Ashok rented this studio, owned their shit furniture, had a bank account. Having nothing in this country, she wanted to at least possess him.

"Sorry I'm your last resort."

"This is not some island, Anita. People are not resorts."

"This city is an island, look at a map."

"Who told you to expect paradise?"

Ashok went to bed. Anita watched a news segment about a bank robber and joined him. Ashok turned to his side. He hated the smell of smoke. The women in his family didn't smoke, the divorcée didn't smoke. The stench could be Anita's alone. Ashok would think of her with revulsion whenever he passed a smoker on the curb. And he would think of the curb smoker when Anita pressed against him, the way she did now, unbuttoning the front of her nightgown, guiding his hands underneath. *Please*, she murmured, almost like an apology.

THAT SPRING Anita got her work visa. She bought a MetroCard, rode the subway to a library in Flushing, and applied for software engineering jobs on a chunky monitor. Application after application she was turned down; the degree she'd worked tirelessly for mattered little here. She could go to school again and redo the degree, an HR rep suggested; but that would cost tuition and take years to complete. So she continued to accept Ashok's allowances for groceries and household necessities and spent them on cigarettes.

"I'm getting a die-vorce," Anita declared, ironing a burn hole into one of Ashok's white shirts. "As soon as I get a job, I'm gone."

"Of course." Ashok sipped his coffee. He had learned to skillfully drift away from Anita's rage. He cooked for himself at nights, and for the friends who visited him, as Anita smoked in the bathroom and played a "Choli Ke Peeche" cassette on repeat. Ashok and his guests laughed at the kitchen table, as if she wasn't there. Anita turned the volume up higher. After the guests left, Ashok took his dinner on the corner of the kitchen floor, as he had done in his mother's house, where there were so many loved ones around and only so many spaces at the table.

"I should get you a damn banana leaf," Anita prodded. "Eat, villager."

"You keep saying you're divorcing me," Ashok said. "I'm learning to eat alone."

ANITA MISSED TWO PERIODS. That she could be carrying didn't occur to her. Anyway she'd lost kilograms of depression weight, and many times in her life she'd been skinny and bloodless. How could she make another person, when there was so little of herself left? Then the smells, undeniable: she couldn't brew coffee without covering her nose. The meat stench from the diner across the street, once tempting, now landed her in front of the toilet, combing bile out of her hair.

On a Monday morning, after Ashok left for the lab, Anita headed downstairs and walked to a corner bodega. She picked up a test and a bag of Fritos from under a sleeping tabby.

Back at the studio she downed the chips and waited for the test results. Two pink lines appeared. Anita took a hand mirror from the medicine cabinet and retired to the bed. She sat with her knees apart and spread herself open before the mirror, as if this way she could see it herself, the horror of a child sticking.

What horrified Anita delighted Ashok. For the first time he looked at his wife with elation. He insisted she eat her meals and bought her strawberry Ensure *for the protein*. He took out a mortgage on a house in New Jersey. He didn't want city children. Public schooling was a lottery system, skewed, as most everything was, in favor of the rich. Now Anita could have her house, and Ashok could still ride to the city by train.

"New Jersey is dinky," Anita protested. The prospect sounded better than two people and an infant in one room, but she had no energy to uproot herself again.

"It's a good neighborhood. 'Diverse,' the realtor said," Ashok said. "There's an Indian family right next door. I spoke to them, the Dixits. They have one daughter. Riya, I think it was. Three years old. And the public school is blue ribbon."

"What good is another Indian to me, my god? And that's false marketing. I checked online. They lost the ribbon in the seventies."

"Oak Tree Road is close. Lots of markets. Maybe you'll like it."

"You always think I'm so simple," Anita snapped. "Go live in that house alone. Keep the child, take it grocery shopping."

Ashok smiled. Anita's reactionary bitterness amused him now. The day of the first scan he took off from work for the first time in Anita's memory. He brought her to the diner for the lunch buffet. Thirteen dollars a head not a problem anymore. Ashok ate three bowls of kheer and two chicken drumsticks. Anita nibbled a tomato slice and threw up in the bathroom. The Sharmas boarded a crowded 7 train to the doctor's office in Manhattan. Anita had no visible bump, so no Good Samaritan stood and offered her their seat. Ashok clutched the subway pole with one hand. With the other he steadied Anita. She refused to touch the dirty steel.

The subway doors hissed. A woman with a coif of white hair and a Ralph Lauren mink coat squeezed in behind Anita. A Pomeranian stuck its head out of the woman's leather handbag and panted, the tip of its pink tongue visible. Anita didn't notice herself reaching for the animal until the owner scolded her.

"You know, miss, you should really ask." The woman glared at Ashok. "Sir, please tell your daughter to ask."

FRIDAY

You're Cordially Invited

Flyers for the service went up around the township the hour before it took place. Tejas Kaushal hung several at the women's threading salon. Parth Rao pasted a stack to the glass walls inside Hema's Dunkin' and taped one over a sign for wake-up wraps. The posters featured Matthew's blurry LinkedIn profile picture, his signature bushy eyebrows scant and gray.

"My toner was low," Tejas Kaushal said.

"Ugly flowers, if you ask me," said Jyoti. She and her husband prompted in the his and hers mirrors of their teak bathroom. "I said, if you ask me."

"But no one did."

The husbands missed Matthew. Their grief was pukka grief. They remembered how he drove Rajesh Dixit to the hospital after his ulcer scare so the ambulance wouldn't rip him off. How he went ice-fishing with Parth Rao. How he, their favorite teetotaler, brought bottles of Jack to their houses; his arrival a convenient interruption to the three-course menu of fights that unfolded between the men and women all evening. Popular first courses included:

- *Am I your bloody servant, man, to wash your underwear all the time?*
- *Do I not work as many hours as you?*
- *Pick up your own damn son from tennis.*

These were followed by threats of repatriation:

- *I'm leaving the country*
- *I'm going back to India, goodbye*
- *I'm going back to my mother's house*

Then those threats hollowed out:
- *I have no mother anymore*
- *No mother's house anymore*

~

TEJAS SENT INVITATIONS TO Matthew's service over WhatsApp and distributed hard copies in the women's mailboxes at the end of his morning run. The envelopes were shimmery and pale blue, plucked from the new-baby-boy selection at Hallmark. Grandmothers reclined on front porch chairs and watched him, sun-spotted and miserable in pastel cotton dresses, tired from the daily care of their bratty, English-only grandchildren.

"For fuck's sake," said Usha Gohel. "My mother was outside, and Tejas put it in her mailbox instead of handing it to her directly. Civility is a dead dog."

"It's in a temple," Devika said, tearing her envelope open. "Matthew wouldn't have wanted religion there at all." (The men knew about Matthew's atheism and proceeded regardless, fearing that, when it was them dead, the women would hold their services in (1) unholy places, (2) unextraordinary places, such as a Target parking lot or a Wawa, or lastly (3) nowhere, no service at all.)

Icing a fresh cut on her cheek with a bag of frozen peas, Jyoti faxed the police department copies of the women's memorial agenda:

MATTHEW'S MEMORIAL SERVICE /
OUR HOURS OF UNAVAILABILITY
located @ the marble temple across from Sushi Sushi Sushi Sushi
12–2 pm: service (Small Hall, NOT Banquet Hall)
2–2:15 pm: break (anywhere)
2:15–3:00 pm: luncheon (rec center; solemn foods only—no sweets, liquor, or meat)

The department faxed a notice back to the women. The investigation into Matthew Pillai had been completed and closed. Thanks very much for their help.

THE UNHAPPY KIND! CIRCA '90s

Leila

THREE MONTHS AFTER the Sharmas moved to Willow Road, Anita gave birth to a baby girl. She called her Leila. It was an easy name.

"We would have set up a pooja, had her kick over rice when she came from the hospital," Karina Dixit said, "but we didn't know her well enough. When we tried, she was nasty and turned down any invitation she got."

"Worse than the white couple from before," Devika agreed. "Your own kind is always the worst kind, no?"

House 24 grew unrecognizable in the weeks after the birth. Weeds overtook the lot. The squash blossoms died. The once pruned garden resembled thrush inside a sick child's mouth. Ashok planted his own seeds, wilting mint and anemic nightshades.

Postpartum depression struck Anita with vigor. Birth thickened her nose and frame. Her hair grew matted from lack of care. She emerged from the house once a day to stroll Leila around the block, as the doctor instructed, and for her personal step count. The women spied her stretch-marked skin hanging in pouches over her jeans.

"She sent them to me to add elastic, then took them back midway, told me she could do a better job herself," Jyoti said.

∼

ANITA DIDN'T SEND her mother her updated New Jersey address or number. Just before the move Anita had called her to share her contact information. But they'd had an argument after Anita offered to send a check to fix her mother's broken fridge.

"Don't take your husband's money," Anita's mother said. She broke into a fit of coughs worse than her standard ones. "Your uncle offered to help."

"Don't ask the ogre for anything. Are you sick?"

"Yes, from wasting my lungs on you."

Fuming, Anita hung up. Somehow her mother found the Jersey landline anyway. The Sharmas received regular scratchy messages on the automated machine, punctuated by coughing fits.

Sunday mornings Ashok tended to the prayer cabinet. Anita sat the baby on her lap. She lit up a cigarette, smoked, and played the messages back on the machine on speaker.

That's your aaji, Anita told Leila. *A witch.*

Dear Anita, the messages began. For eleven weeks they collected. Though Anita wanted to check in on the cough, the mention of the uncle soured her. *Congratulations on the child. Weather is awful. / Dear Anita, still you have not forgiven me. / You will get lines in your face from all the anger that you hold. / Dear Anita, the neighbor ordered a pickle jar from me / Dear Anita, please forgive me / Dear Anita / Stubborn as shit / Dear Anita, you think you are too good for that man, too smart and too pretty. / Dear Anita, today the neighbor brought a new dog. I thought of how you loved the old one. / Dear Anita, think. would you be in America if not for me? Who would have married you here but a drunkard? Look at your father / Dear Anita, maybe yes, it's true what you told me, that even a loser can come to America / Dear Anita, you'll love him, because you will need him / Dear Anita, the cough is not as bad as it sounds / Dear Anita, how many months is your girl what are her measurements? I'm sewing a blouse / Dear Anita Dear Anita Dear.*

One Sunday morning, a new message appeared while Anita played the old ones back. A male voice announced that her mother had passed away from emphysema. Anita's feet numbed. She listened to the message again and her body followed suit. Anita smoked the remainder of her cigarette. Leila cooed in her arms. Ash fell on the baby's curls. She handed Leila to Ashok, went to bed, and spent the next seven days there.

"I didn't hug her when I left," she cried to Ashok, when he came with the baby. He found it awkward to comfort her; he reminded her Leila needed to feed. Anita fed her. She couldn't stop thinking of her mother's arms outstretched in the airport. The varicose veins on her skin. "I didn't hug her, Leila," she said. "I punished her."

∼

WEEKS LATER ANITA landed a software job; during her pregnancy she'd read software books and passed a certification course. She wore her best slacks to the interview, a pair from her college days, though zipping them over her postpartum belly was near impossible. The hiring manager, a mom of three, loved when Anita milked the difficulties of early motherhood—*so tiring, so rewarding*—and offered her a dismal salary that she was too afraid to negotiate.

Anita scanned the Yellow Pages for a daycare, overjoyed. Using a page from Ashok's checkbook she put down a deposit at a cheerful-looking center with a bluebird logo. The school called the landline to confirm details.

Ashok picked up midshave. His face dripped with foam.

"Hold on," he told Anita, who was plucking her eyebrows into thin arches in the upstairs bathroom. "You didn't tell me about any daycare. Is this necessary now?"

He followed Anita out of the bathroom to the ironing board she'd stationed outside. A deep-red shoulder-padded dress lay face down on the board. She'd knocked his shirts to the floor.

"Leila is still so small, not even weaned. Couldn't you wait a little longer? If you pay this daycare, plus taxes, net-net the salary makes no difference."

Anita ironed the dress. "Should I tell the manager to take the job back? Why don't you stay home? As it is you come back so late."

"It takes time from the city."

Anita waved the iron in the air. The box hissed. "I should iron myself! Straighten myself. I should disappear."

Ashok rubbed his temples. "Go, then. Disappear. What else? Should I beg you to stay? Fall at your feet?" He got on his knees. "I'll beg. Begging is what you want. Begging is what makes you happy."

"Get up. Act like a man."

The argument continued until a police officer knocked on the Sharmas' door. A neighbor had made a noise complaint. Was everything okay?

Anita and Ashok united to divert his scrutiny. It was nothing, sir (Ashok). The neighbors are bloody bitches (Anita).

For fifteen minutes the officer gave Anita a firm talk in her dressing gown. The complaint specifically mentioned a woman's voice.

Milk expressed through Anita's fabric. "Who made the complaint?"

The officer was not at liberty to say.

"I won't say anything, anyone has a right to lie. But for my information, who?"

The officer was not at liberty to say.

The shame of the visit cauterized the Sharmas' argument. Anita and Ashok stopped speaking to each other into the next morning. Ashok oiled and combed his hair for work and walked to the edge of Willow Road for the bus into Port Authority.

Anita strapped Leila into a highchair. She pureed rice and boiled spinach in the blender; she didn't trust the chemical Gerber jars Ashok bulk purchased. A *Judge Judy* marathon played on the television. Vandalism. Car repossession. Anita spooned the green paste into a jar and screwed the cap on tight.

Leila cried. Anita unstrapped her from her highchair and patted her back. *Shhh, breathe, shut up. Imagine, Leila, if police come again and take you from me?*

The baby grabbed the front of Anita's shirt to feed. Anita pressed two fingers firmly into her chest and pushed her away. It was gut instinct, a preservation of personal space. Leila's peppercorn eyes glazed over with tears. Anita opened her shirt. *Fine, fine. Eat.* This time Leila refused, her cries of demand now cries of fear. *Judge Judy* ended. *Maury* played next. The man onscreen was not the father.

It was a wet spring day. Anita threw on a cartoon dog show. Leila's tears stopped and she soon fell asleep. Anita strapped the toddler and the puree into the back of the stroller, enough food for two days. Earthworms shone on the sidewalk as Anita walked Leila to the Dixits' house, a note in the bottle compartment. *I need to clear my head.* Anita parked the stroller before the front steps. Gently she squeezed Leila's feet, which she'd dressed in soft sheep-patterned socks. She rang the doorbell and walked away.

The Happy Kind

THE DIXITS were good parents, people meant to be parents. Anita had observed them for some time. The man, Rajesh, was tall and hirsute and worked at an education consulting company in Princeton. He made decent money scrutinizing curriculums. The woman, Karina, looked too old to have such a young child. She lathered her graying braid with coconut oil, as Anita's mother used to. A former postal worker, Karina was now a housewife who painted and volunteered around the township. She took shifts at the library, the women's shelter, the animal shelter. She taught Hindi at the temple and helped children finger-paint religious scenes. The couple had one daughter, Riya, a pale three-year-old suffocated by frocks and lace socks.

Karina treated Riya delicately. If the girl so much as sneezed on a walk, Karina unzipped a fanny pack and spooned orange syrup into the child's mouth. The syrup was sweet; the girl pretended to sneeze for more. Karina never went out without Riya at her side or in her arms. To avoid small talk Anita waited until the two were out of sight before she took Leila on their doctor-mandated strolls.

A few weeks before Anita left her stroller at the Dixits' front door she'd run into them despite her best efforts. Riya sneezed and squealed at the stroller.

"She begs me for a sister," Karina said.

"Sweet," Anita said. "Well, I'll go, Leila needs a nap."

"Why don't you stay, already she's asleep, look," Karina said. "What a nice stage. I wish Riya could have a sister. Already I had her so late. I asked the doctor if it's why she keeps getting sick. Her immune system must be damaged, who knows."

Riya tugged at Karina's braid.

Anita feigned a smile. "Things turned out well, at least."

"Not so well, no. Riya was supposed to have a twin. The twin didn't make it."

Anita nodded solemnly. Why this stranger decided to overshare, she wasn't sure. Now the conversation had veered toward infant death. It would be rude to leave.

"We went abroad for the IVF, see," Karina continued. "Doctors here mint money out of your womb and don't care about your results. So I went. Multiples are common. Me, I get pregnant with twins—"

"Okay—"

"So I get pregnant with twins. First few weeks, all is fine. Then I'm bleeding. I get a scan. The doctor tells me one died. *Vanishing twin*, they call it." She snapped her fingers, as if relaying the events of a tense sports game. "Reabsorbed into the other, like that." She stroked Riya's head. "Drank so much saffron milk, at least this one came out fair."

"Sorry to hear," Anita said. Also: what a brilliant twin.

She looked at Riya, who was picking at the three different Band-Aids through her white stockings.

"Leila can be your sister," Anita said.

Riya stopped picking and looked up. "Really?"

"If you'd like."

Riya coughed into her hands and reached into the baby's stroller. She pressed a finger to Leila's cheek. *Wash your hands*, Anita wanted to command, but why cross Karina, who cooed encouragements at the beautiful child with cheeks bright and spotted with rosacea. Who had money to waste on saffron? Still Anita felt self-conscious of the dusty-looking child in her stroller, who was, much to her displeasure, awake and screaming.

Riya offered to push Leila's stroller for the remainder of the walk, with Karina's supervision. Anita couldn't say no to a child in such a ridiculous purple frock.

"You two take her, ring the bell when you're back. I'm going to rest."

"You come too," Karina said.

"My prolapse," Anita lied. "Things will fall out."

From her foyer window Anita watched the three of them go. What a happy baby Leila was, Karina reported, after they returned to drop her off. Anita thanked the Dixits and shut the door behind. Leila wailed.

~

LEILA WOULD BE better off with them, Anita reasoned, that spring day in the drizzle. As she hurried back to her house she heard the Dixits' door opening, Karina and Rajesh chattering over the stroller.

Back home, Anita packed a hanger and rope into a small black suitcase. In the end she was doing Leila a favor. The landline rang. Karina left a voicemail. *Anita, dear, I've just brought Leila inside, are you okay?* Anita erased the message. She packed her suitcase in the trunk of Ashok's car and strapped herself inside. The rain picked up. She'd drive to a Days Inn, the one next to the strip mall where she and Ashok bought baby supplies. The suites of soft white light faced the highway. Rooms rented for thirty dollars. Anita had pooled enough allowance. She would watch a Blockbuster cassette on the television, then maybe hang herself in the hotel bathroom. The options were endless. She turned the ignition on.

~

FORTY MINUTES LATER, Anita woke to the sound of Karina knocking on the car window.

"You left the garage door open," Karina said.

Anita rubbed her eyes and rolled the glass down. The garage smelled of exhaust.

"Come," Karina said. "The girls are inside. Rajesh is watching them."

The women walked through the wet grass to the Dixits' front door. Karina unlatched it. "Good thing you didn't leave her on some stranger's stoop. They would call the police on you."

"A neighbor already did, over noise." Anita pulled her blouse over her eyes and wiped them. "I'm sorry. I should go to jail. Someone should call."

Karina clicked her tongue. "Don't be such a martyr, ma. Usually no one here ever calls. But your screaming was excessive. Riya couldn't sleep. I had to."

So she was the neighbor, Anita thought, shaken. And what could she say about it now? Karina took her child in. She let Anita use her shower and set out a nightgown for her. She boiled tea and set out warm biscuits.

How lucky it was, Karina repeated, as she poured Anita a cup, that Anita hadn't left the girl on one of the few white neighbors' stoops, the block's American stragglers.

"They wouldn't have understood, child services would come knocking," Karina said. "Your own people understand."

Anita nodded. She drank her tea.

~

"I TELL YOU, in hindsight Karina or someone should have reported that shit," Devika Gill said. "Who did she think she is? Acting like domestic life is such a little life. Just because she had some degree. Just because she *works*."

"I thought about doing it," Usha Gohel agreed. "We thought Anita needed the tough love. But why? The child had Ashok. The child was not our business. Most of us had babies before. We had the blues before. We figured her sadness would pass, the way it did for us. Nobody did anything for us."

FRIDAY

A Communal Mourning

The Matthew memorial service was forgettable. Multiple women slept through it. Those who had complained about the presence of the officers now felt destabilized by their sudden absence. Tucked back in their liminal spaces, they gathered in the temple shoe rack and retrieved their chappals from the shabby oak cubbyholes.

Certain women took too long to identify their slippers. They pressed their hands into the smalls of each other's backs, the bare patches of skin that saree blouses (plain, funereal white) didn't cover, and pushed each other aside. *Excuse me, excuse me. Move, dear.*

"What a joke, this whole thing," whispered Devika, sliding into the foot-shaped sweat stains of her thong sandals. "Not even ashes to spread. Police don't care about a thing."

Aparna, late for a date from her matrimonial site (Nasreen insisted), shoved thick gold earring stems into her nearly closed lobes. "I heard they tried to send the ashes to his wife, and she said no. Even now she doesn't give one-two shits."

"Ex-wife," Karina Dixit corrected. She picked her split ends and sprinkled them onto a frothy spot of carpet.

"Ex, alive, dead," Aparna said. "He'd still want her to have them."

"To scatter in bed."

"To flush down the toilet."

"Like a goldfish."

"I'd rather a goldfish."

The women's whispers escalated into laughter. Soon the room was inconsolable. Fine lines of urine dripped down the inseams of various thighs, and somewhere that wetness turned back into tears. The women checked their reflections in the oblong mirrors running down the sides of the shoe rack. Black eyeliner strung out into tear tracks. Everyone adjusted herself. Some wiped the tracks away. Others considered the sympathetic double-takes they might get in public and left them alone.

Outside the men lined their minivans against the curb at the temple entrance and honked.

Tejas Kaushal
woman pls hurry up ✓✓
leave or I leave without u ✓✓

Other phones chimed with similar threats. The women clicked their tongues. Were they dogs, to be summoned this way? Anyway they filed out to the minivans in pairs. White dupattas fluttered in the breeze. The air was fresh and pleasant, except for the strange trees around the temple perimeter, whose flowers resembled white blood clots and reeked of tart semen. Everyone pressed her dupatta over her nose and mouth. The pairs split off into individual units. Everyone filed into her respective passenger seat, rolled her window up, and turned the radio on.

Tejas clamped his hand over the volume.

"Is now the time, woman?" he asked Jyoti, who'd been bobbing her head to the music. "A man has died."

The car passed Anita's house. The Sharmas' blue Chevrolet sat out front.

"I don't believe that girl," Tejas said. "So much money he gave them. Like a father to her, he was. Slander is how she repays him. A girl can say anything these days and be believed. Are you hearing me?"

Jyoti slid a pair of sunglasses on. "I heard you."

"If he was what she said, would people in the block have let him around their children? Wouldn't we all know?"

"You knew. We all knew."

"Thoo," Tejas spat. "If it's not my daughter, it's not my problem."

∼

IN THE CAR BEHIND THEM, Karina Dixit pulled into her own driveway and slammed the door shut. She changed out of her funeral clothes, showered, and washed the dishes that had been piling up for days. The officers' mugs still sat in the sink, white film on the unsipped coffee and Chapstick imprints on the ceramic rims. Karina dumped the liquid over a bowl of raw chicken bleeding in clingwrap. She filled a fresh mug with Black Label and dialed the precinct. *Another bloody tip for you,* Karina slurred. *Anita was Matthew's Jersey woman; she loved him first and best; when he touched her child she turned her cheek. Perhaps you should investigate that. The rest of us were just parentheticals.*

"It was debasing, embarrassing," Karina told Rajesh later. "So what if I told them? If not for Anita and her daughter, wouldn't we still have ours?"

THE HAPPY KIND, 2000s

A Communal Daughter

THE WOMEN invited Riya Dixit to their homes for sweets and let her watch soaps on television They loved her because she was tall, fair, and beautiful, a walking reminder of themselves as young girls. ("Liars—everyone here was short and ugly," said Hema Rao, as she mixed fish oil into her Dobermans' meat. "I've seen the photographs on their mantels.") As a girl, Riya attended classical dance lessons at the unofficial Bharatanatyam studio in Vritika Shetty's basement. She was poor in school but excelled in languages and flattery, chatting fluidly with the women in Hindi and mastering odds and ends of their respective dialects.

Leila tagged along glued to Riya's hip like a real blood sister. The proximity to charm did not make Leila charming. Mannerless, she addressed the women by their first names and not "Auntie." Because Anita and Ashok did not think to implement parental controls on the television, she watched *Jerry Springer* and asked the women inappropriate questions ("What is sex and do you do it?") and peered into the women's fridges without permission. *Devika, do you have any chocolate milk; Hema, do you have leftover cake, Mummy is intensely dieting.* She came to their houses groomed poorly; though she excelled in school she was behind in life tasks. For instance she couldn't consume a yogurt in a tube without spilling it down her front or open a packet of chips without assistance. Leila, too, watched the women's soaps, but without understanding, demanding frequent pauses and explanations of characters who supposedly killed themselves, then reemerged with surgically altered faces.

"Hema, why would a person murder themselves?" she asked one afternoon at Hema Rao's house, kicking her legs against the couch cushion.

"So they can come back a new person," Hema said.

"What if you're worse than the person before?"

"You're being rude," Riya said. Now eleven, she took pleasure in giving Leila corrections. "Hema Auntie is watching."

Leila didn't mind the corrections. She loved Riya. In the shadow of a beloved girl, she figured the women had no option but to love her too.

("I gave her the leftover cake," said Hema. "Then she got crumbs in the couch cushions. Told me, *this is gas station quality*.")

THERE WAS LESS love between the girls' mothers. Privately and in public, Karina voiced a growing and passive-aggressive disapproval of Anita. She could not move past the time the woman left her child, then a baby and not yet a rude girl, in the Dixits' front yard. *Postpartum blues, bullshit*, Karina told the women. *She assumed I had nothing better to do than raise a stranger's child. In the rain.*

The more Karina got to know Anita through the closeness of their girls, the more she soured on her. *Anita smokes, she stinks*, Karina gossiped at the market. *Anita unbuttons her top clasp when the good-looking contractor comes, I can see from the side window. She wears a horrible electric-pink Target bra. Anita never goes to temple. She stays out late after work. The gym, apparently. She drinks skim milk and feeds her daughter whole. I help her with childcare, save her money and she keeps saying, oh we must have you for tea, for dinner. Then, where is the invitation?*

BY THE TIME Leila was eight, Karina watched her almost every day after school. Anita worked long hours. Ashok commuted from the city and wasn't home till dark. He worked intensely, with his head down. He worked extra hours without fanfare or overtime pay. If another researcher took credit for Ashok's results, he did not raise a concern, preferring to avoid conflict of any kind. Anita complained that he tried too hard and apologized too much.

"This country is about networking and image," she told him one evening. She'd fetched Leila from the Dixits'; Ashok had mentioned the newest young man he was reporting to, an inexperienced researcher who nitpicked the grammar of his emails. "Nobody wants a sorry man."

Ashok changed into his kurta pajamas and prayed at the mandir. He slurped a coffee as Anita invented proverbs to soothe him. "Hard work is a conspiracy," she said, standing over the sink with a coffeepot and a steel bowl, sloshing the liquid back and forth to cool and froth it. "Man, you cannot climb up a ladder if your head is down. There is no top in sight. You will only see how far there is to fall." She slammed her palm down on the countertop.

In her cubicle, though, she put her head down too.

~

AFTER SCHOOL AT the Dixits', Leila passed time watching Riya nurture her Tamagotchi. *A waste of money*, Anita called the device. She tried to instill in Leila an aversion to frivolous purchases. The Dixits, Leila observed, seemed to have no such aversion. Anita often remarked that they could afford a house in a better township, but pinched pennies here instead. Riya had a closet of colorful new clothing; none of it from bargain stores, a wide array of computer game discs.

Riya's favorite was the Sims. Leila sat beside her as she checked the mood meters of the nuclear family she had created, a replica of her own.

"Can I play with them?" Leila asked.

"But they're so happy, you'll ruin them."

Around seven, Anita, sweaty in gym wear, knocked on the door.

"For whom is your mummy trying to look so good?" Karina asked Leila, as they made their way to the foyer.

"For herself."

"Me, I never do a thing for myself, I'm no narcissist. Do you know what that is, Leila?"

"No."

"A person who would eat her face if she could."

It disturbed Leila to think her mother could possess such a wicked trait, though she was sure Karina possessed it too. One afternoon, Leila went downstairs to get a juice from the Dixits' fridge. Karina stood at the door with a delivery person. A shawl Anita had ordered from a catalog arrived at the Dixits' home by mistake. It came wrapped in tissue and was made from pure navy pashmina, a rare splurge purchase. Leila had accompanied Anita to the mall the day she tried the sample fabric on. ("I never buy for myself. Just one thing," Anita said in the dressing room mirror. "It's a good fabric. I used to work in fabrics. One day you can wear it too.") Quietly Leila took her juice and watched as Karina brought the package into the powder room and wound the scarf around her neck. Karina's mouth parted at the sight of her own reflection, in pleasure or surprise, Leila couldn't tell.

~

RIYA DREW UP a system: Leila wasn't allowed to touch her perfect Sims family or any perfect computer-generated family, but she agreed to co-create a character, a man they named Fish. Fish lived alone, slept in a twin-size bed, and worked as an internet hacker. Leila played with him while Riya went downstairs for her hour-long math tutoring sessions. Unsupervised, Leila made Fish flirt with the computer-generated neighborhood women, from the good families Leila was forbidden to play with. Once she gave in to temptation and played as one of the computer-generated women. The Sim walked around in a spacious house in a red tube dress. Her hunger meter dipped low. Leila ordered her to make soup. Because the woman hadn't first read a book on cooking, she accidentally started a fire and died in it.

Riya came upstairs from her math class. "What did I miss?"

Panicked, Leila returned to Fish's house. To distract Riya from the murder she proposed they make Fish a prisoner, for fun. They locked him inside his simple house and deleted the exit doors, the dive board, the stairs to the pool.

Karina didn't approve of the game or of life sentences. *Tell me when you hear her coming up*, Riya told Leila. Leila shoved her for control of the mouse. *Give him to me.* Then both girls heard Karina's footsteps sounding up the stairs and shut the program down. They ran outside to the periwinkle swing set and tree house in the Dixits' backyard. Rajesh had assembled the tree house. There they play-acted scenarios Riya dreamed up and cast: Frumpy Mom (Leila) and Glamorous Daughter (Riya); Cheerleader (Riya) and Unpopular-Nerd-Who-Loved-Her (Leila).

"Hey nerd," Riya said.

"Hi."

"You're supposed to stutter."

"Your dialogue is boring," Leila said. "This time let me be the cheerleader, I'm tired of being on the side. I'm the one who's going to be a real actor."

"Since when?"

"Since I decided."

"But you can't act," Riya declared. "Look at this. I can cry on command. I can fake like I'm sick, and Mom calls off from school."

"I can fake cry, too."

"Okay, go."

"I need to prepare." Leila sat inside the sandbox at the base of the tree house. Pill bugs crawled around the wooden edges and clamped their silver bodies shut when you touched them. Leila closed her eyes and thought sad thoughts, like Anita dying on a treadmill at the gym, or a story she heard on the national news: In California, an eleven-year-old girl went missing while walking her dog. A man had abducted the girl and left the dog, who walked back to the owner's house without her, a black leash dragging behind him. The news aired a clip of the girl's mother crying. She cried so hard that some cries were inaudible. Those cries haunted Leila. But the memory had nothing to do with her. She was not affected enough to muster a tear.

"Okay, I can't cry. How do you do it?"

Riya stooped down to the sandbox, her ashy knees scabbed. "Just put a little sand in your eyes."

Leila did. She spent the next half hour rubbing them clean.

"You lied."

"You listened. And look! It worked." She swiped a finger under Leila's left eyelid. "Tears."

Karina called the girls inside for macaroni and sliced fruit. They ate, and Riya excused herself to finish homework on the computer while Leila sat in a pink-cushioned chair at the kitchen table and completed a worksheet on longform addition, from the practice math book Anita coerced her to do. Karina painted a still life of her rose shrub. After the math Leila excused herself and joined Riya at the desktop computer, worried she might discover she'd killed the Sim woman.

Riya wasn't playing Sims. She was chatting with an AOL bot. Leila heard the sparkling whoosh of a door shutting.

"Watch this," Riya said. "This is so funny. Watch."

> **RiyaBby221:** what is forty-five plus 9
> **SmarterChild:** fifty-four of course
> **RiyaBby221:** sex with me?
> **SmarterChild:** Talking about sex is a lot of fun, but let's move on

"That is funny," Leila agreed, although it seemed uninspired. She worried SmarterChild was a real person, logging the girls' coordinates and reporting their deviance to her mother.

~

"SEE HOW NICELY Leila studies, Riya," Karina said, as the girls worked at the kitchen table. "She's done with her homework and is still studying. Probably she'll go to Princeton, working so hard. And where will you be?"

Riya tore into a cucumber sandwich. "Online."

"So Leila," Karina said. "Your mummy is turning thirty this year?"

"Twenty-nine."

"Is that what she tells you? That's why she thinks she's too young to have tea with an old woman like me. Your father is even older than Rajesh, did you know? When you were in your mother's tummy, I thought she was his daughter. She was so fat then."

Leila never told Anita about Karina's sly insults, or what she'd witnessed with the scarf. She knew it would mean the end of the Dixits' house, where the rooms were quiet and orderly, and bowls of pink potpourri sat above the toilet bowl. Riya's parents had a love marriage, not an arranged one. It fascinated Leila to sit and watch them eating cake rusk and tea after a meal, doting upon each other with quiet affections. *Here is your napkin. Let me wash this.*

It was an easy parallel universe, a gentler existence where nobody threatened to die and/or repatriate, and in exchange for that peace, Leila didn't mind, as Riya did, that the Dixits were intensely religious, that Karina made them pray before they ate tricolored popsicles, or that she was oblivious to what they did on the computer but monitored the shows they watched with stringent parental controls. No *Maury* allowed.

~

ON WEDNESDAYS Karina picked up an afternoon shift at the art supply store, leaving the girls alone for the first hour of after-school care. One day she arrived later than usual.

"My tire is punctured," she told the girls, ushering them into the car. Slowly she drove them to the gas station on her near-flat. It was a warm but overcast day. Karina spoke to an attendant. The girls hung back by the diesel pumps. The oil change man approached from the back of the garage in a grease-stained tank top. He eyed Riya's Limited Too shorts.

"It's a good day, girls. Finally warm."

"Very gray," Leila replied.

"Don't talk to him," Riya whispered.

"Why not?"

"He'll kill us and eat the parts. Don't you watch the news?"

The oil man produced a bag of clementines from a shelf. He spat out the tobacco in his cheek, peeled the fruit, and ate half of the segments. "Want some, girls? Vitamin C."

"No thanks," Riya said.

The oil change man dropped the peels onto the garage floor. "You girls make me sad. You remind me of my daughter." He smiled. "I haven't seen her in years. I have a photograph in the back. Want to see?"

"No thanks." Riya nudged Leila's shoulder. "Pervert."

The man must have heard her, Leila thought, because his eyes seemed to water, and the proud smile he wore when he said the word *daughter* cracked.

"I'll go with you," Leila said. How unfair it was for Riya to see this man as a bad man, this man with no daughter, who ate such tiny fruit. Leila followed him to the back of the garage, determined to make him smile again.

The man's workstation was dark. A fold-up desk splattered with fuel stains sat in the center of a concrete floor. A netted bag of clementines sat on a handmade wooden shelf, next to a picture of a gap-toothed girl with looped black pigtails.

"See her?"

"Pretty," Leila said.

"Your sister looks like her, no? I wish she'd come and see."

"She's not my sister, and they don't look alike," Leila said, annoyed. "I'm the one who came."

"You don't see the resemblance because you're tense." He pressed his fingers against her forehead and pushed her furrowed brows apart. "See it now?"

"No."

The oil man peeled another citrus. The scent purified the air as he swallowed one half whole. Clear juice dripped down his bottom lip. He held out the other half to Leila.

She took it and ate a segment. The door slammed open. Leila felt Karina's fingers on her earlobe. She dropped her clementine on the dirty floor.

"Come, don't go anywhere alone," Karina scolded, and shot the oil man a look like he was a shit stain on a thong.

Leila's face burned. Karina dragged her back to the car. Riya sat in the front, holding a vanilla custard.

Back at the Dixits' house Leila excused herself to the bathroom, too ashamed to face either of them, and washed the oil from her camisole. The stain would not come out. Downstairs she heard Karina and Riya whispering.

"If anyone lays a hand on you, Beti," Karina said, "one hand—you tell me immediately. Don't go off with random men—"

"*I* didn't go, Mummy. Leila did."

"Oh, come. It's you he wanted. What would anyone want with her? Her face is flat."

∽

BACK AT THE SHARMAS', Leila scrutinized her face in her parents' mirror. Anita stood beside her, tweezing her eyebrows.

"Mummy, what does it mean to have a flat face?"

"It means nothing about it is striking," Anita replied. "Who told you that? Give them good."

Leila dragged Ashok's fine-tooth comb over her nose and cheeks. The more she inspected her features the more correct Karina seemed; that Anita suspected someone accused her of flatness only acted as further confirmation. Tearful, Leila retired to the desktop computer and opened her Neopets account. Her animals were starving. She closed out and opened AOL. Riya was online, likely harassing a robot. Leila floated her cursor over the girl's username. She decided to tell a little heinous lie, one that would make them sorry for how rudely they'd spoken about her.

> **LeilaBby221:** Hey. Remember that guy at the gas station
> **Riya2000s:** yeah.
> **LeilaBby221:** u were right. he took his pants off in front of me.
> **Riya2000s:** are you serious?
> **Riya2000s:** ??

Leila thought of the man's daughter in the photograph.

> **LeilaBby221:** no sorry he didn't show me I thought he was going to. Like I thought he was about to
> **Riya2000s:** wow in the future maybe make that distinction

∽

THE FOLLOWING WEEKEND, a distant relation of Riya's died of renal failure. Karina and Rajesh drove up to Albany for the funeral and left Riya with the Sharmas. Though Riya rarely came over, she liked the house, because it was ruleless and (mostly) godless.

Ashok was working that weekend. Anita made lunch for the girls and holed up in her bedroom with a cigarette and a large Russian novel.

The Sharmas' television had no parental controls. Leila and Riya watched reruns of daytime talk shows and reality television without interruption. They watched an episode about a hoarding addiction, then a foot fetish. Halfway through the foot fetish, Riya stood up and got a Cosmic brownie from the pantry. She picked off the rainbow chips and returned to the couch, pushing aside two stuffed Dalmatians in the middle of the cushions.

"You should get a real dog. Or you'll become a hoarder too."

"Mom says Indians don't keep real dogs," Leila said.

"That's a lie. Hema Auntie just got real dogs. Doberman puppies. Hattie and Baloo. She invited me over to see them. Did she invite you?"

"Yes, I haven't gone yet," Leila lied. "Stop getting crumbs on them."

Riya rubbed her fingers on the plastic couch covers. "When will your family take these off?"

"Dad leaves them on in case."

"In case of what?"

"He wants to move back to India. So in case."

"No one ever goes back, unless they were super rich there, with nannies and drivers and cooks," Riya said. "And these are too ugly to return."

"We're rich there," Leila lied.

"Oh yeah? What does your family do?"

"They're actors."

"In what?"

"You wouldn't know. Obscure soaps."

Riya laughed and grabbed the remote. She flipped past PBS, Sandra Lee mixing cocktails, and one of the Hindi soaps that Ashok watched when he was alone. If Anita or Leila walked into the room, he clicked his tongue and shut off the television.

Riya lingered on the channel. Onscreen, a woman with heavily lined black eyes tripped and fell into a suitcase. The villain, equally beautiful, came up from behind and threw the suitcase into a luxury pool and laughed as it sank into the chlorine.

Riya translated for Leila: "The girls are twins, but they don't know they're related. She drowned *her* cause *she* went after *her* fiancé."

"The twin in the water is dead?" Leila asked.

Riya tossed Leila's the remote. "How should I know? Besides, the show is about their brother. The twins are subplots."

"Do you miss your twin?"

"No. If she was born, I'd have to split an allowance."

"Maybe she's still in you. Maybe she'll come out one day."

Riya changed the channel, surfing past *My Super Sweet Sixteen* and *The Nanny* reruns. She landed on *Jerry Springer*, a show the girls mutually loved. The formula felt illicit from the outset, beginning with a domestic dispute and ending with two or more people beating each other onstage: the mistress and the main chick, the incestuous brother and sister, a man in love with his horse, a man distraught that his wife moonlighted as a human buffet.

That day's episode was unlike the others. It was about a happy marriage with fatuous problems. A dowdy-looking teacher feared she wasn't sexy enough for her husband. He was a good man, she wanted to reward him. Production wheeled out a hot tub. A stripper dressed as a nurse shivered inside the water. The teacher ushered her husband to get inside fully clothed and asked the stripper to give her husband a lap dance. The stripper moved her hips in tentative circles, careful to make as little contact with the man as possible. Leila noticed a trance-like look falling over Riya's features; her mouth was open the way Karina's had been in the mirror, in pleasure or surprise. Riya grabbed the two dog plushies from the couch.

"I told you, don't touch those."

"I'm just borrowing them."

Riya disappeared to the bathroom and returned with the animals inside her shirt, lumpy dog-shaped breasts. She pushed Leila onto the couch. The plastic covers squeaked.

"Get off."

"For one second, pretend you like it. Like I'm the stripper and you're the guy."

"You always take the good roles."

Riya rammed her mouth against Leila's and pushed her tongue past her gritted teeth. The TV cut to a drug commercial. Actors played happy diabetics who'd left their symptoms behind and now pranced through flower fields. *Side effects may lead to death.* Riya circled her bony hips into Leila. Her face twisted into private joy. Leila didn't want to feel any, but she did a little. Acknowledging that goodness made her want to die.

The girls didn't hear Anita coming down the stairs or opening the fridge door for the mineral water she took with her afternoon cigarette. Riya sprang from the couch. The stuffed dogs fell to the carpet. Leila observed their beaded eyes and stitched-on smiles. At night she pretended they were alive and under her care.

"Ew, Leila," Riya cried. "Why would you do that to me?"

Anita didn't say a word to either girl. She finished a cigarette, took a plastic bag of prawns from the fridge, and deveined them at the table. The girls joined her without being asked. Together they pried out the dark lines of waste and collected them in a silver cup.

"This is penance, they look like roaches," Leila said.

The Dixits' car rumbled outside. Riya washed her hands, slid on her purple Mary Janes, and left. " Bye, Auntie."

After she was gone Anita pinched Leila's ears. Leila screamed.

"I hardly applied pressure, don't fake it, , actress," Anita said.

"I'm not."

Anita called Ashok. Leila listened from the upstairs landline.

"I want to leave, Ashok. This is a sick country."

Ashok sounded tired. "Anita, these are children. You can't settle this on your own?"

"Your daughter is a sick girl—"

"Okay. She's eight—"

"It is from you that she gets it."

"Okay. It is from me. Sorry, Anita."

"Fuck off with sorry."

"Sorry."

Anita hung up. Leila heard her footsteps plodding up the stairs. She swung Leila's door open and threw the offending Dalmatians onto the carpet.

"Throw these away, I don't want to see them again."

"They're mine."

Leila started to cry. Anita sat at the edge of the bed. She extracted the pills of lint on her tweed skirt and set the fallen dogs on Leila's duvet. "Okay, okay. If you cry like this, so loud, the neighbors will think you're an idiot. Come, let's go to dinner."

She drove Leila to the Burger King drive-thru. It was twilight. Leila sensed her mother's restlessness behind the wheel as they zipped past the township water tower, the miles of electrical wire smudged with crows.

"You're past the speed limit, Mummy."

"Hardly."

Sirens sounded in the distance. Anita pressed her foot down on the gas.

The sirens grew louder. "What idiot are they following, Leila?" Anita asked, but she noticed the cop cars in in her rearview mirror and pulled over. Anita's teeth chattered with nerves. A policeman shone a flashlight into her face, then Leila's.

Anita fished for her license. "Officer, please, I've never gotten a ticket, I never speed. My daughter is very sick. I was rushing her to the hospital."

On cue Leila clutched her gut and moaned. The officer rolled his eyes, took a pen out of his breast pocket, and handed Anita a ticket. She rolled up her window and merged back onto the highway. Dido played on the soft rock station.

"I'm sorry," Leila said. "Are we still going to Burger King?"

"I've just been fined, and you ask me about Burger King."

"I didn't do anything. Riya lied. I know you don't believe me."

"I believe."

"You're mad."

"Yes. Because of you I got this damn ticket. There was food in the house. Always you want to waste money."

"Burger King has a two for six dollars deal right now," Leila said, eyes welling with fresh tears. "You're just mad because we're girls. She made me be the man."

"I don't care if you are girls and girls, boys and girls, girls and boys. Your face, my foot. Is it you who started this stinking game?"

"No."

"Did you want to play it?"

"No."

The sky was dark now.

"I'm mad you let her do it," Anita said. "You chose it."

"I didn't choose it." Though the incident hadn't been wholly unpleasant, Leila shuddered as if it had been. "It just happened to me." She tested out another lie. "I was scared."

"Scared, my foot. You accepted, Leila. You have a mouth, no? Bloody use it."

～

THE NEXT MORNING the mothers disagreed which girl was the liar. Karina stood at the Sharmas' door in a muumuu stained with toothpaste, Riya's twiggy arm linked in hers.

"Anita, in my house, the girls don't even watch television. From where would Riya pick up such things? Hema told me Leila asked her about filth the other day."

"*Mummy.*" Riya pulled the lace on Karina's sleeve. "Can we not?"

Anita fished a cigarette out of her bra. "Maybe we need a new arrangement."

"Nonsense, Anita," Karina said. "I'm happy to take care."

"No need."

"Don't be dramatic. I have come to talk this over, civil." Karina smiled warmly at Leila, who hovered behind Anita. "Why don't you apologize, Beti?"

"Her, apologize?" Anita blew smoke. "From now on, I'll take off from work to watch Leila. Maybe what it is, is that Riya's too mature—"

"Anita, you're oversensitive. I've watched the girls more than you have. Leila has no sense. She followed some old man to the backroom of a gas station. I had to get her, who knows what would happen otherwise? She wants attention, she must be picking these ideas up from somewhere."

Anita's nostrils flared. "From me?"

"What will the neighbors think if they hear you screaming like this, unhinged?"

The threat of gossip swarmed the air between them fruit flies circling rot. Anita sucked her teeth and looked at Riya, who wouldn't meet her gaze. Between the two, which girl would be the guilty party in the women's eyes? And so Anita apologized. *The Incident with the Girls* got settled and buried, as if it had never happened to begin with. But Anita never sent Leila to the Dixits' house again.

"Forget that girl, that day," Anita told Leila, after the Dixits left.

"How do you forget?"

"Just decide! Wake up and think, I have forgotten. Easy."

MATTHEW COMES TO WILLOW ROAD, CIRCA '00s

The Sharmas Alone

After the rift the women noticed the Sharmas isolate themselves. Soon it felt as if they were no longer neighbors at all, as if they had moved to another development, even another state. No one took walks around the pavement in the mornings for her step count. Anita kept Leila out of sight. She never brought her to the occasional functions the women still invited her to, birthdays and house poojas, the market or the Gap.

"The girl grew fast, her body matured too soon," said Devika Gill. "Hormone-laced milk. I read an article about it."

By nine Leila began menstruating. Anita discovered the bloodstain on her bathing suit while Leila showered after a beach day. Distraught, Anita chalked the early puberty down to a fluke. She showed Leila how to stick a pad to her underwear but couldn't bring herself to explain the source of the bleeding. *I'll tell you later, when it comes for real.* Leila struggled to keep the large pads in place, and though Anita instructed her to change them every few hours she forgot or was too lazy.

"Walked around the public school with a red stain on the seat of her jeans," said Vritika Shetty, whose lover worked as a teaching aide at the school. "Stained every place she sat."

Despite her poor hygiene, Leila continued to excel in school. Anita nurtured her talents with zeal.

"All these damn women," Anita told her cheerfully. "Someday you can be a doctor and look down on them."

"I want to be an actor. I can cry on command."

"Okay, still this nonsense. An actor. Don't you want to eat?"

By twelve, Leila started interviewing at several private schools. She took prep classes for entrance exams and attempted tennis as an extracurricular at her mother's insistence. Leila and Ashok stood on opposite sides of the driveway and practiced thwacking a tennis ball back and forth. Because Ashok was self-taught and never bothered with the real rules he applauded Leila's mistakes. He let her strike even after the ball bounced. His pant legs clung to his shins as he played.

"Toothpick legs," said Usha Gohel.

Students of color appeared on the pamphlets of the private schools Leila toured, cradling violins and laughing in labs. Leila rarely saw evidence of their existence in person. Finally a school offered her a partial scholarship, a Catholic girls' school in a richer township. The Sharmas worked and saved to pay the difference. The private school bus didn't stop at Willow Road, so they agreed to chauffeur her, like a big shot.

On her first day, Leila watched from the window of her father's car as the women's children filed onto the school bus. Manu Gill and Arvind Gohel played soccer with a wad of crumpled paper. Ashok's car was old, with windows you had to crank open and no radio. In lieu of music he sang old-timey movie songs, loudly and off key. Though nobody could hear him, Leila grew hot with embarrassment. A cystic pimple throbbed on her chin.

"You can't sing like that when we get there," Leila said. She looked out the window at the Cash & Carry.

Ashok continued singing.

Leila cranked the window open. The township smelled dead and ripe.

"I hate that song. I hate this dinky place."

Ashok stopped singing. "This is home."

An Unofficial Brother

Ashok got a job at a drug company in north Jersey that manufactured rash creams and foot insoles. The pay was better. It would help with tuition.

"It was there that he and Matthew became office friends," Hema Rao recalled. "Met in a breakroom."

Matthew worked as a bigwig on the company's marketing side. Ashok was hired in the research and testing department. Dull work, but at least he wouldn't have to commute into the city anymore. *About time you spent time with us*, Anita assured him. *Find a place that values you, be visible.* Even at the drug company he worked downstairs in a lab. *Like the animals you test*, Anita scolded. *Hidden.*

"Anita could never ruffle him. He was a quiet, thoughtful man," Devika remembered. "Or maybe it was indifference."

Before school, Leila chewed a green apple for her breakfast and watched her father do his hair in her parents' mirror. Hair he was not indifferent about. Each year the bald spot on his scalp doubled in size. Ashok combed over the patch and kept the thinning curls in place with a daub of sandalwood oil.

"Why bother?" Leila asked, biting into her apple core. "By the end of the day, you can see the bald spot again."

"Yes." Ashok considered his reflection and laughed. "Yes, you're right." He set the comb down but continued the practice each morning, a grooming habit leftover from life as a younger man, when he had so much hair it had to be tamed and divided.

∼

"WHO KNOWS WHAT Ashok and Matthew talked about, but at least Ashok was talking to somebody," said Devika Gill. The women pitied Ashok, firmly of the belief that Anita had driven away his New York friends with her flashy displeasures and hatred of outsiders.

Matthew had a mouth like a chameleon. What you loved, he loved too, and with greater intensity. If Ashok heated a Tupperware of idli and sambar in the office microwave, Matthew told him how much he missed good southern fare. If Ashok mentioned the home of his youth, with its outdoor staircase and prowling stray cats, Matthew turned nostalgic, sharing memories of a childhood stint at a grandparent's coffee plantation. Later, when he befriended Anita, who hated past lives and any talk of them, Matthew claimed he could hardly remember *that country*. That he was glad to leave it.

It was an unlikely friendship, but loneliness made brothers out of the wrong men. Ashok in the trenches of research, doing more than what was asked of him for no reward, and the smooth-talking Matthew, who had worked up the business ladder by gossiping and talking loudly and assuredly about drugs he knew little about. Matthew had an admin, a bespectacled older woman who baked him diabetic-friendly biscuits. Peers invited him to summer weekend gatherings out on Long Island. His office window overlooked a parking lot and some semen-smelling trees, but it was an office nonetheless.

Sasha

THAT NOVEMBER, over noon coffee in the breakroom, Matthew mentioned his wife was going on a business trip to Europe. He had no holiday plans except to feed the cats. Ashok extended an invitation to Willow Road, to a small gathering with his wife and daughter.

News of a guest annoyed Anita. "Another rich, freeloading bachelor?"

"I'll revoke the invitation," Ashok said, as he reclined on the couch and watched a soap. Leila watched beside him. Onscreen, two enemy brothers reunited after a long separation and a bout of amnesia. She and Ashok both loved the melodrama, the special effects that resembled clumsy PowerPoint effects. An image of the hero's face circled in from the left, the antihero's from the right. Both images shattered, like sugar candy.

"Does Matthew have kids?" Leila asked.

"None," said Ashok.

"But he's English. The English ruined the earth," Anita said.

Leila sank back into the sofa, disappointed. Guests hardly visited, and she liked when they had children. Riya was now fifteen, and ever since Leila started at private school they spoke less and less. On Facebook Riya appeared in photographs with throngs of friends from the township; from Leila's bedroom window, she sometimes saw Riya entering and exiting cars with bags of Taco Bell and girls and boys she didn't recognize. Leila missed her, but more so wished she was the one orbited by admirers. She spent her private school days talking to no one; at home she played Sims to keep herself company. She built a woman named Sasha, with chunky yellow highlights and a tight lavender dress, and made things happen in Sasha's life the way she wished things would happen in hers. There was a cheat-code for money, so Sasha had plenty of funds. Sasha worked as an actress and lived in a large house with no neighbors. The house had a heart-shaped headboard and a garden with a fountain out back. Sasha had seven boyfriends and five dogs. Each time she acquired a new boyfriend Leila got her a new dog. No mother policed Sasha.

Even so, Leila could never keep Sasha's mood meters up. She studied Maslow's hierarchy of needs on Wikipedia; but Sasha's basic meters dipped low if Leila so much as hovered a cursor over her.

Sasha fell into a depression. Pizza boxes stacked high on her kitchen floor. Her bladder meter rose. Leila ordered her to go to the bathroom and Sasha seemed to malfunction, throwing a fit in front of the pizza boxes. She pissed on the bathroom tiles before she made it to the toilet.

As punishment for the depression, the Grim Reaper arrived to claim a life. Leila saw the scythe in the corner of her screen. She hoped the Reaper had come for Sasha or any one of her boyfriends. The boyfriends survived. The Reaper wanted one of the dogs. Leila had Sasha play rock-paper-scissors for the life of the animal. Sasha lost to the computer. Leila built a shrine for the dog with cheat-code money. He had spotted, pixelated fur, and Leila cried real tears for him, the poor dog Sasha had neglected.

This is why I've said no dog, when death comes what will you do, Anita consoled Leila, stroking her hair. *I'll get you Bourbons from the market.* At the Cash & Carry Anita ran into Devika Gill, who told her she would never buy that game for Manu, the deviant one Leila cried over.

Anita got home and promptly snapped the disc in two. "That smug bitch, Devika."

That was how Leila lost Sasha, her only friend. "I didn't know they could have sex," Leila pleaded. "I swear. Like, that's gross."

"You're lying."

"I'm not."

Of course Leila was lying. She liked making Sasha have sex, first with her collection of boyfriends, but then with anyone who would: the pizza men, the burglars, the Grim Reaper.

~

IF MATTHEW HAD no child for her to befriend, then at least Leila hoped that he and his wife would befriend her parents, and particularly her mother, who desperately needed one. It seemed to her that Anita had no connections, nor any desire to forge them, existing in a private void of her rage and *Friends* reruns. She liked to make comments about which female lead was thinnest or prettiest. Most of all she liked the sitcom laugh tracks and laughed along with them, then remarked forlornly that she had no one to laugh with in her real life. Each time Anita neared the series' end, when characters married and dispersed to the suburbs, she rewound to the beginning. That the neighborhood was full of women to connect with was immaterial to Anita, who could invent new reasons for her self-seclusion at the drop of a hat:

"Rich people are beggars," Anita told Leila. This was one of her reasons. "All the women in this block have more money than us, Leila. Karina and Rajesh just spoiled their daughter with a new Prius. And that stinking Jyoti. She doesn't need to tailor a thing: Tejas is a podiatrist, how much do you think a podiatrist makes, because I can guarantee he makes more than the figure in your mind; just the other day he minted thousands off my ingrown toenail. And they all save by going to public school. Who else is working to send their children to private school, as I do?"

Anita prided herself on being unlike the women. Whereas they were short, with long, graying black braids, Anita stood tall and slinky, a figure she accentuated with kitten heels and cropped hair. Though several of the women had college degrees, Anita considered herself the brightest. All the women were depressed, but Anita believed her depression was somehow deeper and more unique.

The Woman of the House

THE DAY OF MATTHEW'S VISIT, Leila slipped into a gray cotton dress and black tights reserved for rare instances of company. Anita called the outfit *pajama-looking*.

"I don't have better dresses," Leila said. "We're so cheap."

"Kill me off," Anita replied.

In the bathroom Leila jammed a Bump-It in her hair. She had begged Ashok for one after seeing the infomercial on television. He found one on the junk shelf of a pharmacy. She scanned her face for blemishes, frustrated by the enduring flatness of her features, which not even her new hairstyle seemed to improve. Half an hour before Matthew's arrival Leila sat on the bottom step of the staircase and pulled her split ends apart, an inexplicable excitement rumbling through her lower stomach. It was likely this guest would be like the other uncles who occasionally graced this house, with their open-mouth chewing and burping and hem-hawing with Ashok. But unlike the others, Matthew was rich. Leila hoped that that meant he was interesting.

～

THREE POTS bubbled on the stovetop. Anita tended a fourth.

"You think you're paying back some favor, inviting strangers, but I'm the one who pays," she told Ashok. "See how I slave here. No god is doing me any fucking favor." The fumes turned her face pink.

Dressed in his good slacks, Ashok slapped the front of his thighs. No one could punish him if first he punished himself. "I'll die," he offered, brightly. "That will make you feel better?"

Anita considered it. "I'll die first. Go and watch. I will die young like my mother, only." She turned the burners down, content with this blow.

The bell rang at half past, and a man appeared in the Sharmas' doorway, tall and fat, with a large potbelly and a shag of salt-and-pepper hair that obscured his bushy eyebrows. Behind him the sky was white with flurries. Matthew removed his tinted spectacles and used the sleeve of his finely tailored coat to clean the snow that had collected in the frames.

"I was walking the dogs and saw him hand Anita a bouquet of roses from a shopping bag," Hema Rao said.

The flowers, Matthew explained, had bruised on the journey south from New York. Leila watched from the staircase, intrigued. It was a gesture no man, Ashok especially, ever had the foresight to do for her mother.

"For the woman of the house," Matthew said, in an accent less English than Leila had anticipated.

Leila stood and offered him her hand. "Hello."

"O-ho," Matthew said, but did not take it. "I'm sorry—the *women* of the house."

Anita said *no no* and laughed, because Leila was thirteen.

At dinner Matthew drank seven cans of Diet Coke and covered his glass when Anita, who took pride in her fitness, tried pouring him a glass of water.

"Ach, there's no difference, Anita. Both are zero calories. It's all a fitness conspiracy." He patted the bulge of his lower stomach. "As you can see, folks, I am in great shape."

Anita held back a tight smile. "I see."

Matthew rapped a knuckle on his unused glass. "Lovely glassware, by the way."

"Of course they are, I picked them."

Leila turned away, embarrassed by Anita's cruelty, her niche vanities. Matthew winked at her across the table, as if sensing it. "I apologize, I should have brought you wine, but I was afraid the snow would pick up and I'd get stuck somewhere. For next time, tell me, what do you like?"

"Nothing, I hardly drink," Anita said, shaking her head nervously. "Ashok is teetotal."

"Louise will convert him next time. That woman loves her Scotch. Don't tell her I came empty-handed. She'll kill me. She's got those equestrian arms."

Leila sat with her hands on her lap, de-petaling a rose she'd stolen from the floral arrangement. She'd never heard a man speak so fondly about his wife. Matthew hardly shared anything about himself, and yet she felt she had learned everything there was to know about Louise: she was afraid of small holes, rode horseback extensively, and also worked in marketing at a rival drug company in the city. At her insistence, Matthew had worn a kilt to their wedding; when his relatives in India got postcards of the event, his aunt spread rumors that her nephew cross-dressed—at this Ashok laughed. Fifteen years in the States and Louise maintained a Scottish lilt in her voice, Matthew explained, just as he'd kept up his British one.

"Do you hear it?" he asked the table.

"Yeah, it's strong," Leila lied.

"Sure, sure," Anita followed suit. "So. Fifteen years married, no kids?"

The question didn't offend Matthew. "I wanted them, I did," he explained, a pinch of sorrow permeating his voice. "But Louise has migraines. Chronic pain like you've never experienced. She's completely incapacitated for days. If she got pregnant, she couldn't take her medication. It wasn't worth it for me to see her in so much distress."

"Nice of you," Anita nodded, though she seemed unconvinced. "Adoption?"

Ashok tried changing the subject. "Anita, is the heat on?"

"I should have adopted, yes," said Matthew. "Now I'm too old."

The rest of the evening Matthew spoke with rapture. He told the Sharmas an irreverent story about a god who disguised himself as a woman, only for his close friend to unwittingly impregnate him. The god returned to his own body. The fetus lived on in his thigh and had to be sliced out.

The risqué nature of the story made Leila nervous. Usually her parents operated as if men and sex did not exist; Anita fast-forwarded even tame kissing scenes on television. To her surprise, however, Anita neither missed a beat nor resorted to her usual prudishness.

"If men carried, there would be no population," Anita said.

"You're lucky, Anita, you have a child, Anita." Matthew cocked his chin in Leila's direction. "What's this one like?"

Anita assured Matthew that children were labor-intensive and difficult to socialize, and even more difficult to shape.

"Leila, for instance, we send her to a good school, while the women go to the public school, and she spends her free time playing Sims and soaps. She wants to be an actor, of all things."

Ashok cut in. "Anita—"

"Ashok is too gentle. It's easy for a father to indulge. I tell her to be realistic. She could be something big, if she studies."

Leila tore up another flower. She waited for Matthew to commiserate with her mother. Instead, he sided with her.

"An actress? That's plenty big, Anita, a refreshing dream to have, I'm sick of doctors."

Leila felt Matthew's gaze on her but didn't want to meet it, unsure if he was just humoring her, the way adults did to stop small children from throwing tantrums.

He pressed on: He and Louise loved the theater. Frequently they drove into the city watch plays and catch art films. "Just the other evening, we saw a German film, black and white, without subtitles. Neither of us speaks a lick of German but you should have seen us, crying our eyes out on the car ride home. You folks should join sometime."

"I hate the city," Anita replied. "Also art films."

"I'll go," Leila said.

Anita pivoted back to school. Her face was impassive, but Leila could tell she was annoyed that she had assumed such autonomy in front of a guest. "The school we send her is in a good township."

"Can I go to New York, Mummy?"

Anita waved a forkful of potato in the air. "It's so hard these days, Matthew. If you are Asian, South Asian, there's no luxury to be average. Admissions people will think you're all the same. You must do a million things extra, just to distinguish. She tells me it's too early, but when you come from nowhere, no legacy, you start now."

"Leila plays tennis," Ashok said.

"Every bloody Indian plays tennis," said Anita.

"You know," Matthew said, "a friend of mine, a good friend, his daughter acts. As a teenager she went to this class. A conservatory in New York. I don't remember the age requirement, but I believe it was for high school students."

"Has she booked anything?" Leila asked.

"A Monistat commercial."

"Oh my *god*," Leila exclaimed. "Mother, I need to go."

"I can't afford nonsense. For a yeast commercial."

There were scholarships, Matthew continued, and the Monistat girl also attended Yale. He could look into it and send them the details. It wasn't too much trouble, no. Leila seemed talented, he said. Leila wondered why he'd think so. She hadn't said more than a few sentences all evening.

"Think about it, it could be a feather in her cap," Matthew told Anita.

After dinner Anita made drip coffees. Leila passed the cups and saucers around the table. The conversation turned to office politics, into the tedious realm of adults. Bored, Leila slipped away to the living room. *Acting roles for teens*, she searched on her phone. She scrolled for a while and fell down a rabbit hole of local Craigslist activity. Local strangers made bird calls to each other on Missed Connections. *Pipe service R us (Monroe)*; *Female for breakfast (Bordentown)*; *Kyle? It's Marissa from Omegle.*

The small font blurred; Leila dozed off on the plastic couch. She didn't know how long she'd been asleep when Matthew prodded her shoulder.

"Sorry to wake you, your mother says she's left a tray of kheer outside. I can't find the thing."

Leila stood. Had he seen her screen, or her mouth open as she napped?

"It's in the fridge, I'll get it."

She led him past the prayer cabinet. Matthew peered inside the opened doors at the silver dish with the cobra figurine and its multiple heads and dangling red beads, the portrait of Khandoba Shiva riding a white horse. A woman rode behind him and drove a spear into the gut of one of two mustachioed men in the corner frame. Maroon blood trickled from the man's thigh. A sleek white dog bit into the stomach of his accomplice. Leila didn't know the lore, but she understood them to be villains. She shut the doors of the cabinet, embarrassed by the strong scent of incense, the transparency of her family's beliefs.

If Matthew noticed he pretended not to and busied himself with getting the glass tray of kheer from the fridge. Leila stood on her toes and gathered bowls from the pantry. She spooned the slippery noodles inside.

"None for me, please," Matthew said.

"You're sure?"

"My diabetes."

This annoyed Leila; she'd already poured out his portion. Milk crust had condensed over the kheer, yellow and freckled with crushed pistachios. It was a dish Anita liked, and maybe because of that, it was one Leila hated.

"Your friend's daughter, the one in the commercial. She really goes to Yale?"

"The Yale bit was a white lie. Just trying to help your case."

"Thanks."

"I know you have your kheer, but would you like something else?"

Matthew reached into his breast pocket and pulled out a block of chocolate. There was no label on the gold foil it came wrapped in, and the square shape had melted slightly. He unwrapped the foil and held the square between his thumb and forefinger.

"Go on."

Leila didn't understand if he expected her to take it or if he held it out to feed her. Clumsily he pressed a corner to her mouth, as one might shove a medicinal pill past the lips of a dog.

"It's good," she said.

"Louise got it in Europe," Matthew replied. "We only had a little left. I'll ask her to bring more next time. We travel often."

Matthew pulled a handkerchief out of his back pocket and wiped his hands. Ashok carried one too. When Leila was small, she used to cry into it.

Leila thanked him. Her family never traveled. She picked up the two bowls of kheer and walked back to the dining room. Matthew followed her, reopening the prayer cabinet as he passed it.

"Who closed this?"

"Nobody." Leila shut the door with her foot, but it sprang back open, revealing the silver deities with their many arms and heads inside. "Me."

～

WATCHING FROM HER WINDOW, arms-deep in dish suds, Devika called Jyoti Kaushal. Jyoti turned off *20/20*.

"Woman," said Tejas, napping beside her on the couch, "who is calling at this hour?"

"Tell your husband to hold his breath," Devika said. "Who's that man at the Sharmas' house?

"I haven't seen."

"Go look, check from your window," Devika said. "Is he a relation?"

"Do they have any relations?"

"So he's a stranger. All I'm saying is, I would never leave my Manu alone in a room with a man."

MATTHEW, CIRCA '60s

The Pillais, Another Unhappy Kind

"Listen to this trauma-drama loop," said Aparna Naik. Before he developed his semi-English accent, Matthew grew up in a remote village in Kerala, a marshy hub where once missionaries had roamed and advertised the love of a colonial god to the perennially unloved.

"I go to temple, yes, I make Manu go. Sometimes we pray to Jesus Christ, to all powers, for good measure," said Devika Gill. Come holidays Devika loved to curl up on a faux-leather armchair and watch *The Ten Commandments* on ABC. Compulsively she rewound the ending, the pharaoh's wife tending to her lifeless son. "It is terrifying." Devika shivered. "What if I too am doomed, because I am in the hands of lesser gods?"

Matthew's family had decent money in Kerala. He spent his early summers at his grandparents' coffee plantation with his younger sister. Maidservants tended both children. One August the sister died, struck down by a nasty infection, and the Pillais moved to England, a place uninfected with prior loss. There Matthew father took up work at a food processing plant. Matthew liked regaling the women with his family's riches-to-rags tale. *In England he canned baked beans*, he'd say. *In India he studied aerospace engineering.*

("Probably it's not all-the-way true," said Jyoti Kaushal. "He had a flair for drama.")

The Pillais rented a house in East London and enrolled Matthew in a boys' school. He was a meek-faced boy in photos from the time, knobby-kneed with a mushroom cut, a red dot of kumkum on his forehead from morning prayers. *Dothead dothead,* the other schoolboys teased. At day's end Mrs. Pillai dressed in her best clothes and walked twenty-five minutes to the school gate to retrieve her son. He was always the first to emerge from the gates, until the afternoon he didn't come. Anxious, Mrs. Pillai slipped past the gates to search for him. Hordes of boys gossiped on benches. Two cackled on the turf: they'd pulled down the trousers of a third and exposed his small, ashy ass. They took turns spanking the victim. Mrs. Pillai watched with revulsed fascination. The spanked boy made no noise. The spanked boy was her boy. Sunglasses flying, she ran and smushed half-naked Matthew to her ample chest. *Pigs*, she hissed at the boys, in Malayali though it was her own child, his silence, his incompetence with self-defense, who had roused her shame.

The rest of the week the boys collected bags of dog shit from public trash receptacles and piled it in Matthew's locker with a note: *Shit-colored dothead. Mum's titsucker.*

"He told us he pretended he was in on the joke," said Devika.

At Matthew's request Mrs. Pillai began letting him walk home alone. That spring a group of buzz-cut white boys biked around the Pillais' neighborhood. The sight of them unsettled Mrs. Pillai, how they lingered at the lampposts with cigarettes and tiny eager eyes. *I took out the trash and a boy muttered "bitch,"* she told Mr. Pillai. *Ridiculous*, he said, and shook his head. Unpleasant as it was, the boys were all talk. What would they do, kill her? Matthew eavesdropped from the hallway.

"Call the police," Matthew said.

"How ridiculous they'll think we are," Mr. Pillai said. "Complaining about boys biking."

Then the boys came with their matchbox and tossed a lit one into the lot. The flames caught the landscaping. Half the Pillais' house burned down. Mrs. Pillai, home alone, succumbed to her burn injuries.

"If she had been walking to get Matthew, it never would have happened," said Aparna. "That guilt gnawed at him."

Mr. Pillai moved back to India. Matthew stayed in England for school. He grew larger, joined a rugby team; he dated one British girl, then another; he shed one accent, grew another. He changed his name to Matthew and relied on the hospitality of his father's expat friends. The boys laid off Matthew. Why bother with the effort of hating a boy like that? He did it on his own.

MATTHEW ON WILLOW ROAD, 2000s

Mr. Pillai the Benefactor

AFTER THAT THANKSGIVING, Matthew visited the Sharmas once a week. Dried neem flaked off the women's blemishes as they watched his beemer circling into the block from their bedroom windows. Who was this stranger, they messaged each other, so big and broad with his Whole Foods tote, bearing nonstop gifts?

"See, I'm no beggar," said Devika Gill. She ruffled through her handbag for a Costco free sample pita chip.

Matthew brought the Sharmas flowers and Italian wafer cookies, more chocolates Louise picked up in Europe. *Leila loved these last time, so Louise made sure to bring plenty; she has a migraine today, poor thing, she's sorry she couldn't meet you all.* He bought Anita a bottle of dry rose from a vineyard upstate. His presence reminded Ashok of the pleasures of a full house and extended family. Anita too, though she would never admit it. Leila had no concept of diasporic loneliness, but like a Pavlovian dog, she brightened at the sound of the bell ringing, the sign of gifts coming. Matthew discovered a British specialty shop in Montclair and returned with pasties, cans of split pea soup, and Cadbury Flakes for Leila, who devoured them on the spot. The excesses embarrassed Anita and Ashok. Gently they reminded Matthew he was their guest and need not bring anything.

Matthew insisted. "Bad manners to show up empty-handed."

Anita pressed a hand to her chest. "No no, we can't possibly accept."

And then Leila did. "They're martyrs," she told Matthew. She toured him around the house eagerly and subjected him to home videos from Ashok's camcorder, old photo albums loaded with pictures of herself, her favorite subject.

"That's me," Leila said, pointing to a round, naked baby on a quilt. "Look how small I was."

"You're not so tiny."

"I *was*," Leila said. She unwrapped a Cadbury egg and popped it into her mouth. "And I'm still so tiny now."

To illustrate her smallness she pinched the excess fabric of her dress. There was hardly any. Over four months of friendship with Matthew she had shot up six pounds. Anita let out her school uniform.

"She has to go to the gym," Leila overheard her mother telling Matthew. She'd been upstairs, eating an Aero bar and looking up more roles on Craigslist as the adults took coffee in the kitchen. "I'm not saying she's fat, but the way you're feeding her, it's a matter of time."

Matthew dunked a sugar-free biscuit into coffee. "She's a child, she's growing."

"No more sweets. This isn't growth, it's mutation. Know how much I weighed on my wedding day?"

She nudged Ashok's shoulder. "Tell him. That damned wedding day, the anniversary you never celebrate."

Ashok sighed. "Does anyone celebrate Columbus Day?"

Anita cut him off. "Forty-two kilograms! I was twenty-one, so delicate. I still have my blouses from back then. Leila just turned thirteen and she's too large for them."

Leila came downstairs and strode into the kitchen. She snapped the Aero bar in half and bit into the mint-green bubbles. "Mom's an anorexic. And I found an audition."

"What's the role?" Matthew asked.

"An extra in a slasher film. Can you take me, Mom?"

"Can I take you to pretend to be murdered? Have some bloody sense," Anita said. "Matthew, see how her father says nothing. Leila, give me that bar, your third today. Even Matthew agrees, it's too many."

"Let her, Anita, my god," said Matthew.

Anita frowned at his little betrayal.

~

MATTHEW TRAVELED ABROAD for business and returned with international gifts for Leila: tulip bulbs from Holland, loudly patterned neckties from a London trip, a bear-shaped German trinket to hang above the bed, to ward off nightmares.

He went to Paris and returned with braggadocious stories of raw beef and the slender women he flirted with.

"Parisians know how to live, you know," he told the Sharmas, as if delivering to them a great axiom. "Even the hotel gave me, a teetotaler, the finest complimentary champagne. The company dollar, no, Ashok?"

"No." Ashok sipped water from a steel cup. "The company never spends an extra dollar on me."

"Parisians are racist," Anita declared.

Matthew snorted. "But how would you know, have you ever been?"

These tense moments had become more frequent, but out of politeness to Matthew, Anita and Ashok never allowed them to boil over until after he left. In private, Ashok and Anita fought over their daughter's spoilage. Eventually it became tedious to hide it, like the time Matthew returned from Dublin with a fine silver claddagh for Leila. Matthew held the ring next to her finger. He turned the crown inward and outward.

"This way means your heart is owned, this way means it's available. How will you wear it?"

"Outward." Leila slid the ring on her finger. "Mom never took me to that audition."

"A Craigslist slasher film isn't quite right for you. We'll find something better."

"Matthew, I'm sorry, jewelry is too much," Anita said. "Leila, don't take that."

"A girl should have a nice ring," Matthew said.

"For what? If she needed one, we'd get it for her. Ashok came here with one suitcase."

"What's wrong with having more?"

Anita narrowed her eyes. "So, when will you bring Louise?"

"Next time, Anita, next time. She's having a terrible migraine now."

Before he left, embarking on the long drive back to upstate New York, Anita arranged a bag of fruit and leftovers to take to Louise. She took the best apples from the fruit bowl, a generous Tupperware of whatever she'd cooked for the visit, and a green chili pepper.

Leila pinched the end of the pepper. "What superstition is this?"

"Mohini," Matthew said. "A femme fatale myth. Long hair, white saree, lures men in, drives them mad. I would let her catch me, Leila, if it wasn't all bullshit."

"Usually I don't believe such things," Anita said, coolly. "But I had an uncle who went insane."

"If a woman who looked like Mohini wanted me, who am I to say no? She'd have been lucky if she caught me younger; I was quite the looker back then."

"Yes, I'm sure, look at you now, only," Anita said. But Leila thought her mother's face looked cruel, its beautiful features twisted into the sharp lines of a soap opera villain, the plump bottom lip tucked under the thinner top, biting back laughter. Matthew could wield his wealth over Anita, but she would always win in the domain of her face.

Anita's laughter spilled out. Matthew fished for a Polaroid in his wallet, himself in his younger years.

"You keep a photo on hand?" Anita teased.

Leila felt a shift in Matthew's affable demeanor. He was searching the wallet frantically now. Then and there Leila feared her parents' friendship with him would end, the stream of presents and the promise of Monistat connections over. *I want to see*, she said, and stood on tiptoe to get a good look at the photograph. She hoped young Matthew had been handsome, that her mother would be forced to retract her nastiness. At the sight of the Polaroid her heart sank. He was just as ugly then as he was now, even without the slight wrinkles along his forehead and no gray hairs.

"Handsome, right, L?"

"Yes."

Anita laughed again. "I'm sorry, Leila, you're such a bad liar."

Matthew stuffed the photo back into his pocket. "I'll be going, folks."

Anita handed him his superstitious fruit bundle on his way out. The next visit he dismissed her offerings, as revenge for the slight. "Louise doesn't eat leftovers. The woman wants her steak, not your cooking, Anita. And the apples rot in my kitchen. Not even the cats touch them."

Matthew and the Men

THE MEN CIRCLED Matthew's beemer in the block, admiring its make, curious if they could recruit a benefactor into their homes, too. At Hema's Dunkin', Parth Rao fixed him a coffee with five Splendas and invited him to a cricket game at the local tennis court. Matthew obliged.

"Played a bad game, then took the whole team to dinner at Houlihan's," said Hema Rao.

At the post-cricket dinner, Tejas Kaushal invited Matthew to a bhajan at the Tropicana in Atlantic City.

"No compulsion, of course, the neighbors always throw my flyers away, they do not understand Krishna Consciousness," Tejas said. Matthew told Tejas he believed in the cult of god but respected the discipline of personal reverence. Throughout his life he had dropped in on church services and listened to passionate sermons. Sonorous calls to prayer had stirred him on trips to Morocco with Louise.

"Of course I'll come," he said. "For the music."

Meanwhile, the women chitchatted in the market:

"Who is this man? Anita's having an affair?" whispered Devika.

"He's too butt-ugly for her," said Hema Rao. "The other day I let him pet the dogs. Personally I wouldn't let him touch me if you held a gun to my face."

"Anita outsources her parenting to a stranger as usual, and lets him spoil her child," said Karina Dixit. "She used to think I spoiled Riya, the bloody hypocrite."

Nasreen Farouk hummed in assent. "A generous man, though, no? My meat fridge broke down the other day. He'd stopped in for lunch. On the spot he ordered me another."

∼

AND SO THE neighborhood fell in love with Matthew, despite his unconscionable ugliness, the tone-deaf mentions of his tax bracket, and his staunch atheism. He patronized local businesses and bought coffees at Devika Gill's convenience store. He had tea with the Gills and played cards with young Manu. He taught Arvind Gohel how to focus his lazy eye and brought him to a top-tier out-of-network optician. (For weeks the child roamed the neighborhood in an eye patch, optimistic for a future with a better face.) Matthew took an adult dance class at Vritika Shetty's basement, the first man ever to attend, then had coffee with her and her bungling lover in the upstairs kitchenette. He walked Hema's dogs. On all his neighborhood ventures he encouraged Leila to tag along, worried her mother had isolated her in her private school. She didn't speak a language beyond English; she should get to know her real neighbors, her real community, he insisted.

"Stop, I've never stopped her," Anita said, aggrieved by the accusation. "She'd rather watch reality TV."

"I'll go to the convenience store," Leila said. "Can we get Twinkies?"

So Matthew drove her.

"Bhai." Devika smiled at Matthew as the two walked in. "Manu wants to know when you're coming next."

"Tell him soon, we'll play Happy Families."

Leila set a bottled Frappuccino and a Twinkie onto the counter. She said hello to Devika and waited for Matthew to swipe his credit card.

"You said nothing to Devika Auntie, just hello," Matthew said, back in the car. "Why?"

Leila opened her Twinkie. "What's there to say? We have nothing in common."

"You're the same."

"No, I don't want to be like the women," Leila said. "They're petty and small."

"Oh? What do you want to be?"

She told him about her ideal future self, her differences: she wanted to attend a prestigious school, live in a city like Los Angeles, appear in multiple commercials and daytime television; to become a person who could dissolve into someone else. Before school, she'd write these mantras three times on a piece of notebook paper and burn it with flames from the mandir. She wondered if god noticed that she never prayed for the happiness of anyone else.

"Not that I believe," Leila added, because she knew he did not.

"Don't worry. God's too busy to worry about your altruism or lack thereof."

"I guess."

"The other things, the commercial things, we'll work on it, I know some people. We'll have to convince your mom."

Leila slumped back in her seat. How a man in marketing knew of people in the entertainment industry, she wasn't sure, though it seemed plausible enough. "That won't ever happen."

"Sure it will. In the meantime, there's things you can do if you want to get famous."

"Like what?"

"Louise and I just saw a fantastic play in the city. A conman becomes a doctor. The actor wrote it himself. Before commercials, you should write some plays. That's the first way into the business."

"A play about what?"

"I don't know. Your mother is so strange, I feel for your father sometimes, dealing with her, the horrible things she says."

A Play About What?

MATTHEW WENT ON a business trip to Prague. Leila found days without him slow and devoid of excitement. By serendipity, the drama department of Leila's school sent an email out about an annual playwriting contest. Leila forwarded him the message.

Matthew
Got your email, L. It's a sign,
what did I tell you? ✓✓

Leila
Yeahh I probably won't win though ✓✓

Matthew
That doesn't matter, in any case I'll send it to
my people ✓✓

Leila
Omg rly??? Ok I'll enter ✓✓

For dialogue Leila recorded her parents' recursive arguments in a notebook, certain these would receive sympathy. That would be enough to win; so long as she could exploit the family's unhappiness, it would be worthwhile.

WIFE: *You abduct me, then never appreciate me*
HUSBAND: *abduct? You did not have to stay*
WIFE: *Not one anniversary have you celebrated*
[Husband slaps his thighs, his forehead, his face.]
WIFE TO CHILD: *Child! Look, your father is a crazy man. He broke my mangalsutra once. Yanked it clean off my neck. The beads are in my dresser.*

The scenes didn't feel riveting enough to Leila on their own, so she added an extra flourish of detail, like someone striking the other's cheek or jaw or abdomen. She buried the notebook of exaggerations in the bottom of her sock drawer, like the terrible secret it was. Anita never looked there, but on the hunt for one of her missing work socks she happened to check it Leila was walking up the staircase with a Toblerone in hand when she saw her mother through the crack of her bedroom door, crying over the open notebook.

"It's fake," Leila insisted. "It's not you."

"This is how you repay your family who pays for you. What you share in the school we pay for."

"I'm sorry."

"Fuck your sorry."

Leila had no counterargument. So she threw a tantrum, running, in socks, to the bus stop, nearly knocking over Hema Rao, who'd bent over to pick up Hattie's waste. She ran past Riya Dixit, midstroll with a lanky boy Leila didn't recognize, until she reached the bus stop. Coach buses arrived every hour and shuttled commuters to New York. Leila counted the change in her pocket. Seventy-five cents. Anita's car pulled up around the bend.

"I'm leaving," Leila said.

Anita rolled her window down. "Sure. Need money?"

"No."

Anita reversed.

"You're leaving?" Leila said. "What if something happens to me, like somebody takes me? I'll probably get killed by the morning."

"People have more important things to do than to take a brat."

Leila got into the passenger seat. Instead of going home Anita drove her to Hot Breads. The two drank tea in paper cups and shared a slice of pineapple cake.

"You know, your father is the one who makes me fight like that, the way you wrote it, I never used to be so angry," Anita said. "Probably you are so unhappy, so dramatic, because he is so old. Old sperm makes for mental problems. What do you think would happen, if you got on that bus and left?"

"I would have quiet," Leila said, sullen. "I would be happy."

Anita licked her fork. "You're a smart girl, a spoiled girl, what do you have to be unhappy about?"

LEILA'S SCRIPT WON the contest. The school held a small ceremony and reception for parents with triangular sandwiches and coffee. Ashok was so happy he saved the program, and afterward the Sharmas went to pray at the local temple; a divine thanks, they brought red apples from the Cash & Carry as offerings. Better not to buy from the temple, Anita said, where selfish volunteers upsold you. Gods, she told Leila, were sensitive and mercurial, happy to take back their gifts if you didn't show enough gratitude.

Anita rang the temple bell. She pressed her head to the ground before a deity and wiped the smell of feet cheese from her forehead. A gaggle of children in pigtails and bowl cuts rang the temple bell and barreled past and tripped over her sundress.

It was a nice day. The Sharmas finished their prayers and drove to the shore. By the time they arrived the sun had dimmed, the salty air almost too cold for comfort. Anita walked to the ocean. She lifted her sundress and dug her feet into the sand until her ankles disappeared. Leila sat on the sand beside her. She let the waves wash up the prickles of hair on her shins. Ashok took photographs on a Kodak, in the same dress pants he had worn to the ceremony.

"Come, man," Anita called to him.

"I'm not dressed."

"Just your feet, old man."

He lifted his pant legs a few inches and tiptoed across the wet strip of sand, stopping when he reached foam. Leila stood and took the camera from him. *Careful careful*, he told her. A handful of waves crashed against him. Little ones. A little one amounted to something bigger and soaked his knees. Ashok laughed, a rare and pure sound.

Broadway

Leila
Hi matthew. Just wanted 2 know if you got my script. ✓✓
It won btw ✓✓

Matthew
Hi L, sure, I've got it, yes you told me, congratulations again.
No time to read yet ✓✓
I'm back saturday, have a surprise for you ✓✓
Cleared it with your parents: you, me, and louise, a broadway show ✓✓
So you can see how it's done. ✓✓

L EILA STRAIGHTENED HER hair with her mother's iron and sprayed her extremities with flowery perfume. She tied one of the turquoise neckties Matthew bought her around her neck. She wanted to impress Louise; Matthew had painted an air of sophistication about her that lay carefully outside Leila's comprehension. *She's not like the women on your block,* he told her, in a lengthy phone call the night before the show. *Not like your mother, who goes on about her education but still processes the world like a simpleton, in binaries of beautiful and ugly, love and hate, skinny and fat, her mind a narrow hallway; how sad, Leila, to be trapped inside it. I read your script, I'm worried you're going to be trapped , too.*

Leila had a chance to be different; Matthew said. He wanted her to associate more with women like Louise, who read the news in the mornings, who operated from authority but never cruelty, who gave not only one shit but two about what happened in the world outside her face and body. *A woman who does not think, in every circumstance, how am I a victim of it?*

The frankness hurt Leila, but she didn't say anything. Matthew had been so sensitive when Anita ridiculed his Polaroid.

~

DOWNSTAIRS, ANITA FRIED pappadums for the guests. She eyed Leila's fried hair. "What's this show you're seeing?"

"*Chicago.*"

"About?"

"The wives murder their husbands and get famous."

"Okay. You were on the phone for an hour last night. What all has your uncle told you about his wife?"

"That she's not concerned with whether people are ugly or fat. She cares about more."

"Cares about what?"

Leila didn't know. "Globalism."

"What he means is, his wife is ugly and fat."

The bell rang. Matthew stood in the threshold of the front door in a tan trench coat and boots. He embraced Leila warmly and handed her a box of Matryoshka dolls he'd picked up in Prague.

"None of you look older than when I saw you last," Matthew said.

No one laughed but Ashok, who was polite in that way. Matthew shook his hand and attempted to kiss Anita on the cheeks. *How they do it in France*, he said, but Anita, unfamiliar with the gesture, disgusted by the saliva of strangers—she would not share a smoothie straw with Leila at Hema's Dunkin'—tilted her head away from him.

A woman lagged behind Matthew. She resembled his exuberant descriptions of Louise but was also different, like a dress that appears perfect in an online catalog but in person reveals itself to be cheaply made: her eyes were not big and blue as he said, but little and gray; her cheeks were ruddy and bloated as an alcoholic's; her frame was wide, as Anita predicted. She didn't meet anyone's eyes as she issued inaudible *hellos* and offered only the tips of her fingers in a handshake.

"Louise, hello," Anita said. "So nice of you to let Leila join. She's so excited, she did her hair for it. It's not too much trouble?"

"I didn't do my hair, it's just like this," Leila said.

Louise offered Leila her fingertips. "Of course not, it's our pleasure. Matthew does this sort of thing all the time."

Matthew waved away the pappadums that Ashok put out onto a plate. "We'll miss the matinee," he said. "You all should come—there are no tickets left for this afternoon show but we'll drive you to the city. You two can hang around by yourselves, and we'll all join up for dinner after. I've made reservations at an Italian spot. It's an early one; we'll get you home soon."

Leila imagined her mother in the car, prattling on about Ugly and Fat. "No, they're busy."

"I hate the city, a hideous, disgusting place," Anita said. "Ashok's working today."

"On a Saturday?"

"The school fees eat our heads, his job is not as easy as yours."

Leila gave her parents perfunctory hugs goodbye and followed Matthew and Louise outside. On the concrete path to the driveway Leila tripped on a stray landscaping rock and fell on her knees. Her tights ripped. The skin of her knee shredded and oozed with blood. She felt Louise's fingertips on her shoulder.

"You're all right?"

Leila crossed her knees to hide the torn tights. "Yeah, sorry."

"You should be more careful."

On the car ride Louise operated as if Leila wasn't sitting in the back seat. Quietly she told Matthew about a difficult client at work, one of the cat's exorbitant veterinary bills, a payment on an investment property. *Yes, I know, yes, I know*, Matthew mumbled, in annoyance. Leila expected him to be enamored by his wife. Instead he turned the jazz station up higher.

Halfway to the city, he turned around. "Good back there, kid? You're quiet."

"Yes."

"Was it your mother mentioning your school fees? Did you hear that, Louise? Making money a child's problem. I told you about Anita."

"At length, yes."

Matthew reached into the glove compartment, took out an envelope, and handed it to Leila.

"Look at this, L."

Leila opened the envelope. Inside was a freshly developed photo of Louise in a black cocktail dress, holding a martini and smiling with yellow teeth. She stood sandwiched between other martini-wielding Manhattanites. A man snaked a hand around her waist.

"This woman just helped chair a whole benefit, raising money to build a school in the tiniest village you can imagine, L."

"Wow, yeah, I probably can't imagine it," Leila said. "Louise, what was the village?"

Louise sounded startled to be addressed. "Oh, somewhere near Matthew's hometown, I can't quite remember the name."

"I heard you're an equestrian. What do you like about horses?"

"I don't know," Louise replied. "They've always bore my weight."

"How did you and Matthew meet?"

"In a train compartment. I was very lonely."

"Did he really wear a kilt at your wedding?"

This softened Louise. "He told you that, did he? He's lying; he wore it for two minutes and took it off."

"Louise was a knockout," Matthew interrupted. "You should have seen her. Her dress was cut so low, her breasts were so nice, no one paid attention to what I wore."

"Stop, she doesn't want to hear about that," Louise said, the softness evaporated. "You always do this. Look at her, in the back, so embarrassed." Louise opened the window and covered her face with her blouse.

~

THE SHOW DAZZLED Leila; the slender dancers and light sleaze. Matthew sat between her and Louise, who kept her face covered during the first few musical numbers. She excused herself to the bathroom, where she remained for a long stretch of time.

Leila picked the hole in her tights and whispered. "Matthew, is she okay? Is it my perfume?"

"She's fine." Matthew patted Leila's hand. "She told me she stepped out for air."

Intermission. Leila went to the bathroom. The line was endless. Louise was still absent when Leila returned to her seat. Louise remained absent for the rest of the musical. The curtain fell; the audience clapped. Matthew leaned close to Leila's ear.

"Louise had a migraine, she had to go."

"Where did she go, is she in the car?"

"She went to a friend's place to rest. Let's get dinner."

"Alone?"

"She'll stop by when she feels better, she'll come for dessert."

"She told you?"

"She told me, yes." He poked at the scrape on Leila's knee. "We'll stop at a pharmacy on the way. Get you new tights."

It was pouring outside the theater. Leila and Matthew ran down two avenues to the pharmacy, then to the restaurant, drenched and laughing. Louise did not arrive through the salad or the spaghetti or the profiteroles. Matthew paid the check and led Leila to the parking garage where he'd left the car.

"It's late," Matthew said, after they reached Willow Road. "You go inside without me. Tell your parents we didn't want to disturb them, Louise and me. Don't want them to get the wrong idea, right?"

"Right." Leila waved goodbye. Matthew's car receded into the distance. She went inside and brushed her hair out in the downstairs mirror. Anita's reflection appeared behind her. She took the brush from Leila's hands and combed.

"You'll lose hair if you use such a hot iron next time. And you still can't manage a knot," Anita said. "How was Louise, the big shot?"

"Good."

"Too good to come in and say goodbye?"

"She thought you were sleeping. She didn't want to wake you."

"It's eight o'clock. How thoughtful of her."

"She also had a migraine."

"Delicate doll."

They retired to the living room and watched television. An episode of *Gilmore Girls* played. Onscreen, Lauren Graham arranged Pop-Tarts on a tray and garnished them with a red apple.

"I hate these white women, Leila, skinny no matter what. What all god has given them, while I struggle? Rory looks so innocent, though, like porcelain."

"She cheats on a lot of her boyfriends," Leila said.

Skinned Goats

LEILA SET ASIDE the strangeness that transpired with Louise, not knowing what to think of her midshow disappearance to the apartment of her unnamed friend. The friend was likely a man. While perusing the Cash & Carry biscuit aisle, Leila overheard Aparna Naik and Karina Dixit gossiping about Matthew's open arrangement. *How does that man dip it inside her, knowing she's infested with the germs of another; probably because he never does dip it, and* that *is the reason there's no progeny.* Leila could not picture Louise, fragile as she was, infested with anyone. But remembered the photograph from the benefit, the man's hand around her waist.

Leila pushed Louise and her potential infestations aside. She made an online profile on a casting website and submitted herself for roles, inspired by her lone theater experience. She took a selfie on the camera of the family computer, turned up the saturation on her face to hide the zits and plainness, and input her details:

> 13 years old, can play 13-17
> skills: has a passport

Soon after, she found a casting call for a leg warmer advertisement:

> Seeking talent, 13-17, for leg warmer advertisement
> Must be located in NJ
> Must provide your own transportation to-and-from shoot location
> No compensation.

Leila submitted her photograph. The poster responded within the hour: Could she audition tomorrow in South Jersey? The address was an hour away by car. Anita would never agree; Ashok was working that weekend, and Matthew had a flight to London.

The women would sooner report her to Anita than take her. But Riya Dixit had recently gotten her license. Leila had seen the student driver sticker on the Dixits' cars. Riya no longer stood at the bus stop in the mornings with her Juicy Couture necklace and rib-length hair, brassy from a bad dye job. The bad color became her. Everything did. The puberty that came too early for Leila arrived late for Riya, lengthening her. She'd begun to teach dance in Vritika Shetty's basement, where she'd first learned it. She continued to charm the women, now with commiseration: *How did you marry a man you hardly knew, Auntie? How do you manage the lacto-ovo-vegetarian days, how do you manage all these children?*

In the afternoon, Leila made her way to the Dixits' house, where she had not gone in years, and knocked on the door twice. Riya opened the door, contour on half of her face.

"What's up?"

"I need a favor from you," Leila said. "Are you busy? Can I come in?"

"Sure. No one's home. And I have to head out in thirty minutes, I have a date."

The Dixits' foyer had been redone from years ago, the old worn furniture replaced by dazzling new pieces, the linoleum floors swapped out for marble. On the mantel sat a portrait of Sai Baba with his palm outstretched; a fresh garland hung from the edges of the frame. Next to it were pictures of Riya in various states of adoration: squatting in a dance performance, posing with a strawberry ice cream in a group of girls on the beach in Belmar.

"What time is your date? Can you drive me somewhere on your way?"

Riya flopped down onto the sofa. "Where?"

"An audition in South Jersey."

"Audition for what?"

"A leg warmer infomercial."

"Can't your parents?"

"They don't know I applied."

"Is it legitimate?"

"Completely."

"I don't know." Riya folded her arms. "I can't have another person in the back seat. You want to be in a leg warmer infomercial that badly?"

"I do."

"That's very sad. What about Matthew?"

"He's traveling now. But he'll take me to other ones when he's back. He says he knows people."

"Vivek and I see him around here all the time." Vivek, Riya explained, was the boy she had been seeing for the last several months, the one Leila saw her around the neighborhood with when she'd attempted to escape on a Coach bus to New York. Riya had let him dip it inside her once or twice. He did so respectfully. The Dixits didn't know about that part, but they knew of him and loved him. He mowed their lawns and brought them meatless Taco Bell. The other day, Riya said, after he picked her up from Vritika Shetty's dance class, he noticed Matthew staring at her from the Sharmas' driveway.

"Like a creep," Riya said.

So a boy loved Riya, enough to dip it inside her, and only a creep could take interest in Leila. "It's not like that. He wears tinted glasses," Leila said. "Maybe you got confused. Maybe he wasn't looking at you."

"Maybe." Riya shrugged. "I have to get ready. Sorry about your audition."

Leila walked home and deleted her submission for the infomercial. She opened Chatroulette and flipped through the rolodex of strangers with her volume off. The first stranger held his penis in his hand. The next held up a sign reading FLASH ME, BOOBS AND WHAT NOT. The final stranger had hung a dummy from the ceiling, so lifelike Leila mistook it for a real man. *Help him*, the stranger typed. *He never got laid.* Leila closed the window. She opened a private tab and searched: *penis, what does sex feel like, what does sex feel like if you're in love.* The results reminded her of sitting at the sticky tables at Kwality Meats, watching the butcher-boys skinning goats.

A Bad Time for Us

SHORTLY AFTER LEILA turned fourteen, Ashok lost his job.

"Anita asked me for my astrologer's contact information," said Devika Gill. "He told her they were entering into a bad time. She had a pooja to reverse it. Nothing worked."

"What can a priest fix? Without money, life is awful, abnormal," said Jyoti Kaushal.

Hema Rao hummed in assent. "It is why you, Jyoti, stay married to your stinking podiatrist, his salary," she said. "The happy kinds hoard the money."

"I'm deeply unhappy," said Jyoti.

Though they were no longer co-workers, Matthew continued to frequent the Sharmas' home, but the tenor of their relations was irrevocably changed. Ashok seemed embittered by the presence of Matthew, his cursory mentions of bootstraps and connections. At the first few vague suggestions, Ashok nodded intently, but eventually he fell silent and excused himself.

"Not one of your connections has known shit," Anita complained to Matthew, her hair in foils of box dye. A green timer ticked down on the stove. She'd be a chocolate-auburn hybrid in twenty minutes. "There's no one else you can ask?"

Matthew spooned a heap of rice onto his plate and licked his fingers. "I've been asking, I told you."

Leila rested her head on her placemat. "Life's trash."

"Bollocks," said Matthew. "When I was your age, L, the boys beat me in school. Called me dothead. A criminal burned my mother to death."

Anita hiccupped, not to be one-upped. "I was poor. And my three siblings died, one after another. Like cicadas." Anita stewed, dissatisfied with this metaphor. "Like rats. I still remember when they brought the bodies to the house, laid them on the table where we ate."

Leila thought she saw Matthew roll his eyes. She watched him house another plate of rice and wondered whether the traumas he relayed, like the recommendations he made to her father, were real.

"Matthew," Leila said, "remember that program in New York, the one the girl in the Monistat commercial went to? You never sent it to me."

"Funny you mention it," Matthew said, and swallowed his rice. "I looked into it, and you had to be fourteen to start." But now Leila was fourteen, and a new session of the teen conservatory started in a month. No auditions were required, only a deposit. Not wanting to strain the family at this time, he'd put a deposit down on her behalf. Classes started on Saturday mornings and ran through the evenings. He could drive her there and back. No need for NJ Transit.

"A belated birthday gift," Matthew said.

Anita shook her head. "It's a bad time for us. I don't want you paying for me."

Matthew frowned. "It's not for you, Anita, is it?"

"Of course, I know that," she said, blushing. "Of course."

MATTHEW LEFT AND Ashok went to bed early, without speaking to his wife or daughter. Anita rinsed the color from her hair and poured herself a glass of wine downstairs, from one of the bottles Matthew brought over. Leila, who seldom cleaned, took the broom out of the cupboard, swept, and begged:

"It's not you taking the money, Mummy, it's me."

"Why do you want to go into that hellhole of a city? Imagine my life, living with a man like your father, in a place like that! My mother would call and tell me to leave him. I'm a good person, I did not. Otherwise who would take care of him? He hardly talked to me. He boiled his rice, phoned his mother, and went to bed. He liked another old woman. I went to the library. The librarian watched me typing a résumé. What was there to put? Who had I ever been? I didn't know I was pregnant with you. Then really I would become nobody."

"You make everything about you."

"Yes, everything should be about you, only."

"I'm sad, Mummy."

"How should I feel? You're sent to a good school; you're fed, thanks to me you are not ugly. Hopefully I'll be dead soon; you can stay with your father, who cannot fold underwear—"

"I do nothing, I am nothing!" Ashok shouted, from the bedroom. "Have you finished, Anita?"

"Okay, victim. You never say no to her," Anita said. "Leila, you want to spend time with your family, or some old man in some stinking acting class that goes nowhere? Your choice."

Some Stinking Acting Class

"Of course Leila picked the old man," said Aparna Naik. "She would have given up a limb to be in a foot fungus advertisement."

The Sharmas asked Matthew to revoke the class deposit. He promised he would. The first Saturday of classes he left them a voicemail—*I'll be there in an hour, the money is paid, there's no refunding it, it's a done deal*—-and parked at the curb of the house, to fetch Leila without stepping inside.

On the drive to the studio in Chelsea, Leila hung her head out the beemer and let her ponytail flap in the wind, like a dog's ears.

Matthew parallel-parked outside a tall and nondescript office building. "Your studio's on the seventeenth floor, up there. Tell me when you leave for lunch, and I'll come meet you."

"Okay. What will you do all day?"

"Don't worry about me, I'll see a friend."

Leila took a narrow silver elevator up to the seventeenth floor. The studio resembled a bleak office space, dim with long gray carpets. A receptionist stacked conical white cups on top of a water cooler. Leila took a seat in the lobby and waited.

The morning portion of class was dedicated to movement. Leila and eight other self-serious teenagers dressed in black lay flat on the cold gray floor of a dance studio that reeked of feet. Leila had not worn black, the teacher reminded her politely, a twentysomething-year-old woman with one off-off-Broadway credit. Leila promised she would next time. The teacher smiled; of course it was fine, but in the real world of the theater, there were no next times.

The teacher blasted instrumental music and asked the class to shut their eyes, scan their bodies, and move as and when the sound moved them. Unmoved, Leila squinted one eye open and watched a boy next to her convulsing, as if in the middle of an exorcism. Perhaps her mother was right. She should abandon this doomed dream of narcissism and focus on school. After body scans the group moved on to a diction class. With wine corks wedged between their lips they practiced transatlantic accents.

Come lunchtime, the group decided to go to a noodle joint around the block. Leila tagged along, trailing behind the convulsing boy.

Leila
Hi matthew out to lunch with my class actually ✓✓
I'll be at the pickup spot at 6 ✓✓

Matthew didn't respond. Leila assumed he was busy with the friend he'd gone to see, perhaps a woman he was dating. At the end of the day, she couldn't find his car in the spot they'd agreed to meet after class. Leila called him. No answer. She paced around a few blocks before spotting his car next to a corner store.

"I was looking all over for you," Leila said, climbing into the passenger seat. On the dashboard sat small circles of brie, parmesan crackers, egg salad flecked with capers and dill, and an individual-sized bottle of prosecco.

"This was your lunch," Matthew said, with a dour expression."

"I'm sorry."

"Well, eat it now, don't let it go to waste. And I thought you might want to try a little prosecco, as a toast. Before you go home and subject yourself to your mother's cooking."

"You usually eat it with gusto," Leila said. "I'm not very hungry, we had noodles. And I shouldn't be drinking. It'll make me look old."

He started the car. "Okay, then."

"Wait, were you waiting for me all day?"

Matthew didn't respond.

Out of guilt Leila chewed a waxy circle of brie. "Do you have any water?"

Matthew twisted the wine cap open. "This should do it."

"Mom will smell it on me, she'll know."

"Your mother doesn't know anything. Have you ever seen her read a book? Pour it into the coffee thermos, put it in your cupholder."

"Why do you hate her?"

"I don't. I just love you."

The thought of him loving her, the off-handed comfort with which he declared it, addled Leila. Her parents, the only humans obliged to love her thus far, were rarely so maudlin.

The six weeks of classes swept by. Saturday mornings, Leila clambered into Matthew's car as the women in their orthopedic shoes and brightly colored nightgowns strolled past. Matthew waved at them, his friends. But in the privacy of the car he shit-talked them.

"These gossips," he said. "Miserable women."

Leila felt him waiting for her reply. And though it felt antithetical to a feminist existence, it was awkward to sit in silence under the pressure of his love for her. He'd paid for her classes. He chauffeured her to New York waited for her at odd hours. So she insulted the women for him, her lifelong neighbors and elders.

"That's Nasreen, she's so cheap," she'd say. "That's Karina, I once saw her steal a scarf. The bitch."

∼

TWO MIDTIER AGENTS WOULD attend the final acting class, a showcase. The teenagers were asked to bring headshots and résumés and prepare one comedic and one dramatic monologue to perform.

In the back of Matthew's car, Leila clutched her headshot tightly, a school album photo she'd blown up to bigger dimensions. Matthew drove past the Dixits' house. Riya had been accepted to Rutgers, and Karina and Rajesh got out of their car with celebratory Party City bags of favors. Riya emerged next, then Vivek in a backwards baseball cap.

Matthew adjusted his mirror. "That boy is a twig," he muttered.

"I think he's good-looking."

"A twig. That girl, your neighbor, is very cute. Her mom told me she got into college. Invited me to a party today, but I told her it's your last class. What's she studying?"

"How should I know?"

"You're friends, no?"

"No."

"Karina said you just visited recently. Asked her for a ride somewhere."

"I don't know what you're talking about, Karina is getting old, she must be confused," Leila said. "And anyone can get into state school."

"Okay, elitist." He turned the radio to the nineties station. ". . . Baby One More Time" played. Matthew chuckled to himself. "Funny story, this song."

Leila did not ask him what the story was. He chuckled louder.

"Funny story," he repeated. "Have you seen this video? A friend of mine had to leave the room whenever it came on."

Leila did remember the video: a young Britney celebrated the bell ringing at the end of a grueling school day and asked repeatedly for an amorphous baby to strike her, presumably on the face.

"Why?"

"You know."

"I don't."

"Hot and bothered, he was."

"Oh." Leila stuck her head out the window again. "What a pedo."

Matthew stopped at a rest station just before the Lincoln Tunnel. "My sugar is low, I'm going in, I'll only be a minute," he said, and locked Leila inside. He returned with a McDonald's bag and tossed Leila an English muffin. "Sustenance for your showcase."

"Thank you." She unwrapped the silver foil. "I don't eat sausage."

"Eat. I promise you won't be reborn as a cow. Or go to hell—whatever the women warn."

"Hell is Christian. And sausage is pig."

"Fine, I'll eat it. It'll spike my sugar, but I'll eat it." Matthew rapped his knuckles against the glove compartment where he kept his passport, spare cash, and a fanny pack of medication. "If I get ill, my medications are here, call 911 and inject me."

"Okay, stop, I'll eat it."

"Thank you."

The sausage was sweet and gamy. Leila ate ravenously, then threw up in the bag. Sick landed on her headshot. Softened by her effort, Matthew offered her cleaning wipes and stepped out of the car to dispose of her sick. Leila heard the trunk pop. Matthew returned with a Bergdorf's shopping bag.

"A surprise for you, L."

Underneath the tissue sat a neatly folded black dress with a golden zipper up the side, identical to the one in Louise's benefit photograph.

"All black for your showcase."

Leila thumbed a deodorant stain on the fabric. "Is this Louise's?"

"I got the same one in your size."

"I'm already wearing black."

"There's agents coming to this, you look cheap now. Change."

He wouldn't unlock the car door. He didn't want her going to the rest stop bathroom alone. They were short on time; it was a bad stop, muggings and what not; there'd be drugged-out women in the stalls, shaking and strung out on methadone.

"Sad," Leila said.

Matthew continued: Women crying at their reflections, swishing Listerine in the mirrors. Trafficked women banging up gumball machines, begging a stray ball to fall out without having to slip a quarter in and looking for new girls to traffic. Leila was perplexed. The trafficked women, so busy with gumballs, why would they push the same sordid fate onto a new crop of girls? Weren't the men the traffickers?

Oh yes, Matthew agreed. Men accomplished all manners of terror. But it was women—mark his words, it was women—who did worse, who had more evil inside them. Leila should trust him on that.

"It's like your mother," he said. "Eats the misogyny, then regurgitates worse than it ever went down."

Leila's stomach churned again. Too self-conscious to get sick in a public restroom, she agreed to change inside the car. Matthew looked down as she stripped off her black cotton shirt. She had on her best Target bra. White with a silk rosebud center. The dress Matthew bought was low-cut. She had to take the bra off to wear it properly. Her nipples puckered and darkened in the cold. She spotted a pair of tinted glasses in the rearview mirror.

"Are you looking at me?"

"No." Matthew turned his head. "Why would I want to look at a child?"

Now she was insulted he didn't want to. "Cause I'm cute. Don't you think? Look at me. I'm cute too."

A Temple-Free Holiday

The two agents who came to Leila's show had clapped politely at the end of her monologues. They accepted her Cloroxed headshot with the contact information on the back. Weeks passed. Neither reached out to her. Dejected, Leila signed up to audition for the school musical. She spent the beginning of Christmas holidays working on an audition song and refreshing her inbox for representation.

Matthew had flown to the UK to see Louise's family. She had not seen him since the day of the showcase, the exchange of the black dress. Since then he'd responded to her messages infrequently.

Leila
Hi ✓✓
you mad at me? ✓✓
I'm so sorry about the other day. Ty for the dress✓✓
Hello??

Matthew ✓✓
busy✓✓

Leila
I'm so sorry. ✓✓
I don't know what's wrong with me. I know you weren't looking at me ✓✓

what can I do? ✓✓
Hey I am really really sorry :-(I'll do anything ✓✓

On Christmas Day, *Dil Se* played on loop in the Sharma living room. Leila tried not to look on her phone and sat on a couch opposite Ashok, reading the subtitles.

"Why does no one kiss?"

"Government censorship," Ashok replied.

Everything else was appropriate viewing; mass rape and suicide bombing. Malaika Arora's pipe bomb detonated onscreen.

Anita oiled the dead ends of her hair at the kitchen table. "How sad that Shah Rukh Khan dies with her."

"You are missing the point, Anita." Ashok said. "It's a statement, she's the victim of a mass violation."

"I know, professor. There's no reason for some young innocent man to die too. There's a limit to everything."

"Your aphorisms are tiring, Anita."

"Leila, never marry an old man. He'll lecture you. Get ready for temple. Your father must see his girlfriends."

"Anita, please."

The Sharmas spent Christmases at a temple in north Jersey. It was built decades ago, and Ashok loved the classic architecture, a collection of ornate towers, vestibules, and pillars flanked with gilded wire-bound nymphs. He also loved that it was far from the community temple, where the women talked smack and served bland rajma in the small hall. Here you could meet people *who did not know you from Adam*, he liked to say, and in the basement, priests' wives sold oily vada on paper plates. Ashok teased them about the sourness of the batter.

Leila was indifferent to the temple, where throngs of worshippers walked barefoot on the marble, and strangers stepped on her toes without apology.

"I'll get changed," Leila said. Before she could make her way up to her bedroom the house phone rang. She ran to the kitchen to answer it.

"Hello?"

"Leila!" Matthew said, jovially. "I'm back from holiday. Tell your dad I'm coming over tonight."

"So you're not mad at me?"

"Tell him I'm cooking."

"We're going to temple."

Leila heard a teakettle or cat hiss in the background.

"You must be the mad one, Leila, if you'd rather sit shiva than see me."

"Hold on."

Ashok had already put on his good kurta.

"Sometimes people have to be with their own families, Leila," he told her.

But Matthew had none left, Louise was still in the UK with her family, Leila implored. Christmas wasn't their holiday anyway. Remember the criminal who burned Matthew's mother to death?

"Fine," Ashok said, and watched the television in silence.

Upstairs in the master bathroom, Leila discovered Anita dry-shaving her legs. Her mother wore a powder-blue dress with padded shoulders.

"Can I borrow something to wear, Mummy?"

"Sure, you do what you want. We said no to that class, and you go anyway. Your father, for all he does for you, he says no to this, and you do it anyway."

"Matthew has nowhere to go."

"How much pity you have, for outside people. For your people, zero."

Leila ignored her mother and stepped into her closet. She parsed through the work blouses and dug her fingers into a deep-mauve V-neck sweater. The sweater was inexpensive; Anita prided herself on her ability to make cheap clothes appear luxurious with the understated fact of her beauty. Leila slipped it on. The neckline hung low; she had no cleavage to hold it up.

Anita glossed her lips. "Low shirts are for desperate women."

"It's your shirt, Mummy."

"I'm a desperate woman. For what are you getting so dressed up?"

Leila hung the sweater back up. She could not shake the recollection of Matthew's tinted eyes in the dashboard. Like a stone she had turned that memory over and over until the discomfort went smooth and it became pleasant to hold.

MATTHEW ARRIVED WITH a Whole Foods tote that clinked with glass. He kissed Leila's cheeks.

"How are we, kiddo? Heard anything from your showcase?"

"Not yet," Leila said. "But I'm auditioning for the school musical. Want to hear my song?"

"One second," Matthew said. "Let your mummy open her gift."

Anita shook his hand. "Nice to see you." She took two bottles out of the tote. One was Old Monk Rum, the other a dark brandy.

"Top-notch stuff," Matthew said.

Ashok lay on the couch. "We don't need so much alcohol, these days there's too many bottles in this house."

"A family of martyrs this is," Matthew replied. "Anita can drink them."

Matthew insisted on cooking. He made spaghetti and fish; he had an unofficial Italian grandmother in Montclair, he said, who'd taught him how to do it right. He made a great show out of the simple act of boiling pasta, rolling his sleeves high and embarrassing the Sharmas with the sight of his soaked armpits. Garlic burned in a pan with tomato paste and anchovies.

Anita lit a beedi. "This man," she whispered, to Leila. "So much drama for a bloody pasta."

Matthew picked up the pot and sniffed the inside. "Who washed these? Smells like Auntie's fish curry."

"Leila," Anita said, "go help Uncle scrub that pan. I have never cooked fish in it, but apparently there's a smell."

Leila squirted soap into a Brillo pad.

"So," Matthew said, behind her. "What's your audition song?"

" 'Big Spender.' "

"Mature. Might be a shock to those nuns."

"Well, my voice is mature. Do you want to hear it now?"

"Leila," Anita exhaled. "Don't torture him, please. Didn't he suffer through that class already? And have any agents said shit?"

~

THE SPAGHETTI WAS OVERCOOKED; the fish bland and oily. Anita opened the brandy bottle and inhaled. "My dad loved this. So I avoided it."

She poured herself an inch.

Ashok sighed. "Some people, one sip and they drown."

The liquor was strong, and though Anita hadn't had much, it quickly went to her head. "See, Matthew, how these two conspire? I had Leila so young, I had no fun. Ashok never pays attention."

She poured herself another inch. "I don't even have affairs. I deserve one good thing."

Ashok rubbed his eyes. "You deserve if you hydrate."

"He's afraid of my genes," Anita said. "Drinking made my father ugly. He grew chins. I should go slow."

Anita closed her eyes and hiccupped, lost in a private reverie. The top button of her dress came loose. Matthew watched her attentively. It embarrassed Leila, how comfortably her mother came undone, the interest she commanded so easily, even from a man who bad-mouthed her.

Anita swirled pasta around her fork without taking a bite. "We had a house with two rooms, no bigger than this kitchen. The women say they were poor, but back home they have maidservants and drivers. Nobody was poor like me. Papa collected ticket stubs for work. He drank until the room spun. My mother made pickles. Her brother had a garment shop. I worked there."

Leila tried to interrupt. Absorbed, Matthew shushed her. "Listen."

Anita continued. "I'd come home and tell him, *Papa, your brother-in-law pays me bullshit. He tells me you're a drunkard. That you're less than a man, because your daughter does everything. A household on a schoolgirl's shoulders.*" Anita hiccupped. "My mother—good-for-nothing, she was. Marrying me off to this—" she smashed a knuckle into Ashok's biceps—"old man. Anyway, she said, *Beti, what am I to do? The drink ate your daddy's brain. Is it my fault? Just bury and move on.*"

Ashok rubbed his temples. "Okay, Anita."

"I asked my daddy, why drink? Why would a handsome man pick ugly? He said he had bad memories. But a leech doesn't suck only the bad blood, it sucks all of it. Liquor did that. *You idiot*, I told him. And one afternoon I came from the shop in tears. For the life of me—oh! Hopefully there's not much left—I don't remember what made me so upset. It's redacted ink in my brain. Papa was home. He poured me brandy. He was right about nothing, but he was right about liquor. Whatever bad memory I had, I forgot."

"Okay, Anita." Ashok cracked his joints. The room slumped under silence. Matthew took Anita's outstretched hand. Anita retracted hers, as if electrocuted.

"If a man has a problem, Anita," Matthew said, "it does not mean it is yours to carry too."

Ashok stuck a fork in his pasta and acted as if he couldn't see Anita commanding sympathy. He hated such ostentatious shows of emotion; he never felt possessive or coveted attention. If anything bothered him, it was the food she wasted in her lachrymose performance.

Leila took Anita's plate to the sink before her father could polish it off. She didn't notice Matthew following her to the kitchen until he leaned over with a dirty dish, a soft bulge in his pants.

"Sing a verse for me, from your song."

Leila sang. She had no vocal control, Matthew said, and he rested his hands, thick with suds, on her diaphragm.

"Suck in tighter." He pressed into her. The sensation comforted Leila, who felt accomplished to have instigated some goodness at last.

Anita's footsteps sounded down the hall. Matthew stepped backward and pushed Leila into the sink. She dropped the Brillo pad.

"Stop, stop," Matthew said. "Do you want to upset your mother? Didn't you listen? Already she's suffered so much."

After he left, Anita discovered the Brillo pad in the sink and screamed:

"What monster leaves Brillo pads here? Ashok, it's always you!"

"I'll die, Anita," Ashok replied calmly. "Then you'll be happy."

"Don't say such horrors in front of your daughter."

"I'm a horrible man."

"Watch. It will be me who goes first. Leila, get the salt; your father's casting nazar on us all."

Leila spooned chili and salt into her palm and shook it in front of her father's face. She sometimes did the same for Anita, when she looked too good in public and feared the women would wish acne on her.

Ashok waved Leila away. "No, I want the evil eye."

"Martyr," Anita said.

"Please stop involving me in these hysterics," Leila protested. "I'm a child."

"Excuses, excuses," Anita said. "Being a child does not exempt you from life."

Yes, Beti

"Someone must have cast the evil eye on them, because then Ashok died," said Aparna Naik. She stood on a rickety ladder inside the Cash & Carry and pried dead flies off a gold sticky trap. "It happened without warning."

It chilled the women to think back to Ashok's cardiac arrest. Devika hooked her finger on her mangalsutra and counted her blessings. Her husband was a cheater, a liar, a narcissist, but at least he was alive.

"The universe is sadistic," she said, and tucked the necklace back into her blouse. "I don't want to jinx it."

Paramedics reported that Anita was in the shower when Ashok fell. It was twelve thirty-nine on a Sunday afternoon in the first blush of spring. Earlier that day, Ashok had picked up potatoes from the market and forgotten milk. ("The one man who came to the market, bless him," Aparna Naik said.) Before he left he'd turned on the AC but forgot to close the windows in the house. The excess humidity gnarled Anita's hair into tight curls.

Ashok came home around ten. Anita inspected the potatoes. Five or six were soft with age. After a brief and final fight with her husband—*Cheapskate, the AC was on, what useless man brings spoiled potatoes*—she went upstairs for her second shower of the day. Leila was in the backyard, reviewing her script from the school musical. She was a chorus member with two lines. She marked up the emotional beats with highlighters, as she'd learned at the conservatory. LET'S GO TO THE MALL, the first line read. The next: YEAH!

Leila colored the words at random. There was no emotion. She plucked a flower from the rosebush Ashok used for prayers. The ragtime ice-cream truck tune sounded in the distance. Hattie or Baloo howled. Leila ran inside the house and took a five dollar bill from Ashok's wallet. She skipped past him downstairs and tapped him on the head.

"I stole from you," she said. "Make me a turkey patty melt?"

Yes, Beti, he said, but Leila was already out the door and did not hear him.

Riya Dixit stood at the front of the ice-cream line, holding hands with Vivek. Behind them, Devika gripped Manu's reluctant hand. *Mummy, Mummy, let g*o, he whispered. The truck charged four dollars for his chocolate cone.

"Scammer," Devika spat, at the pimply ice-cream man. She had only three dollars on her.

Leila turned out her pockets. "I have extra, Auntie."

Devika recalled feeling the urge to smack Leila. "Manu is not spoiled like her, he has principles of abstinence," she said. "I didn't need some blasted handout."

That memory haunted Devika. As she fantasized about smacking the girl over ice cream, her father was home, dying.

"But she didn't know—who could?" Devika said. "I watched her order a lemon ice pop."

Paramedics said Ashok had been in the kitchen when it happened. Frying Leila's patty melt. ("You see, spoiled. Manu is years younger and does it on his own," Devika said.) A white ribbon of fat spluttered in the oil pan. His chest sweltered and dulled with ache. He fanned himself and reached for a pepper shaker. His blood flow slowed and stopped. The patty melt burned in the pan. Upstairs Anita heard a dreadful thud. Somehow she knew it was a body. She ran downstairs in a towel.

"I have never died, so I cannot imagine the moments before," said Hema Rao. "I imagine it's like when the hangover is too much, and you kneel before the toilet and plead, *god, don't make me vomit.* But the sickness is cemented. No prayer will keep it from rising."

Anita dropped to her knees, soap-covered and dry-mouthed. With no real CPR knowledge she tried to resuscitate Ashok. Death couldn't happen here, in this place he hated, she thought. With this woman he hated. Anita took Ashok's hand, first held in a wedding hall, and wove his fingers with hers. She stroked his wrinkled knuckles. Ashok's eyes, unfocused, drifted past Anita's pleading gaze and glazed over. Anita slapped him across the face to provoke him back to life.

"Hey, idiot, wake up," she cried. "Motherfucker. Awake. Please."

Paramedics arrived. There was no resuscitation, one told Anita. She emitted a banshee cry of grief that sounded around the block and raised the women's leg hairs.

"Some moments stay with you, even if they're not yours," said Nasreen Farouk.

Every woman remembered what she was doing the moment the scream broke out. Nasreen was eating fried takeout on her Formica table. Aparna Naik was dog-earing a page in her monthly issue of *Vogue*. Vritika Shetty was receiving oral sex from her bungling lover.

"Horrifying," Vritika said.

In the cul-de-sac, Leila dropped her lemon ice pop and ran home. A stray cat huddled around the spot of concrete where Leila's popsicle melted and licked the drip clean.

The Dixits and Kaushals stood out on their driveways and stared at the ambulance and cop cars looped around the Sharmas' house. Everyone wore the look of intrigue and relief one got watching terrible things happen to other people. Vivek wrapped an arm around Riya, who whispered something into his ear. He kissed her forehead. Leila ran past them and into House 24, where she found her mother in a dress of suds, hunched over Ashok's body. The kitchen stank of burned meat. Leila took one look at her father's glassy eyes and felt her own vision cross. *It can't happen here, Leila*, Anita cried. *He hated it here. Hated me.* Leila watched on, fascinated, as her mother pressed her mouth down on Ashok's one final time and huffed her oxygen into him. In all Leila's life, she had never once seen her parents kiss.

/ THE SHARMAS AFTER MATTHEW

The Division of Youth
and Family Services

THE OFFICERS had closed Matthew's case, but after Karina's tip about the Sharmas ("More substantial than the laddus," said Nasreen Farouk) they made a report to some child services agency or another and handed it off to them.

"All this bullshit would have been over, the heat lifted, but Karina had to open her mouth," an anonymous grandmother said, fanning her face outside. "What was it she said? *When he touched her child, she turned her cheek. Perhaps you should investigate that.*"

Anita waited for the Division of Youth and Family Services visit. In the interim the Sharmas mostly stayed locked inside with the blinds shut and tried to behave.

"She will lose that girl, I think," said Nasreen Farouk, clicking her tongue at her canteen register as she handed a takeout bag to Karina Dixit.

Karina slammed a ten-dollar bill on the fat-soaked countertop. "And maybe she deserves to."

～

LEILA WAS SITTING on the concrete steps that led up to her house and eating the whipped cream off a Wawa smoothie when Karina Dixit pulled in to her driveway with a Kwality bag. Leila removed her dirty sunglasses and went back inside, shutting the door behind her before Karina could see. She used to think that girls who survive tragedies are chosen for Reasons of Great Importance. Court payouts. *20/20* interviews. How disappointing that she enjoyed no such fanfare, that she had suffered meaninglessly for three years, another trite and tiresome abuse account.

Since Matthew died, life had been no better than it had before. Leila had been stuck home while the neighbors planned his memorial, drinking Wawa and flushing the carpenter ants that had been infesting the house down the toilet. A few times she'd texted Adrian, the college boy from the town over, but her messages stopped going through. Earlier that week, after the officers first descended on the neighborhood, Anita discovered Leila's porn search history on the home computer and dropped extra dollars on a Verizon Family plan to monitor the numbers in her contacts.

Leila complained to Verizon's help line. *Minors should have privacy, should have free will*, she said. *I'm not sure that's how it works*, a customer service representative responded.

Leila hung up. She'd been careful, saving Adrian's name under a woman's. Isha. It was Matthew who had suggested that trick to her, to use it for him. *Put me in as Emma, our strategy of secrecy*, he'd told her, after his friendship with Anita soured.

Anita never cracked the Emma code in time, the code that mattered. But when she discovered Leila messaging "Isha," she barged into the bathroom. Leila was sitting on the floor of the shower, washing her hair with a beige plastic tumbler and bucket and pumping diluted Pantene conditioner into her palm. Anita had filled the bottle with water to make it last longer.

Anita rammed her fist against the frosted glass. *I thought you were done with this behavior. This deviance. Do you not see police in town? Who is Isha?*

"No one." Blood thrummed in Leila's ears. "Mother, can we not afford a new conditioner? Are you so frugal?"

The two devolved into an argument about consumerism, and Leila felt certain she'd diverted the suspicion. The next morning, as she brushed her teeth, Anita called Leila's contacts and blocked Adrian, the lone male voice who answered.

"What did you *do*?" Leila shook the staircase banister. Spearmint foam dripped onto the hardwood.

"Shut up, woman," Anita replied, in Marathi. Anita only spoke Marathi to Leila when she wanted to gossip about people without them knowing. Also when she wanted to punish her. Leila's understanding of the language was limited to its little cruelties: *I-will-rip-rip-and-tear-you*; *come-downstairs-and-bloody-eat*; *beggar-woman*; *madwoman*; *eat-shit-woman*; *see-what-I'll-do-to-you-woman*.

"No mother would do for you, woman, the things I have done to protect you. You think Karina would have done it? Devika? Jyoti? Hema? She doesn't even speak to her sons. Just her dogs."

"It's too late to protect me."

"Kill me off, then," Anita said. "I told you not to go with that old man. It was you who wanted to. This audition, that audition."

What had been fraying between them snapped. Leila rushed down the stairwell. Anita scampered up. Leila grabbed a fistful of her mother's dyed hair; Anita pinched her ears under a painting of poinsettias. Nails dug cleanly into forearms.

Anita ugly-cried into the stairwell. "Monster. I work so hard, keep my credit score so high, and still I have given birth to one."

~

IT HAD BEEN A TERRIBLE week. Unable to go to town or call anybody without scrutiny, Leila watched reruns of *America's Next Top Model* in the basement. There was one makeover episode she liked rewinding, in which a girl gets extension tracks that resembled Maggi noodles, so painful she cried. Tyra praised the girls who didn't.

After a few hours of television Leila came up for air. She joined Anita in the kitchen. The two laid a mat on the granite floor and snapped the ends off string beans.

"See, when I cook, I cook homemade, healthy," Anita said. "Karina, who can't keep her mouth shut, drowns her food in ghee. You know she once called the police on your father and I once, just for fighting?"

"You don't eat anything you cook," Leila said. "You're on your Persian cucumber diet."

"That's because I give, give-give. Do I ever take? Can you believe she went to that bloody memorial?"

"I think I am chemically depressed."

"That too, is my fault?"

"I didn't say it was."

"There is such a thing as subtext. Save your sad for when the social worker comes, look sad about what Uncle Matthew did."

Anita set the beans aside. She fished a beedi out of her bra and sauntered to the back door, slid the glass open, and blew smoke through the mesh. "Let them know you have a happy life here and would be happy no place else. And you *are* happy, you are."

Leila sat at the table. A carpenter ant walked across her sticky floral placemat. "Would they really put me someplace else?"

"Who else could put up with you? No mother would do it, this thing I've done for you. Even you—if you were a mother, even you would not do." She said this without looking at Leila, who sat on the floor, dressed in a cropped shirt and lace shorts Matthew had bought her.

Leila understood her mother wanted thanks. "But what did you do?"

"Nothing." Anita bunched up her sundress and dried her eyes. So Leila had been touched. Who had not been? "I buried and moved on. You want to get sucked into the black hole."

"What did you bury?"

Anita lit another cigarette. "Wear your gingham dress when the people come. You look less slut in squares."

SATURDAY

Heather

THE DAY OF THE VISIT, Leila watched five hours of reality TV in the basement and came up for a glass of strawberry SlimFast. By now the Sharmas had been on edge for so many hours they had no edge left. Anita chewed betel leaf on the couch, her laptop open to the Verizon Family page. Through the foyer window Leila spotted a red Nissan creeping into the block, a car she did not recognize.

"Leila." Anita's square teeth were stained red. "You're still trying to call that boy, even after I blocked him?"

Leila sipped her SlimFast. "I don't know what you're talking about."

"I can see it on my account, right here."

"This is emotional abuse."

"This again. Imagine living my life, idiot, if you think this is abuse. A bloody liar you are."

The Nissan parked in the Sharmas' driveway.

"I literally never lie."

"Aiyoh, see? Another lie."

A knock sounded at the door. Anita spat out the rest of her paan in the trash. SlimFast spilled down the front of Leila's gingham dress as she raced the door. Through the foyer window they could see that the DYFS woman had parked her Nissan over a chalk evil eye Anita had drawn that Tuesday, hands and knees pressed into the hot pavement, while Leila heckled her. *What does this help, Mummy? Evil was already here.*

The car door opened. The woman, Heather, was short and heavyset with a clipboard pressed against her chest. Her thin copper hair was pulled back into a practical nub.

Anita ushered Heather down the front walkway. The woman's heel snagged on a weed growing in the cracks between the stones.

"Fuck," Anita whispered, in Leila's ear, when she reached the threshold of the front door. "Did I not tell you to pull those? Or you are too busy with your reality TV?"

The two squabbled so quietly and intensely that they didn't notice it at first—the women watching.

All around the block the women were watching.

Devika had opened both garage doors; inside, she and flat-faced mama's boy Manu reclined on yoga mats and drank lemonade next to the lawn mower kerosene. Hema Rao jogged around her yard with the Dobermans, their tongues hanging heavy and red with heat exhaustion. Jyoti Kaushal watched from her door window in her horrible green dressing gown, one hand pressed against her baby bump, a copy of *People* in the other.

A fallen eyelash clouded Leila's vision. She blinked away the irritation. When she opened her eyes, the women were nowhere to be seen: no garage doors open, no green nightgowns and gossip magazines; no dogs panting. She'd imagined them walking. She wondered how many truths she had imagined. Maybe it was wish fulfillment. To think that the women, shuttered behind their own blinds, cared enough to look at her at all.

∼

HEATHER REQUESTED a quick house tour. Leila trailed behind Heather while Anita walked briskly ahead, so that she could make sure the prayer cabinet was closed and that toilets had been flushed, that blood hadn't dripped on the rim of the seat.

See, this bitch left her shoes on, Anita told Leila, in Marathi.

Heather pressed her clipboard closer to her chest. She opened the fridge and inspected the cans of SlimFast. "Who drinks these?"

"Nobody, they were a gift," Anita said. "From a very offensive friend."

Carpenter ants swarmed the strawberry liquid Leila had spilled on the kitchen floor.

"We're getting an exterminator," Anita explained. "I keep a clean house, but the neighbors are dirty and their filth drifts over. The Kaushals just had this problem, no, Leila?"

"Yes," Leila said. She stared at the ants swarming, too embarrassed to look at her mother fussing over this woman in a way she'd never seen her fuss over anybody—would Heather take tea? Water? Coffee? Sorry sorry.

"No, no need," Heather said. "Leila, let's talk in private?"

"Sure, sure," Anita hummed. "You two go into the living room. I'll just be here in the kitchen."

"We won't be long, Mrs. Sharma, you can go upstairs."

Anita kneaded her hands together and smiled. Her teeth were still red from betel leaf.

"I'll be here, only. It's my house."

"We won't be long."

Anita nodded, then turned to Leila. *This bloody bitch*, she said, in Marathi, leaving the *bloody* in English. *Ordering me around in my own house. Opening doors. And you—watch yourself, idiot. Think this bitch is here to help? She could do with a SlimFast.* She left "SlimFast" in English too.

Heather and Leila sat in the living room on opposing sofas. Heather patted the plastic wrapping of the couch and cleared her throat. When did it begin?

Leila knew Heather wanted her to tell a very sorry story, like the girls in the SVU episodes, who exist only to tell very sorry stories.

"When did what begin?"

Heather frowned. Leila didn't have to be shy. Heather had helped dozens of girls before.

"Help them with what, exactly? Whatever it was, it's over now, and he's dead. The neighbor who told you hates us."

Heather helped girls younger than Leila. Girls who had to use dolls and point to diagrams to talk about what had been done to their bodies. "And you're, what, sixteen, right?"

"Right."

"Well. Well, I have talked to girls as little as three."

Heather said this with percolating impatience, but Leila saw tenderness in her expression too. Leila wanted to tell her about the dream that woke her all summer long, a dream of driving down the interstate, down the Jersey Turnpike. It was Matthew's car but there was no Matthew inside. Just Leila in the driver's seat, jetting past billboards advertising luxury watches and medical malpractice lawyers and into the city alone, where she had spent so many overnights with Matthew.

The Matthew parts didn't interest Leila. They were horror without variation. What she most wanted to tell Heather was how light and free it felt to drive alone. Although merely a dream, it was a lightness she hadn't felt for months. The math of pleasure was unfair: it took a man five minutes to cum, and maybe fifteen to die, but that lightness was a feeling Leila wouldn't have again in real life for many years, and maybe never again. Leila wanted to tell Heather all of this, but when she looked at the social worker's face, that tenderness she'd seen before she didn't see anymore. Heather yawned, peered at her clipboard, and asked her again; she had a job to do: How did it begin?

THE SHARMAS WITHOUT ASHOK, 2010s

He Was Not a Bad Man

After the cardiac episode, Matthew met the Sharmas in the white hospital lobby. He arrived unshaven, with bloodshot eyes and jeans, his careful demeanor askance. Leila slumped over in a chair and cried between her knees. For an hour she waited for a doctor to reverse time, or undo the pronouncement the paramedics had made, like when you discovered a goldfish belly-up in the water and mistook him for dead when in fact he was only sleeping, overfed, or fraught with bladder disease.

Anita had made the call to Matthew. Initially told Leila not to. *That fool of a man, ate our meals and never helped your father*, Anita said. Then she saw a sick patient on the other side of the hospital wing defecate onto the floor and called him herself.

On the phone, Anita told Matthew she could not face her fate alone. When he arrived, she could not look him in the face.

"You can leave, sorry for the trouble," Anita said, staring at the lines of orange-and-yellow-tape on the hospital floor, a map for the sick young and the sick old.

"Of course I'm staying." Matthew rested a hand on Anita's shoulder, which she instantly brushed away. "Let me take Leila home. You don't want to have her sitting around seeing people shit on the floor."

"I'm not leaving, I want to see Dad."

Anita rubbed her eyes. "A body is not a person."

So they waited. Matthew drove the two of them home. Leila rode in the passenger seat. Anita cried in the back.

"I heard the sobs from my window," Jyoti said. "Like animals dying."

"He was not a bad man," Anita said, to no one. "To him, I was the bad man. Now I'm alone."

"Nonsense," Matthew said. "Look around, how can you be alone?"

That night Matthew slept on the sofa. He gave Anita a pill to sleep deeply and took one himself. *Sorry, L, not for children*, he told Leila, who wanted one too.

The phone rang around three. Leila picked up. It was her great-aunt or a grandmother, Leila couldn't tell; she'd talked to each only a handful of times. They spoke little of each other's language, and communicating with her felt to Leila like pulling a too-small blanket over her body. Cover one part and another became exposed.

This time the great-aunt or grandmother was lucid. "My soul hurts," she said, and ended the call.

~

MATTHEW STAYED AT the house for days. Like a maidservant he bustled in bags of groceries, discarded the trash, locked the doors at night and made toast in the mornings, though no one had an appetite.

The first few nights he brought Leila water and sat with her as she cried in her bedroom. Every hour, Anita slammed the door open and hovered at the threshold to check on them. The fourth night she fell asleep.

Near sleep herself Leila startled, awoken by a warmth on her lower back. A chubby thumb kneaded small circles into her pajama shirt, then her bare skin.

"I won't get into bed," Matthew whispered. "When I lost my mother, I thought it was my fault."

No one asked about his mother or his faults, Leila thought. Now his fingers were higher, between her shoulder blades. The warmth was pleasant, but he was so ugly, no wonder Anita had laughed at his Polaroids.

"I got you tickets to another show next month, to get your mind off this. You need to move on."

"My mind will never be off this, I will never move on. I don't want to think about shows."

"Give it time. And I've already bought the tickets."

"I don't want to go. Mom will be alone."

"Your mother loves you, sure, but wants you to be miserable like her. She is— what? Thirty-seven?"

"Thirty-six."

"My god, thirty-six. At that age a woman should grow up and realize she has lived her life. It's your life that I care about."

Leila brushed his hand aside.

Did she ever consider, Matthew continued, that Anita would be happy without Ashok? How many times had she complained about him, spewed insults at him? He'd read Leila's play; clearly even Leila knew it.

"She goes on and on about her plight in life, her arrangement to him," Matthew said. "She tells you she had no choice, no agency, and you believe her. Don't drink that Kool-Aid, Leila. Absolutely she had a choice."

He hated to see Leila sad, he said. He pressed a hand to her back and rolled the dead weight of her body over, so that she was facing him. He rubbed circles up her stomach and pinched her nipples.

"See? That means you're excited," Matthew said. "Like you were in the car, but more. You've probably not been excited like this before."

"I'm not excited whatsoever. I'm cold, I'm tired."

"Let me make you happy."

"I will never be happy again."

"Just wait." He bent his shaggy head and pressed his lips against her chest. He left them there for a long time, expectant. His hair smelled of sebum. Leila wanted to crawl out of her eyes. She wondered if she should make a noise, some indication of satisfaction that would keep him from going on longer. She made a noise. It compelled him to go on for longer. Matthew pressed two fingers between her legs. Leila made a standing ovation noise; his fingers cramped, and it was over. *Change your underwear before you sleep*, he said. *That one's soaked.*

Leila fingered the fabric. "It's bone dry."

The Sharma Women

MATTHEW RETURNED TO New York. The Sharmas' house immobilized. Laundry stopped thrumming from the basement. Dirty bras piled up in the sink with the dishes and were worn regardless. Soon there were no groceries in the fridge beyond bananas and Persian cucumbers, which Anita cried into as she cut. *He was so happy to die*, she announced, unbidden. It was difficult to be around her like that, and Leila retreated upstairs to sit in her father's closet, to thumb the patterned ties he wore, the unwrapped candle on a top shelf, a housewarming gift from an old friend he lost touch with, though he'd kept the candle forever.

She wept, but nothing made her weep harder than seeing Anita weep too; Anita whose grief was more grandiose than even she had expected. She wept at the table, in the bathtub, urinating in it.

~

"BUT HADN'T ANITA waited for singledom all her married life?" said Jyoti, under the threading needle at the eyebrow salon.

"For so long I heard her arguing with Ashok, telling him he held her hostage," Devika agreed, flipping a magazine in the next chair over.

"She would say, *old man, old man, old man*," Karina chimed in. "For so long she set a placemat for grief. Then when it arrives, she cannot eat opposite it. Poor girls. But who knows? Maybe it is in their karma, probably it is."

"My god, women," said the salon proprietor, thread through her teeth. "You have let your faces grow so fuzzy."

~

THE WOMEN RANG the Sharmas' bell with oil-stained fingers and condolences.

"We dropped trays of okra and lemon rice," said Jyoti.

"Your okra was overcooked," said Hema Rao.

Karina and Riya dropped by with kheer. Butter pats swam under the foil.

"I'm sorry for you, Auntie," Riya said.

Karina nodded. "It is terrifying, having husbands so old and infirm. I should know."

Anita lifted the lid of the aluminum tray. The vermicelli congealed under a pool of yellow foam. "I don't eat so much butter."

Leila accepted the tray on her mother's behalf. How nasty she could be in mourning, as nasty as in normalcy.

"So what?" Anita said. "These women don't care about your father. They just want to fatten me."

~

ANITA DROVE LEILA to the Cash & Carry to replenish the empty fridge; their first excursion in weeks. It was a golden summer afternoon. Usha Gohel's pimply nephew scanned their items. As Anita bagged them, Leila pushed the green shopping cart past the oil aisle and returned it to the stack outside the market. Hema Rao's truck was parked nearby. Hattie and Baloo panted in the driver and passenger seats. Leila walked down the strip mall path. In the window of the ice-cream store next door to the market, Manu and Devika split a tall glass of pink falooda. Leila opened her phone. She reread her father's final text message. It was about the patty melt. *Ur food is ready.*

Aparna Naik came outside and straightened out the Cash & Carry carts, a spliff tucked behind her ear. Behind her, Leila could make out Riya's bony shoulders. She carried a large bag of fruit.

Leila waved. "Hi."

"Hi." The sun wavered. The older girl looked uncomfortable, her gaze shifting from the left to the right.

"Congratulations on Rutgers."

"Thanks."

"What's your major?"

"Chemistry," Riya replied. "Did you come here alone?"

"Mom's inside."

"How is she?"

"Terrible."

"At least you have Matthew," Riya said.

"But he's a creep, didn't you say that? How can it be a good thing?"

"I'm not even sure, anymore, if he looked at me," Riya said. "And it is a good thing. Most people are left with nobody."

SATURDAY AFTERNOON

A Loose Girl

"Matthew befriended other young girls, he told us. He didn't tell us he was a sick man, but he told us. We thought it was a sweet thing, a fatherly thing," said Devika Gill, sipping a lemonade on her front steps, eyes glued to the Nissan in front of the Sharmas' house. "As a graduate student in London, he rented out a room in the house of one of his professors. Pakistani man, with twin daughters, very sheltered. He introduced them to McDonald's. Unsheltered them. That's all I know."

"And then they moved away, and he rented from another man, from Hyderabad. A terrible thing really, what happened to that daughter," said Jyoti, sitting in the lawn chair next to Devika.

"What happened to her?" Devika pressed.

"Matthew said she was a loose girl, he tried to stop her from sneaking out to a concert, but one way or another she went, she ended up pregnant, you know, and then they sent her away. Then the mother, in shame, drowned herself. Matthew found her body."

Devika covered her mouth. "My god. Yes, I remember now. He showed me a picture of her from his wallet. He liked fair girls. Remember he bought Leila that pale foundation? So thick, like a clown. Thump her on the back and her face would fall off the front. I wondered, should I say something?"

Jyoti interjected: "I wondered, should *I*?"

Devika cut back in. "But it was me who said to her, maybe six months after Ashok passed, you know, I'm a sensitive person—you'll look old, dear, if you slather it on your face like that. Like an old escort. She said 'Thank you, Auntie,' and left. Later I got a text from Anita: *r u calling my child a whore?*"

THE UNHAPPY KIND, 2010s

Comic Sans

Months passed and softened the sharp bite of grief. Leila tried to drop out of the school musical, too depressed to continue. Anita encouraged her to carry on. *"Unnamed chorus role" will go on your college record, you went to the practices, now finish the show.* The night of her performance, she lip-synched, fumbled her two lines, and sucked ice cream out of a prop float. Anita had to work late ("Your father used to give me allowances, now he has left me as the single earner"). Matthew came to the performance in her stead.

After the show, he handed Leila a bougainvillea bouquet. "So talented, L."

"I messed up my lines."

"No one noticed."

"Of course they did."

"I'm telling you, you were great."

On the walk to the car Leila swung the flowers up and down, cheerful again. "Tell me what moments of me you liked best."

"You had two lines. I'll tell you at dinner. I told your mom she was welcome to come if she's finished working."

"Where's dinner?"

"Madeleine's. The French place near your house. Have you been?"

"No, how bougie."

"Only the best for you, L."

THE RESTAURANT WAS small and dingy, its gray-blue walls patterned with peeling Eiffel Tower print. On the back wall the proprietor had accented the space with a portrait of a Scottish Fold cat wearing a bow tie. The hostess showed Leila and Matthew to their seats. Retirees drank cosmos and ate chicken in a split cream sauce at the table over.

Matthew cracked the menu open. "Time to show you how the Europeans do. This is fine dining, L."

Leila studied her menu. Entrées were listed in Comic Sans.

"This is my daughter," Matthew said, to the chipper waitress who came to take their orders. "A pâté to share, please. And a glass of pinot grigio."

The waitress left.

"I'm not eating blood," Leila said. "And I thought you didn't drink."

"Pâté is liver. The wine's for you, if you're careful about it."

"I'm your daughter now?"

"It's easier this way. I don't want anyone thinking there's anything funny going on, that you're my date."

"I have a backpack under the table. You're so old. Who would think that?"

Matthew set his menu down. Leila sensed his energy souring, as it had when she skipped lunch with him in the city.

"So," she said, "what was your favorite part of the musical?"

"The two leads were quite pretty. The blonde, especially."

"What parts with *me* in it, I mean."

"You were good."

She could tell he was restraining some truth and burst into tears. "I wasn't good, I didn't even want to be part of it. I wanted to quit."

The waitress came around with the pâté and a carafe of wine. After she left the table, Matthew poured half of it into Leila's lemonade glass. It would help her tears, he promised. As for the show, he did have one critique, and it wasn't her fumbled lines. When boys appeared onstage, unfortunate souls who volunteered from other schools, she'd scampered to the side.

"You're gun-shy, L."

"Gun-shy?"

"Don't let these old folks hear me. Afraid of *penis*."

The retirees had moved on to chocolate cake and small glasses of port. "I'm not gun-shy. And you're not much younger than them."

"You should become better friends with your neighbor. What's her name? Riya. She's not gun-shy. She has that twig boyfriend of hers." Matthew pried a mussel from its shell. His tiny fork clattered to the carpet. "What do you think they get up to together?"

She remembered what Riya had said, about Vivek respectfully dipping it inside of her. "How should I know?"

Matthew opened another mussel and refilled Leila's lemonade with the carafe. "Here, finish it before the waitress sees. She's coming."

Leila drank quickly. A floating warmth overtook her.

"Riya is prettier than you, but I prefer you."

He said this naturally, so without desire, that Leila, the warmth in her ears now, curled her fingers around his. A garbage compliment, sure. But how nice it was to be chosen. Matthew squeezed her fingers. "I mean, she's a knockout. But you're special. You have no self-regard."

The floating sensation stopped. "Excuse me?"

"Ah-ah! It's good—the only good thing your mother's ever done."

Matthew squared the check and they walked outside to the car, one of the last three left in the parking lot. The evening had turned amber. Matthew put his arm around Leila's shoulders. The bouquet of flowers wilted at her side.

"I'm not gun-shy."

"Prove it, kiss me," he said, matter-of-fact as a business proposal. His sour tongue shot past her lips, through her teeth. It lasted all of one second. Leila wiped her mouth on her sleeve. Matthew drove her home. He greeted Anita at the door. He told her to put the bougainvillea in water.

After he left, Leila went outside for a walk in the neighborhood, the richness of the meal weighing on her. It was late but still humid. A horde of maple bugs swarmed the purple flowers Nasreen had planted around the base of her elder tree. Leila stopped to watch, mesmerized, forearms freckled with goosebumps of disgust.

She heard panting and whining. Hema, Hattie. and Baloo were out for their night walk. The dogs strained against their leashes to greet her. She held out her palms to be licked.

"Sorry about them," Hema said. "Look at these bugs. I checked, they're harmless, but how awful. She takes such good care of the plants."

"It's said she does it alone, no one helps her," Leila said.

"You can help her," Hema said.

"Okay," Leila said, but she'd only wanted to make the kind observation and then do nothing. "Do you think I have self-regard, Auntie?"

"Get a dog," Hema suggested; with a thing to care for Leila would not think so very hard about herself.

The Audition

After the musical and the Comic Sans dinner, the days dragged on. On Willow Road, Leila killed time in a chatroom. Anita pounded on the door. Leila hadn't defrosted the chicken in time or folded the laundry. Should Anita alone be cursed?

Leila closed the chatroom. "I'll help cook."

"No, I don't want help," Anita replied.

"Let me."

"No, I'm not cooking anyway. I'm busy."

"With?"

"I have to kill myself."

Anita slammed the door and left. Leila returned to her chatroom. A thirty-five-year-old male stranger asked her for her age, sex, and location.

Eighteen, she lied, *f, NYC.*

Sick, he wrote.

What are you reading? I just started Wide Sargasso Sea.

I have an erection, the stranger replied. Leila heard a crash downstairs; a clatter of ceramics, a body-sounding thud. Her heart raced. Imagine Anita had made good on the threat. Police would find Leila's search history and see she'd spent the final moments of her mother's life online with a stranger and his purported erection.

Leila ran downstairs. The sound, she discovered, was only the frozen chicken, dropped onto the granite in a rage.

She picked up the bird and set it to soak in a bowl of warm water, then returned to her casting profile. After the failed leg warmer infomercial audition she'd barely used it. Leila submitted herself to five auditions. The website wouldn't let her apply for more. For one hundred dollars, however, she could upgrade to gold-member status.

> **Leila**
> Hey. I'm still disgusted by what you did at Madeleine's ✓✓
> And in my room when you stayed over ✓✓
> Hello?? ✓✓
> Where are all the acting connections you promised me,
> the people you knew? It was all talk ✓✓
> Can I have one hundred dollars ✓✓

At the mention of money Matthew became responsive. He sent Leila links to Craigslist advertisements for open roles.

> **Matthew**
> Check these out ✓✓
> They require pictures. Fine for me to submit your
> headshot?? ✓✓

Leila clicked through the links. Someone was looking for a female model to lie naked on a table, covered in canapés for party guests to eat. A student director sought a girl, *ethnic but beautiful*, to get killed roadside in his ten-minute horror film. A third ad called for women forty plus to act as an employee in a human resources sexual harassment video.

> **Leila**
> These are shit ✓✓
> I am not forty plus✓✓

> **Matthew**
> Ok, how's this one ✓✓
> <u>Girl, 14-17, to pose on front of self-authored math prep book. All ethnicities welcome. Must be local.</u>

> **Leila**
> Ok. Send my photo to that. ✓✓
> And the student film. And I still need the $100 ✓✓

From her bedroom she recorded and submitted a self-tape for the horror film. It involved two lines, *no please no*, followed by a high-pitched scream. Anita burst the door open.

"What the bloody fuck?"

"I saw a roach."

~

THREE DAYS LATER Matthew called. The horror film was a bust, but she had a callback for the prep book. He offered to drive Leila to the audition in Plainfield. Anita watched through the front door mesh as Matthew pulled up the driveway. A plume of cigarette smoke clouded her aquiline face.

Leila rushed downstairs. "Is he here?"

"Yes. I don't understand why you're still wasting time on this."

"I'll get roles. Make money."

"As a mother I'm telling you. Nobody wants to see you onscreen. There is hardly anyone like you on a screen. And if they are, they're the prettiest girls. Or tokens. Do you want to be a token?"

"I do, actually. And I'm a pretty girl."

"Sure. What else? Nothing more? Nothing else?"

"I'm uniquely desperate."

Outside, Matthew rolled his window down, waved and tapped his watch.

"Unique?" Anita said. "Who put that in your head? This plain man? There are billions of girls just like you."

STILL SATURDAY AFTERNOON

Girl Smiling with Chili

"Unfortunately for everyone, she got the part," said Karina Dixit. She thumbed through her trash for the advertisement she'd discarded earlier that week. Leila in her thick black glasses, now covered with the Dixits' coffee grinds and eggshell bits.

"It was a fluke, but her ego ballooned after it. She auditioned for more. *Girl on SAT Book*, *Girl Smiling with Chili*. She handed the magazine out to all of us, even though they didn't pay her." Karina crumpled up the photograph and threw it back into the trash. "One lunch voucher, max."

THE DEPRAVED KIND, 2010s

Fire Safety

LEILA SENT THE advertisement to the two agents who attended her conservatory showcase. *Hi, you may not remember me, but here is an addendum to my monologues. Also I do scripts.* The email went unanswered. The sheen of joy Leila felt over the advertisement wore off. She fell into a depression and took long, aimless walks around the block. The women's unkempt stalks of grass spackled her sandals with a pollen resembling house fly eggs. August sweltered. Everything reproduced. Maple bugs absorbed the base of Nasreen Farouk's tree.

Leila opened her sock drawer and took out a notebook. Inside were the notes from the play she'd written a year ago, inspired by Anita and Ashok's private fights. It shamed her, and yet she carried on making notes for another one, a tasting platter of Anita's traumas—her engagement, her marriage, her dead siblings. Anita discovered that notebook too.

"I am just a regular person," she complained to Matthew over the phone. "And she makes me into some poor character, herself some star."

~

TO LIFT HER SPIRITS Matthew submitted Leila for one last-ditch audition. An education company was casting a teenage girl for a school fire safety video: the girl lights a Bunsen burner in the chemistry lab and leaves it unattended. It tips over and burns the school down.

On the drive into the city, Leila's throat scraped with sickness. Matthew stopped an ATM near Rutgers to get change for the tolls. Leila waited in the car and stared out the window, at the bank and the daycare and Very Delicias bakery with its Bible-shaped cakes and buttercream verses. All three establishments were built from the same red brick. A mother in sweatpants carried her toddler on her hip and jaywalked leisurely into a Dunkin' Donuts. A few minutes later she emerged with a pale caramel drink, screaming into a cellphone. *Never see me again! Never!*

The pain in Leila's throat intensified.

Matthew returned and stepped into the driver's seat. "Poor bloke, whoever she's badgering." He looked in his rearview mirror. "You're shivering."

"My throat hurts, and I have a migraine."

"Well, toughen up. I made dinner reservations after your audition. It's a late reservation, all I could get. We may even need to stay over in the city."

"I have chills. Can we please go home? Forget the audition."

"You look fine. It's a bad impression, Leila, canceling an audition. You could be blacklisted."

"Over a Craigslist fire safety video?"

"You're not sick," he said. "A migraine isn't the worst thing. I'm the one in medicine, I would know."

"Aren't you in marketing?" Leila stretched her hand over the glove compartment. "Look, I'm trembling."

"Rubbish, you're being dramatic."

At the intersection Leila rolled down her window and vomited. It splattered against the side of Tejas Kaushal's car in the neighboring lane.

"Fuck," Tejas said, and swerved past.

Matthew pulled over. He took a bottle from his dashboard, shook out a pill, and instructed Leila to swallow it with Diet Coke. For a few minutes he let her rest, engrossed in his phone.

"Feeling okay now, drama queen? Now it's out of your system."

"I guess so."

"I just reserved a hotel room. Eighteenth floor, great view of the village. We'll tell your mom we had a flat tire. Tell her Louise came."

"Why doesn't she come? What does she think of you spending all this time with me?"

"She has a migraine, a real one." He applied a thick layer of cherry Chapstick to his mouth. "And she'd rather not think about it."

As he spoke, a wave of drowsiness overcame Leila. She slept through several exits and woke up in the parking lot of a mall with another shopping bag on her lap. Inside was a fitted gingham dress and a pair of nude heels.

"Change," Matthew said, pointing to her orange sweatpants. "I don't know why you don't wear that black dress I got you."

"Louise's dress."

"You look like a dowdy prisoner in those pants, of course you're not booking more roles."

"I am a dowdy prisoner."

"A prisoner. That's what you think?"

He drove on in silence, blinking excessively to produce fake tears. Leila ignored him. The drowsiness hit again. When she woke up, she could see the Manhattan skyline in the distance, the dark arch of a tunnel, an immovable stretch of traffic.

Leila poked Matthew's neck from the back seat. "Did I miss the audition?"

He didn't respond.

"Let's end our warfare," she said. She leaned closer to the driver's seat and prodded his oily cheek with her index finger. "Can we please go home? I'm not well, seriously. And can we possibly get chicken nuggets?"

"You're fine," Matthew replied. "Meanwhile, and I didn't want to tell you this, I didn't want to bother you with everything you have going on, but my doctor says I may die in a year. Heart issues." He popped open the glove compartment again, took out another container of pills and rattled them. "I need to take these just to stay alive. Meanwhile you're here, faking sick."

Leila removed her finger from his cheek. "You're right. I'm faking."

THEY MISSED THE fire safety audition but went to dinner. Leila did not stomach more than a clear broth. Matthew called Anita. He told her he and Louise had taken Leila to a play, then dinner. The tire had gone flat; Leila had an upset stomach; it was best to stay over, yes; they'd gotten Leila her own room, adjacent to theirs, no trouble at all. They'd be there in the morning, all three of them.

The next morning Leila's migraine still hadn't subsided. Matthew brewed coffee in the corporate hotel pot, wearing nothing but his linen shirt and a pair of briefs. Leila turned on the television. How terrible to look at him in this casual state of undress, as only a lover might. On Disney Channel, a pop star led a double life as a regular person.

"She's cute," Matthew said.

Leila shut off the television. "You ruin everything."

Matthew poured Leila a cup of coffee. He tossed her a cell phone.

"Your phone was buzzing nonstop," he said. "I set it on silent, so you could sleep."

Leila opened her messages.

> **Anita**
> Hi. When will you be home✓✓
> No answer? Busy eating fancy with the old man and his horse wife? ✓✓
> I said I would come join you. He told me you did not want me. ✓✓
> I wish I had a son. I wish I had someone. U r not a family person ✓✓
> Pls tell me if u r ok. I said I would come ✓✓

"Did you tell my mom you didn't want her here?"

"My god, she mischaracterizes everything. I told her she could come."

He took a seat on the hotel armchair and leafed through an issue of a celebrity magazine. On the cover was a photograph of a thirteen-year-old reality star in shorts and a crop top. FROM SWEETHEART TO NIGHTMARE, the headline read.

"Look at this," Matthew tossed her the issue. "She is out of control."

"She's just wearing shorts."

Leila tossed her bed covers aside. Spots of blood were drying on her sheets and underwear.

"We'll get you a pad, L."

"Can we just go home? Can you please put on pants?"

"We have a matinee today." Matthew picked up the magazine and flipped to another page. "I got tickets online. You were out like a light last night, shivering. You begged me to come to bed, to keep you warm."

"I don't remember that."

"Yes. You tried to touch me," he said. "Your hands wandered near my nether regions."

"I never did that. I would never, ever do that."

"I wouldn't be so sure. Like I said, you were out of it."

"Shut up," Leila said, but her pulse quickened. What if she had indeed done it, and couldn't remember? "I never did that."

"It's nothing to be ashamed of. I like that you go after what you want."

"Why would I want you?"

Matthew shut his magazine. He let out a strangled noise, dry-heaved, pressed a hand to his chest, and slowly collapsed onto the floor.

Leila turned on the television. "You call me a drama queen." But Matthew remained in a rigid heap, and from where Leila sat she couldn't tell whether the hairs on his chest rose or fell with breath. Perhaps his doctor really did sentence him to him to death, and now it was happening here. Leila lifted the dead weight of Matthew's right arm and looped it around her shoulder. "Please, get up."

Matthew didn't move.

Leila searched his shirt pockets for the pill canister he showed her earlier. It wasn't there. Also she palmed a twenty.

"Matthew, wake up. The matinee. If you die, I can't go."

Leila pinched his armpit fat. He opened his eyes.

"You don't care if you hurt me," Matthew said. "I'm dying, and you tell me you don't want me."

"I'm sorry. I want you just fine."

Matthew brightened and peeled her comforters off. "Your legs are sore, you have cramps," he said. "I'll massage you, then we'll go home."

Leila tensed. At the very least he could have been a handsome creep. And yet there was plenty good he did for her, like this room on the eighteenth floor of a hotel, with two soft beds and an expansive view of the park. The city appeared green and gray, and even from this height Leila could make out the bikers riding, the poodles walking, immaculate floofs on their heads.

Anita
Bloody when are you coming. That idiot doesn't respond. ✓✓

"You're a daughter to me," Matthew said, fingers still working. "You're so sad, I can tell, no self-regard, no self-esteem. So I keep helping you. I don't get any pleasure from it."

The show would last three hours, not including intermission. Leila knew she would not be home until dark. "Can we shop instead?"

Matthew smiled. Of course they could. They packed their bags and took a cab to a department store on Fifth Avenue. He bought her a fine fur coat and a bandage dress and paraded her around the beauty counter, pressing ointments into her palm and samples of blush into her cheeks. He was not so bad, Leila thought, softened by the finer things, his careful attention. He was a generous person with one unfortunate quality. Most people had several. After all he would be dead soon, like his doctor said, and why ruin the end of his life. She could tolerate the bad parts in the meantime.

That evening, when they reached Willow Road, Leila slammed the car door without thanking Matthew or saying goodbye. Inside the house she called for Anita, who didn't respond. She hid her new clothing in her closet and turned on the television, to one of her father's soaps. There were no subtitles. She wondered what moments would grab him. What ridiculous plot might amuse or move him. Lovers pressed against each other in verdant fields. They had slender noses.

"Leila!" Anita cried from upstairs. "Shut that channel. Your dad had bad taste."

Leila threw the remote. "You hated him, Mummy. You wouldn't let him stand without forcing him to slouch. If he was walking, you'd want it to be with his head down."

STILL SATURDAY AFTERNOON!

A Bloody Chauffeur

AN HOUR PASSED, and still the social worker hadn't left the Sharmas'. Devika Gill poured another lemonade and brought it outside. "To take so long can mean no good."

"Listen, Matthew never told *us* he was dying," Jyoti said. "She should have opened her mouth, she should not have acted so helpless—maybe then, things could be different."

"Too gullible for her own good, meanwhile Anita was working nonstop, no attention to spare. To be frank, we thought she took Matthew for granted. He chauffeured that girl to school and back more times than I can count."

"In that beemer, like a rich girl," Aparna agreed.

"It's not Anita's fault, you know, it is miserable to make a living alone, but then don't point the finger at us: how could *we* know?" Jyoti said. "If the girl had a problem with Matthew, then why did she keep asking for money, like it was commerce? She still wore the clothes he bought her. Acted like a terror, a tart. I pitied Anita. Coming from where she came from, only to deal with this this spoilage. Did you see Leila was wearing the gingham dress just today? How was her mother to know she was unhappy with the situation, when she herself flaunted it?"

THE DEPRAVED KIND, 2010s

Why Suffer Like Me?

IN THE WEEKS that followed the hotel trip, Leila woke up sweating in the middle of the night, racked with the fear that maybe she'd touched Matthew while she was unconscious, as he said she had. Maybe she too was a deviant. To test her theory she watched pornography in all possible categories. Stepsiblings and exacting landlords. Anime and performative choking. She watched impassively and compulsively. What had the casting calls for the roles looked like, she wondered. How much were the actors paid? Had they received a meal voucher for the day?

She watched on the home computer and deleted the history. One evening, waiting for Anita to pick her up from school, she watched on a library monitor. It was her hundred and fourth video and the scenes had become monotonously awful. Even from an anthropological standpoint she could no longer pay attention and preferred the comments sections. *I have terminal cancer, this is my last month to masturbate, strange that you could be reading my comment when I'm dead*, one user wrote. *This country needs a moral reboot. In the meantime, does anyone have a good Totino's pizza roll recipe?*

RIP, this porn star hung herself. I will fap one out in her honor, read another. Leila googled the porn star. Her Wikipedia page was written in the past tense; indeed she'd hung herself. Leila was so absorbed by the tragedy of this stranger she didn't notice the librarian stepping inside.

The next day Leila and Anita went to the counselor's office. Leila sobbed. *I'm so sad, please don't expel me, my father is dead, I'm depressed. I still get straight A's.* There would be no expulsion, the counselor said, speaking mostly to Anita, but Leila should attend five therapy sessions.

Shameless, shameless shameless, Anita chanted on the drive home from the meeting.

"How hard your father worked, to send you here. Imagine if he was here for this. He would have died of the embarrassment. From where did you get that coat you're wearing?"

"I borrowed it from a friend. And you're a misogynist. Harping on about shame."

"Are you a beggar, to borrow? I'm a realist." Anita pointed to Leila's protruding gut. "No chest, you're just showing *that*. Cheap people will be drawn to you. Is that what you want, murkha? Wrong-quality people?"

They passed thickets of trees and an old church. The bluish stained glass windows that glittered in the yellow evening sky. "I remember when Karina, that bitch, had the nerve to come to my house all those years ago, after I found you and her daughter in the middle of filth. Do you know even after that she called me? She said, *Maybe you should send the girl to therapy. Maybe she is a deviant.* I gave her good. Now I'm wondering, was she correct?"

Leila held back tears; she remembered the confrontation in the front door, but she had not known about any kind of call. "I'm a deviant."

"My god, don't be a martyr."

~

THE IN-NETWORK THERAPIST on Anita's health plan, Dr. Marin Elheart, had 2.9 stars on Yelp. Anita left work early to accompany Leila to the first session. Leila sat quietly as her mother's manager spoke sternly on speakerphone. Anita had missed a meeting and forgot to notify him in advance.

"Sorry," Anita said told him. "What else should I say? My husband is dead. My daughter is sick."

The call ended.

"I'm not sick."

"And yet we're off to the doctor, to a therapist no less, a scammer." She fingered a pain in the back of her jaw. "I'm having tooth problems, but when do I have time to get help, who helps me?"

The doctor's office reeked of Pine-Sol. Childhood suicide posters lined the wall. On the waiting room table sat a fish-shaped bowl of soft clementines. Dr. Elheart, haggard in a red pantsuit, insisted on first speaking to the Sharmas together. With light vocal fry she asked about Ashok, about finances. She frequently deployed phrases Leila imagined her reading in pamphlets, like *cultural sensitivity.* Anita answered quietly, her gaze locked on the deck of tarot cards on the doctor's desk.

After the three of them talked, Dr. Elheart spoke to Anita alone. Leila waited on a chair in the office lobby. She did not want to read a suicide magazine and watched *America's Next Top Model* clips on her phone instead. In one clip from a makeover compilation, the judges had a Black woman with a gap tooth get her teeth pushed together. In another season they pushed a white girl's gap further apart. Both tooth surgeries were permanent.

Anita left Dr. Elheart's office blowing her nose into her blouse. "Next time, come with your idiot uncle," she said. "What does that bitch know? How can we trust a doctor who is obsessed with astrology? She asks about my marriage, my sign, this, that. Says I should see her weekly, so desperate to line her pockets. Am I crazy to do something like that?"

"So I'm crazy. And you're into astrology too."

"When did I say, Leila, you're crazy? Always you want to stir some drama with me. That's all a mother is good for! A dump. Do you think I'm not in pain too?"

But in the parking lot, Anita held the passenger door open for Leila, and she stopped, without being asked, at a Burger King.

"Just go, get better," she said, passing Leila a bag of nuggets and fries. "Why suffer like me?"

Sick Leave

"MATTHEW TOOK HER to that doctor. Then, he started pulling her out of school, for various sicknesses," said Jyoti Kaushal. "The first time it was food poisoning. She ate meat left on the buffet platter too long."

("Not from my establishment, FYI," Nasreen Farouk said. "A knockoff.")

All night Leila hardly slept. She got up for water and later to vomit. Anita held her hair back, half-asleep; she had to leave early in the morning for a conference in Delaware. For days she'd rehearsed her presentation in front of Leila.

"That's enough," Anita said, over the toilet bowl. "You'll ruin your hair, that's enough."

At six A.M. Anita called the women to keep an eye on Leila. Jyoti was busy; Devika was out of town. Hema had back-to-back shifts. She dialed Karina's number.

"Hello, speaking?" Karina said.

"It's Anita. You have my contact saved."

"Anita. Something wrong?"

"I'm sorry to disturb you so early. Leila is ill today, I'm afraid to leave her alone. Could you watch her?"

"I'm volunteering today," Karina said. "What about Matthew? Why do you act as if you have no one?"

~

"SO MATTHEW WATCHED HER, sent a doctor's note to the school," Jyoti Kaushal said. She procured a stack of notes from an empty Royal Dansk tin. "But he dramatized them."

"Jyoti would know, Tejas was the doctor signing off on them, even though his specialty is warts and feet," said Hema Rao.

"Tejas never examined her, he trusted Matthew's assessments, why would he not?" Jyoti said. "So he signed off on them. And she faked the illness, too. Why would she want to go back to school, all the shame she had?"

She smoothed out a copy of a note:

To the Headmistress—
This is Leila Sharma's Uncle. I left you a few messages. This is to say that Leila's very sick, likely with appendicitis, and can't come to school tomorrow. TBD about the rest of the week, we'll see how she goes. I'm her emergency contact and practically her guardian, her mother asked me to call, you can check with her to confirm, but practically there's no need. Dr. Kaushal is signing off, attached.

—Matthew Pillai

~

ON HER THIRD sick leave with Matthew, for fake appendicitis, Leila scrolled through casting calls and instead came across a screenplay contest for high school students, facilitated through a nearby university. A sixty-page episodic drama, a $1,000 cash prize, a $250 entry fee. She had time to work on a script; four days for the scratch in her throat Matthew swore was appendicitis, eight for a bump on the head he told the school was a full-blown concussion.

Leila wrote a script inspired by Matthew. In it, a fiftysomething man's wife prefers her horse to him, and he spends his spare time bonding with a teenager he meets in a park. The man used phrases like *nether regions*. While working, Leila took breaks to check the Craigslist missed connections, where she took solace in the existence of people lonelier than her. *You were at the dog park with the worst-behaved terrier I've ever seen.* She checked Facebook. A photo of Riya popped up at a tailgate, scarlet *R*'s on her cheeks. Leila clicked on her profile, her photo albums. Her photos with Vivek had been deleted.

Anita called from work a few times, fretting. At Matthew's instruction, Leila pretended her hyperbolic sicknesses were real.

"Now a concussion, when already she is so sick in the head," Anita told Matthew over the phone. "I should take off."

"Don't take off, Anita, you're so close to a promotion. I have the time, I can afford to. I'm taking her to a specialist today."

~

AFTER ANITA LEFT for work in the mornings, the women saw Matthew load Leila into his car and drive off too.

"Sometimes Anita didn't know Matthew had called Leila out sick from school," said Hema Rao. "He told Anita he was taking her to school."

Matthew drove Leila to a Residence Inn twenty minutes from school. Leila found his shirts hanging in the closet, his sweaters and suppositories and insulin pens in the cherry-stained drawers.

"Do you live here now?" she asked.

"Of course not, I rented it for your care alone," he said. He opened a cabinet of painkillers. "Your house has no good medicine. I looked in the cabinet: generic brand, generic brand, generic brand. Louise agrees, she wants you to get better."

By her fifth fake illness Leila had finished a draft of her script. She checked her grades portal at school. There were numerous incompletes.

"I need to go back," she told Matthew. "I miss human contact."

"You see the therapist, that's contact."

"She's an idiot, she spends most of the time talking to you."

"You'll catch up on the tests."

"No. I live here like an amoeba, going to the fridge and back."

Matthew glanced up from his work laptop, where he was busy drafting an email. "Then you'll go to school tomorrow," he said, shrugging. "I'm not holding you hostage here."

"Really?"

"Of course, you'll go back tomorrow."

"Thank you." She turned on the television. Matthew sent the email he'd been drafting.

> Dear Headmistress:
> Matthew again. I'm taking Leila to therapy, as per your mandate, but she's in a bad state and must miss her history test Friday. The therapist

met the mother once and is concerned. I'm considering stepping in as an emergency guardian.

What's more, I'm concerned about Leila's mother, too, and I write to you in confidence. She is the only parent left to this girl and works most of the day. She drinks more than she eats; I have seen her occasional alcoholism up-close, and she's hardly ever home to care for her own child. She is increasingly absent and unhinged. I am doing all I can for this family. One man can only do so much.

—M. Pillai

THE NEXT DAY Leila showered and put on her school skirt. She poured herself a bowl of cornflakes. Anita had an early meeting; Matthew offered to drive Leila to school. He sipped tea as she dug a spoon into her cereal and scratched her shins.

"Why are you scratching like that, L?"

"It's nothing, it's eczema."

"It looks worse than that. It's a bad rash. Sorry, L, you can't go today, not like that."

He called Tejas for another doctor's note, this time for severe skin disease. He drove her back to the Residence Inn and took a conference call in the kitchenette. Leila sprawled out on the carpet in the living area with her textbooks.

Matthew's call ended. He came to the living room with a tube of cream. "For your chest rash."

"I don't have a chest rash. It was my shins, it's just eczema."

He needed to apply it to her chest, or the rash would spread there. "Let me take care of it, and you'll go to school tomorrow."

"No, there's no eczema there."

Matthew conceded and returned to the kitchenette. Leila resumed studying. She was working out a math problem when she heard wheezing at the dining table.

"Matthew?" Leila called. "Is something wrong?"

Matthew wheezed again. "My heart. It's getting even worse; my doctor said it's comorbid with the diabetes."

He fished in his pocket for a small white canister. Leila poured him a glass of water.

He swallowed. "I have a wife, a stunning one. I'm not the kind of man you think I am, L. You have a serious skin ailment; if you don't listen to me now, you'll see, it'll spread. It'll ruin your skin. I was just trying to help. I don't know how long I can help, if I'll even make it to a year. Three months would be lucky. My lungs are bad, L. And you lie to me, you tell me you have no rash, you don't need cream."

"I thought it was just your heart you were dying from," Leila said. "It's your lungs, too?"

"Yes."

She let him apply the cream. After it was over, she wrote the experience into her screenplay but stopped halfway. It was hardly interesting, a man touching a girl, and it reminded Leila of a slasher film, in which everyone exists to die.

While Matthew took another conference call, Leila tapped him on the shoulder. "Can I have two hundred fifty dollars?"

He forgot to put the call on mute. "What?"

"You owe me," she said. "I never had a skin disease, I never had eczema there. You owe me. If you don't pay me, if I don't go back to school tomorrow, I'll tell someone what you did." She spoke clearly and plainly, with a rage that surprised her. "In fact, give me five hundred."

She stored the envelope of cash in her sock drawer. The next day, she returned to class.

Old Man Money

For a month after the cream incident Leila avoided Matthew. She returned to school as a regular attendee and submitted her finished script to the contest with half of the money Matthew had given her. The other half she saved.

She couldn't avoid his utility for long, nor his money. A week out from Mother's Day, Anita's tooth pain intensified. A wisdom tooth she never removed as a teenager had erupted and infected her gums. She had oral surgery and afterward ate soft foods and prescription Percocet. Anita loved the Percocet.

"It wipes my mind, it keeps it fresh and clean," Anita said, dazed. "Like bleach."

With Anita drugged and dazed, she and Leila got on well. The two watched *Friends* and flipped through magazines on the couch.

"She is so fat," Anita would say, of one skinny starlet. "*I* am so fat."

"All you care about is bodies, Mother."

Anita yawned and pointed emphatically at a model in a sleek red gown. "What a nice color," she said. "I always wanted a saree in this color. But your father was cheap."

"I'll get you one, for Mother's Day."

"Where will I wear it? The supermarket?" Anita laughed, then fell asleep under a lumpy quilt.

Leila
Hey are you free today ✓✓
Let's go shopping in the city. The department store on
fifth avenue ✓✓

Matthew
Yes, of course, so good to hear from you. Be there in an hour ✓✓

Leila adjusted Anita's quilt and kissed her on the forehead. "I'm going shopping with Matthew," she said. "Be back by six."

～

LEILA STRAPPED HER SEAT BELT on. Matthew kissed her wetly on the cheek.
"It's nice to see you, L."
"We're going straight to Bergdorf's, right? I need to get a dress."
He started the engine. "Whatever you want."
It drizzled on the way to the department store. Leila's phone buzzed; Anita had awoken from her Percocet nap:

Anita
Pls no gifts for me on that fat man's money. ✓✓
Just come home, have dinner. that's enough ✓✓

Matthew parked in a garage near Fifth Avenue. "So, what restaurant would you like to go tonight, L?"
"None, let's just get Mom's dress and go home." Leila rummaged in the pocket of her jean jacket. "I have two hundred fifty from last time, but that's not enough. Can I use your Mastercard?"
Matthew frowned. "I thought we were getting a dress for you. That's why I agreed to come. Now you're telling me it's for your mother? She's an emotional abuser, L. I need to draw a boundary. I'm not setting foot in that store."
"Okay." Leila took the card and went into the shop alone, into a cloud of floral and amber perfume samples, the throng of wealthy women having routine good days. Leila scoured the dress section. A tall evening-wear mannequin wore a dark-red sequin dress with a slit up the side, close to the color Anita admired.
Leila emerged from the store with a bag in hand.
"Finally," said Matthew. "How much did you spend?"
"Two thousand."
"Jesus."
"Well, I paid two fifty of it. What's the problem, aren't you rich?"
"You're getting spoiled, L. Let's go to dinner."

"No, I told Mom I'd be home by six."

Matthew was irritated. "I waited for you for hours, my sugar's low. Let's eat."

"I took fifteen minutes."

"If I don't eat something I'll die. As it is, your mother is blasted on Percocet, she won't know six from Adam."

~

MATTHEW GOT A sticky table at a noodle shop. He ordered beef broth and flat rice noodles, slurping loudly to cover the sound of his flatulence.

Leila looked at the time on her phone. "Can't you eat faster?"

"This is life or death, L. Why don't you order something?"

"No, I want to go."

Matthew slurped another noodle. "The dress you got is too young for your mother. It's inappropriate."

"She's in her thirties."

"Exactly."

"You're in your fifties."

"It's different for me."

By the time he dropped her home it was dark. Leila found Anita at the dinner table, her drug daze over. Dirty pots and a thava with crisp brown dough filled the kitchen sink.

"You said six," Anita said.

"I'm sorry."

"It's fine. I cooked, I can't even chew, but I cooked for you. It's fine. You'll always pick him."

Leila set the bag on the table. "I got you a gift."

"I don't want what the fat man buys," Anita said. "Your real mother. Maybe you should have been born in his house."

"Maybe."

Overnight Leila heard Anita argue with Matthew on the phone, dregs of panic in her voice. *Why were you so late? What is that makeup all over her face?*

The Antecedents

The following Monday, Leila received an email from an account she didn't recognize.

EmmaXXX
L, please message me here for a bit ✓✓
Someone from work overheard you at the residence inn,
the call wasn't on mute ✓✓
They saw some messages on my laptop, got the wrong idea ✓✓
Need to lie low for a bit ✓✓

Leila
Ok what if I need something ✓✓

EmmaXXX
Not a good time to need anything ✓✓

After that exchange he went dark, with Leila and all the women of Willow Road.

"He offered to help us paint Dad's room, and I haven't heard from him in days," Aparna Naik said.

"He missed a cricket match with Tejas, and no notice," Jyotis said. "I heard he was almost let go from work. They found personal communications on his server."

"Communications saying what?" Devika Gill said.

"Who knows."

"My thinking is, Anita must have told him not to answer you. I asked him if he could watch Manu the other day. No response. It's not like him. Meanwhile if Anita wants something done for her child, she snaps her fingers and he comes running."

"I, too, want a sugar daddy," Aparna sighed, bagging dill in the market. She watched a news report on the corner television. A Florida man had been arrested for stabbing his wife, a nurse, in the thigh outside the hospital where she worked. Then he ran her over with his car. Because she was on his insurance, she was transported to a lesser facility for care.

Karina Dixit hoisted a value pack of red onions onto the checkout belt.

"Just like Anita, to be out for herself. Matthew's been so busy taking care of that girl's endless sickness, of course he'd run into trouble at work. When does he have time to go in? And do you know they stay out overnight? I've seen them come back in the mornings. Good thing he's a good man. What kind of mother allows it?"

Behind Karina, Anita stood with a basket of lychees and Cadbury Flakes.

"Your daughter's in college, done, all set at state school, easy," Anita said.

Karina turned. "My god, I didn't see you. Next time, act civilized, speak up."

"Easy to spew shit when your stomach is full." Anita left the basket behind, grabbed Leila by the hand, and led her to the car. She pressed her face into the steering wheel and stayed there for a long time.

"Karina Auntie is so ugly," Leila said, knowing this would lift her mother's spirits. "She's jealous of you, she looks like an old witch."

Anita left her face on the wheel. "It isn't like that, is it Leila? Even she said Matthew isn't a bad man. I would never forgive myself."

"Of course he isn't," Leila said. "Karina has the evil eye." She peeled one of the lychees she'd taken from the store and offered it to Anita. How pathetic she looked.

~

IN MATTHEW'S ABSENCE, Leila somehow missed him, accustomed to his excesses, the deluge of restaurants. She reread her screenplay, about the old fiftysomething and his teenage friend. It would be three weeks before she heard back. Imagine Matthew had died of his various conditions. Out of guilt she considered withdrawing her submission, but her curiosity about the outcome—*maybe she would win*—won out, and she left it alone.

Anita reveled in the lack of Matthew.

"It's a good thing," she told Leila, as the two snacked on cucumbers at the kitchen table. "You were getting big from whatever he feeds you. Don't have that face. I'm telling you because I care. A mother who doesn't won't tell you the truth."

On Anita's cucumber diet Leila lost five pounds. Standing in the bathroom mirror she pinched the fat of her abdomen, which protruded like a tiny, judgmental frown. Her mother, however lean, had the same frown. Dedicated periods of Special K diets and low-carb starvation diets hadn't dissolved it. Anita liked to rail about these bellies. She said the women of the family had them because their ancestors were poor and legitimately starving, that the resources meant to nourish them had been swindled by a country of queens. *Colonialism lives in your fat cells*, she liked to tell Leila—a body like yours remembers how little it once had. Now it holds everything it gets. How unfair, Leila thought. Why did her body have to remember? She just wanted to be hot.

"Mother," Leila asked, reading online, "are you sure that's a fact?"

Then, with no announcement, Matthew returned to Willow Road. He came to the Sharmas' on a Sunday. He wouldn't reveal where he'd been lying low or what had prompted his disappearance from the neighborhood.

"I was traveling," he told the Sharmas. His cheeks appeared sunken and unshaved. There was a sickly pallor to his skin. He opened the pantry, stocked with Special K and SlimFast. "Leila's gotten very thin."

Anita shooed him out. "Thanks for dropping by."

Matthew
What is she feeding you. She is incompetent. Must be drinking too much. ✓✓

Leila
Where were you, did you lose your job. I look great btw. ✓✓

Matthew
I was soul-searching. Looking at places. ✓✓

Leila
Places for what? ✓✓

The Little Dog

A COLD WAR RAGED between Matthew and Anita. Matthew swayed Leila easily, by landing her an early-morning audition for "Girl Dead in Cornfield."

"So easily a child sells its loyalty," said Hema Rao. "That's why I keep dogs."

After Leila left for the audition Anita pulled an old Yellow Pages from under the sink and read it for a while, as she used to do in Queens. She drove to the park and smoked outside, watching the children screaming. A woman with a curly lapdog approached. Anita lowered her cigarette and smiled, preparing to feel its soft warm fur under her fingers. The woman frowned and pointed to a sign with green lettering: NO SMOKING HERE.

Anita drove home. She put the Yellow Pages back under the sink and stumbled across her and Ashok's old leather address book. There was his handwriting, tight and overwrought, in the magenta pen from his lab. He listed family, the number of the old apartment super, friends from school, doctors. And then in her own handwriting Anita had jotted down three numbers: Maria's, her uncle's, her mother's. Each line had a squiggle running through it, also in her penmanship, her own crude attempts to obliterate the digits.

Anita poured herself a glass of wine and watched an old soap. She hated when Leila played them; they made her long for Ashok. She shut it off and dialed her mother's line. She imagined the new residents living in that old house with the love swing, the basin to wash your feet, the ghost of a little dog next door. The line rang. Anita half-waited for the reedy crackle of her mother's voice. The dial tone beeped. Anita left a message behind:

Amma—

You won't receive this. Today a dog like the neighbor's one approached me. He had a small pink tongue and sweet black lips, a smile as big as a thumb. I wanted to lift him to my lap. He had such fine eyes, like stones.

She left several others:

Amma—so you forced me to marry old and now where is my husband?

Amma—I am suffocated in this neighborhood of old women. Everyone brings her mother here to watch the children. I cannot ask you. So I have asked some man. Leila loves him more.

Amma—something I told nobody. In New York I once took money meant for groceries and took myself to eat in a diner. I ordered salmon. Waste of money. So unseasoned. The world grew hot. Back in the station sickness shot down my toes. I had to sit so as not to faint. Two security women came and fanned me with transit maps. "Maybe she's pregnant," one said, and I started to cry, because how shameful the possibility. The other woman said "Don't cry. It could be a little gift. I had my first at eighteen." I went home and threw up in the studio. The salmon was just off.

Amma—Leila is a teenager now. Maybe she should have been born in a better house.

Amma—she wants a dog. I can only think of the neighbor's dog passing. The bad memories bury the rest.

∼

"LET'S GO TO THE SHELTER," Anita said, when Leila returned from her audition. "You always wanted a dog."

Leila brightened. "No way. I thought you hated the smell?"

"I can endure anything. Get in the car."

Anita turned on the radio. "Do you know, Leila, I used to live across from a Pomeranian. I cooked for it. Have I told you that story?"

Leila put her sunglasses on. "No. What was his name?"

∼

THE SHELTER VOLUNTEER wore a thick green sweater with a waving black cat on the front.

"We'd like to see the dogs," Anita said. The volunteer led the Sharmas down a narrow metal hallway lined with cages on both sides. A pit bull howled. Leila squinted at his placard: SPOT, seven months old, sixty-eight pounds, a frilly pink smile. Another was AIDEN, a bully mix, ninety-seven pounds.

"He was purchased on Craigslist, the buyers thought he was a Labrador," the shelter volunteer explained. "Gave him up as soon as his muscles came in."

"I can't handle a big dog," Anita said. "Anything smaller? Look at him, my god."

She pointed to the cage between Spot and Aiden, where a little lap dog napped. JERRY. He opened his round brown eyes at the commotion and barked.

"We want Jerry," Anita told the volunteer.

The volunteer pointed to the card on his crate: ADOPTED.

Anita took out her checkbook. "How much?"

"That's not how it works."

Anita put her checkbook away. She pulled her blouse over her nose. "It stinks in here."

"You can endure anything," Leila said.

"Let's see the cats."

The cat room was lined with local newspapers. CAR OVERTURNED, DRIVER TRAPPED IN CRASH read one headlines. Milk crates of kittens sat stacked on one side; opposite them adult cats slunk behind thick glass. Anita took a liking to a gray tabby kitten the shelter called Yum-Yum, who was missing half of his tail. The volunteer let the Sharmas to play with him inside a large green bathroom. He was badly behaved, and the volunteer yanked his scruff to demonstrate discipline. She invited Leila to try it too, but the looseness of the skin unnerved her. Who was she to control him?

Yum-Yum flashed sharp incisors and swished his half-tail.

The volunteer returned the kitten to his crate. Yum-Yum shut his eyes and peed into his litter.

"Housebroken!" Anita gushed. "But what happened to his tail?"

The volunteer tapped the glass of a full-grown gray cat with electric green eyes.

"That's his mother. He came out with no littermates. She tried eating him right back up, we stopped her at the tail."

"My god." Anita shook her head. "Who would do that?"

The woman offered Anita a clipboard with adoption papers.

"We'll go home and think."

Leila followed Anita to the parking lot. Think, she knew, meant no. In the car Ashok's old Hindi music cassettes were jammed in the cupholders. Two were intact; one had tape coming out the end, as if Anita had either been listening to them or destroying them.

"So we're not getting anything?"

"You have your PSATs coming up, who will take care of it but me, Leila? And your hair stinks, I can smell it from here. You smell like the dogs."

"It's the Pantene 2in1 you keep filling with water, I need Herbal Essence. I'm so sad about his tail."

"He'll survive."

They argued about Leila's greasy hair. What a waste it was, this shelter trip, Leila said. Why go if Anita never intended to get a dog? *I don't want to bring another animal into this house*, Anita countered. *I should have gone to the city with Matthew*, Leila said.

Anita wiped her face with the collar of her dress.

"I'm sorry," Leila said.

In silence they turned back onto Willow Road. There was Matthew's beemer, only this time parked in front of the Dixits' house, next to the Prius that Riya had borrowed to visit from college. The Dixits' front door was open. Leila could make out his large shape shaking hands with Rajesh, hugging Karina and Riya goodbye.

The sight of it incensed Anita, who would not stop talking about it all through dinner preparations.

"And to think, Karina bloody gossips *about me*, tells everyone at the temple, the Cash & Carry, the threading salon, how strange it is that he's so close to us. She tells them she never let the oil man near her daughter, her daughter the queen."

She handed Leila a knife to slice an eggplant.

"These women want to drink the juice out of you. And Matthew is not a bad man. You told me yourself, have you not? Hasn't she said so too?" She took over the eggplant and dropped mustard seeds into the oil. Leila watched them crackle and pop.

"How can you have a dog, you don't do one work," Anita said. "You don't pack your lunches, you cannot slice an eggplant. What happened to Girl Dead in Cornfield?"

∼

LEILA WENT TO bed after dinner. Anita stayed up late, watching *Friends* reruns. At midnight the phone rang. Anita paused her episode, "The One with All the Cheesecakes." The number was an international one, her mother's line. Anita listened, goosebumps on her forearms, as a male stranger left a voicemail: *Who is this? I am blocking this number—never contact this line again.*

Honorable Mention

Leila
What were you doing at the Dixits house ✓✓

Matthew
I can't see other people? Are you so jealous? ✓✓

Leila
It's concern not jealousy ✓✓

Matthew
Calm down, miss gun shy ✓✓

The checks turned blue, but Matthew didn't reply. Leila decided to punish him. After school she changed into a pair of heels he'd bought her at Bergdorf's, black-and-tan stilettos, and headed downtown on the bus. She would find a man to have sex with her. The whole affair would sicken Matthew. He'd leave her alone and the neighborhood too. Her cover would go as follows: She was eighteen instead of fifteen. It wasn't her mother buzzing wildly on her phone; it was nobody. She came from nowhere; had no backstory, anyone could inhabit her and assume the controls.

But it was daylight, and she had no fake ID to enter a bar, so she settled on a tea shop and began to complete her homework at a table. A barista came around. Leila had to order something to use the seat.

"What tea is good for sadness?"

"Peppermint," the barista said.

"I'll take a pot."

Two cups later Leila noticed eyes on her from the opposite table. There sat a man who looked to be in his late thirties, with dead gray eyes and a pinched face. Leila pulled her shirt down and buried herself in her precalculus homework. The tea burned her mouth. She got up for her water. The man stared at her ridiculous shoes.

Leila gathered her books and slid her backpack down next to his open seat.

"May I sit here?"

He eyed the textbook in her arms. "I wish I'd been as studious in college."

"I'm a freshman," Leila said, automatically. She set the book on the table. It was a precalculus textbook, but the professor wanted to believe her, and that mattered more than the truth of her age. They talked for a while. Leila inched her foot up his pant leg.

Why didn't she show him her dorm, the man suggested? He took a bite of his cranberry scone. The crumbs dribbled down his chin.

"Oh, I would, but my roommate's in."

The man said he knew of a place, a country hotel behind the garden. Leila left her tea behind and followed him down two narrow winding streets, palms sweating. Imagine he discovered her lie. Imagine he was an ax murderer. Imagine dying in these trashy stilettos she could not balance in. He opened the brass door to the hotel. She spied a glint of white gold on his knuckle, a wedding ring, and took off sprinting in the other direction, blistering in the heels. She took the bus back to Willow Road, in a state of elation, with the shoes in her hand. So this was self-regard! She walked around the neighborhood, past Manu and Arvind playing water guns, and checked the mailbox before going inside the house. A large envelope was addressed to her, from the university playwriting competition. *Thank you for your submission*, it read. *Your script has received honorable mention.* Anita was thrilled—now surely Leila was Princeton-bound!—and took the girl out to dinner.

"Did you hear, Leila, that Jyoti Kaushal is pregnant?" Anita tore off a piece of bread at their Cheesecake Factory table. "Another horrible citizen is baking."

Adrian

THE NEXT DAY a +91 number flashed on the Sharmas' landline, Ashok's sister in India. Anita was sitting on the kitchen floor, her hair wrapped in dye foils, shucking squash for a detox cleanse.

Leila studied at the countertop. She watched Anita balance the telephone receiver against her aluminum head. The sister's tone was jagged and mournful. A flat in Ashok's name had to be sold. Squatters had moved in; the deed was left in Anita's name. *Mhm, mhm, mhm,* Anita murmured. The call ended. Anita slammed her vegetable peeler and the receiver onto the floor. Skin and pulp flung into the air.

"*Everything* your father's left for me to do, Leila. Lazily, he dies. Still, I must work like his dog."

"I'll go with you."

"Aiyoh! You've missed so many school days for your illnesses. They'll make you repeat if you miss any more, just to pocket the tuition."

That night, muttering complaints and her hair smelling of bleach—she'd forgotten to rinse the dye out in time—Anita booked round-trip tickets for a week and a half of travel. She refused to ask Matthew for childcare; think, she told Leila, of how the women would talk after that scene in the market.

Anita dialed the women.

"I'm fifteen," Leila said. "I don't need a babysitter."

Anyway the women were unavailable:

"I have my dealer and father over," Aparna Naik told Anita.

"Tejas won't allow," said Jyoti Kaushal, fraught with morning sickness.

On and on, until Anita knocked Karina's door.

"Once again I need a favor," Anita said, almost kindly, "as I don't want to leave my daughter with any man. I'm sure you'll help this time."

∽

RIYA WAS HOME on break from college the week Leila stayed with the Dixits. She seemed altered to Leila, the delicate features of her face bloated and speckled with acne. Instead of chitchatting with the women, teaching or attending dance classes, she spent the bulk of her days sleeping upstairs in sweatpants. If Karina asked Riya to do a minor chore, she complained of a vague stomach ailment and slept. Leila watched Karina shuttle Motrin and pink bottles of Pepto-Bismol up and down the stairs. *Come to temple, Riya, it will make things better*, Karina said, but she was careful never to say aloud what the problem was.

Karina gave up. She drove to temple alone. Only when she was gone did Riya saunter downstairs. She buttered toast and joined Leila on the couch for *My Super Sweet Sixteen* and *MADE* reruns. Riya enjoyed episodes in which people labored to transform and failed. A tomboy became a beauty pageant queen but lost the pageant. A band geek became a salsa dancer to win his best friend's heart; at the end of the episode, the friend accepts his pink rose but rejects him: *I see us as really good friends.*

This outcome thrilled Riya. "That's so funny," she said. "He thought it would all work out."

At seven Karina came home from temple, lit incense at the mandir, and turned on a channel where a guru advertised a spiritual deal on loop. Wire him fifty dollars and receive blessings. Call now, the advertisement commanded. Karina listened. She waited on the line for a while before giving up and playing Ganesh prayers on a cassette tape. As if on cue Riya complained of a pain in her throat and excused herself to her room. Karina instructed Leila to pray alongside her, in Riya's stead.

"Ganesh is the easiest god, the god who will do what you want," Karina said.

∽

TO SEEM POLITE Leila helped Karina in the kitchen. Using the silver mortar and pestle reminded her of being young and preferring the peace of the Dixits' house to her own. Leila poured a teaspoon of fruit salt into dhokla batter and watched it sour and foam. Childhood felt extant. Karina arranged the yellow cubes onto a plate.

"Leila, take this to Riya, make sure she eats," she said. Her stress over her daughter's melancholy dissolved her usual animosity. Riya put too much pressure on herself in school, Karina confided in Leila; now she was on academic probation. She socialized but missed classes; when she attended, she failed.

"Kids these days endure nothing," Karina said. She should never have let her waste time dating that boy Vivek. "He wrung the beauty out of her and left her like a kitchen sponge. Your uncle Matthew referred us to a therapist, someone he says you saw."

"She has 2.9 stars on Yelp, she talks more to Matthew than she does to me." Leila checked the therapist's Yelp. "Now it's 2.5."

"I told him, Riya is not like Leila, she doesn't need a doctor."

Leila took the plate of dhokla to Riya's room. Riya opened the door in a stained sweatshirt. She narrowed her eyes.

"Tell her I'm not hungry, tell her not to spill my business."

In the evening Karina went to temple. Riya and Leila watched television together. Rajesh didn't come home till late, and when he did, he shuffled through the house quietly, like an inoffensive ghost.

"Your phone keeps going off," Riya said. "Who keeps texting you?"

Matthew
How are you baby? Thinking about you. Send me a photo. Heard you're with the Dixits. I told your mother I would have taken care of you ✓✓

Leila
Thx for thinking of me. Why are you advertising that stupid therapist ✓✓
She's a quack, you just shit talk mom ✓✓
Riya has self-regard fyi. ✓✓

Matthew
Her parents asked for help. What are you insinuating? ✓✓
Let me know if you need anything ✓✓

Leila
Sure ✓✓
Send me $50 I'll order takeout there's just stale dhokla here ✓✓

Matthew
What is this, baby? I don't see you anymore. You don't respond to most texts ✓✓
It hurts me. I've given you thousands by now, no more ✓✓

Riya stretched her legs long on the sofa. Real leather, no plastic wrap. "Who is it?" she repeated.

"No one. Why are you asleep all the time?"

Riya picked at a toothpaste stain crusted on her sweatpants. "I'm tired."

"When do you go back to school?"

"Soon enough," Riya equivocated. "I'm going to QuickChek, do you want anything?"

"Cheddar fries."

Leila listened for the drone of Riya's car pulling out of the garage and watched a mindless half hour of television.

Leila
Seriously you're not sending the fifty? ✓✓

She hiked up her skirt, slid her underwear to the side, and spread herself open in front of a phone camera. The first five shots were blurry and bushy. Number six came out obscure but presentable. Leila applied a sepia filter to the image. She was so focused she didn't notice the front door creaking open and Riya standing in the kitchen, peach rings and hot fries in hand.

Riya sucked the hot fry dust from her fingertips. "Are you taking a nude? On our good couches?"

"It wasn't a nude."

"Show me, then."

Shamefaced, Leila blurted out the photo was for Matthew. Once that truth came out Leila was unleashed, sharing graphic details no one wanted to hear, like a sad, drunk stranger perched on a stool of a community bar. She told Riya about the hotels, the fake doctors' notes from Tejas, that Matthew was dying; it was taking him longer than expected but he was doing it; it was cruel to deny him what he wanted in this last interval of his life.

Riya picked again at the stain on her pants. "You're serious?"

"Why wouldn't I be?"

"Remember the oil man, what you said he did to you?"

Leila had a flair for the dramatic, that was all. Riya just had to be sure. Especially because it was Matthew. Riya had read him wrong at first. She'd thought he was a creep, yes. Now she knew he wasn't the type. He loved his wife. He'd been helping the Dixits communicate with her dean and keep her in school.

"But if it's true, that's horrible, of course," Riya said, yawning. "I'm beat."

She went upstairs. *If it's true.* What was she insinuating, Leila thought? What had she gained by telling a person? The person had yawned and gone to bed; the darkest drama of her life was just as she feared it, tedious and exhausting. A creeping sense of panic overwhelmed Leila. If Riya told anyone, Matthew would be locked behind a cell door and die there, never feeding his cats or lavishing Leila with good chocolate again. Leila swallowed what little concern she'd felt for the older girl that day she saw his car parked in the Dixits' driveway, Riya in his damp embrace. If Riya didn't know by now that he was the type, it meant Matthew had spared her, like a trinket behind glass, too valuable to touch.

～

ANITA returned from her trip with a knee cramp from her eighteen-hour economy flight.

"How was Karina, the bitch? And her princess daughter? She looks like a burnt potato these days."

"They were fine," Leila said. Riya had not told anyone. She silenced a call from Matthew, who'd been invigorated by the nude photograph, forwarding Leila audition links and a promotional email from her old acting conservatory, which offered a new commercial and voiceover class for teenagers with parents willing to shell out four thousand dollars. The course was taught by a casting agent who successfully got a student a cameo in a Lifetime movie about eating disorders. *Want to do this, L?* Matthew wrote. *I'll put down a deposit.*

This was tempting, but Anita was right, Leila was no good at acting. College was the surefire way to escape Willow Road and leave him behind. The screenplay honorable mention was a nice line on her résumé. When she saw a flyer on the school bulletin board about a PSAT prep class taught by Princeton students, she unpinned it and pocketed it.

Anita peeled an egg at the kitchen counter. She beamed when Leila handed her the flyer.

"Glad you are seeing some sense."

Prep classes met at the public library, a frosted glass building tucked behind trees and upscale eateries. After school, Leila took an elevator to a fourth-floor conference room. Enrolled students took practice tests and handed the completed Scantrons to disheveled undergrads dressed in argyle. Each student was paired with an undergrad to go over answers. Leila's tutor was a senior named Adrian, a short but not unattractive history major with uneven black stubble along his chin.

"Looks like you're stuck with me," he said, peering at her Scantron. "Leila Sharma. Where are you from?"

"Norway."

"The shade! I just didn't realize Leila was an Indian name."

"My mother picked something easy to pronounce."

"That's sad."

"It's such a waste of brain space to think about these things, names, belonging," Leila said, to impress him. "There's more interesting things to think about."

"Such as?"

"Oh, I don't know, I don't think interesting things. But they're out there, I'm sure."

He graded her Scantron. "What would your difficult name be?"

"I'm difficult as it is."

Adrian handed over Leila's answer sheet. "No corrections. I'll read your essay now."

"It's illegible."

He read it anyway, stroking his stubble for scholastic effect. "This isn't bad. Do you write a lot?"

"Plays."

"About what?"

He must have noticed she looked nervous. "Bring one in next time," he said.

Leila said she would, thanked him, and picked up her bag. Adrian watched her closely. "You sound older than you are, has anyone told you? On paper, that is," he added. "On paper you sound older."

∼

MATTHEW'S BEEMER was parked outside some shrubbery behind the library. A box of Shalimar sweets sat on his dashboard.

"Why do you look so happy, L?"

"I'm just happy," Leila said, biting into a magenta ball of rosewater. "Can't I be happy?"

Leila
Heyy, you coming on Saturday? I have a psat class and mom can't drive me ✓✓

Matthew
Looking forward ✓✓

Leila
Cool. Can you order this outfit for me??
This one www.sexxydollzzfashion.com ✓✓
I need to look good ✓✓

Matthew
Can it wait?
I've been preparing a surprise for you, have to save up ✓✓

Leila
Fine ✓✓
I'll get another ride, don't come ✓✓

Matthew
Ok, I ordered. Please do not show your mom. She said no more clothes. Delete this message ✓✓
Please delete ✓✓

SATURDAY, AFTERNOON POOJA

A Pooja in the Afternoon

Karina Dixit pinned her saree in place and rubbed black powder into the partition of her scalp, where the hairs were disappearing. While the women watched the Sharma trainwreck, Rajesh let a priest inside Riya's prayer service, the fourth one they'd held in two months to bring her home.

Karina watched the two men speaking conspiringly in the kitchen, *Bride's Toilet* behind him. The priest was squat and hairless except for his fine gray mustache. Streaks of talcum lined his forehead, like children's hopscotch.

"You're the mother?" he asked Karina.

"So I am."

He set up Riya's portrait at the mandir, squeezed wicks into rusted diyas, and set flames to each. The priest set a garland of carnations around Riya's photograph. To Karina's surprise the bell rang. A few women dropped by to pay their respects. Usha Gohel and her ratty son, Arvind. Nasreen Farouk and the Naiks, the father with flowers from his garden. Midservice, Rajesh took Karina's hand in his and squeezed it tight.

THE UNHAPPY KIND, 2010s

The Second Home

THE WEDNESDAY OF her final mandatory therapy session, Leila strapped herself into Matthew's passenger seat. He drove in the direction of the office, then continued straight.

"You missed the turn, we'll be late."

"I told her you're sick. Don't worry, you don't have to go again; she'll tell the school you went five times. I have a surprise for you."

He drove past the twin horses of a P.F. Chang's and a billboard for a medical malpractice agency, then turned onto a back road leading up to a corporate-looking apartment complex. Leila followed him up bare concrete steps and past steel residential mailboxes. They crossed an older woman dressed in a pashmina and walking her Pomeranian. The dog had eyes like beads. The women knew Matthew by name. She asked him how his move was going.

"May I pet him?" Leila interrupted.

"Of course," the woman said. "So this is your daughter, Matthew, the one I've heard so much about?"

"Yes ma'am," Matthew replied.

"Looks *just* like you."

The dog humped Leila's leg. The woman picked him up and carried him away.

Leila followed Matthew into the building. The taupe hallway carpets reeked of cigarettes and disinfectant. "What a bitch, why did she say I look like you?"

"You don't?"

"No, I'm pretty."

"Charming as ever."

"You moved here?"

He didn't answer as he unlatched the door to an apartment. Leila walked inside, where it still smelled of disinfectant. There were two beige bedrooms and a forest-green kitchen. Charcuterie dried on a marble island.

Home away from home, Matthew explained, whenever Leila needed one. This was the place he'd been looking into when he disappeared from the neighborhood. He leaned against the marble countertop and slid her his phone. A stopwatch appeared on the lock screen. Matthew had calculated it: if the traffic lights didn't lag, this apartment was only seven minutes and forty-three seconds from Leila's school.

Leila followed Matthew down the hallway to the smaller bedroom. The walls were empty save for a vanity mirror. A life-sized corduroy bear sat on a bed, green ribbon tangled around its neck.

"Like it, L?"

"It's fine."

"It's your room."

"I have a room. And a house. What about your house upstate?"

Matthew's linen shirts littered the carpet. Hermès pants hung over an ironing board.

"I've been living here."

"How long?"

"The past three months."

"What about Louise?"

"We're separating. She met another man."

"But you're open."

"Not anymore. I couldn't tell your neighbors, your mother. I don't want anyone to know."

He sat at the edge of the bed. The springs creaked. His tears were earnest. Leila hugged him.

"Do you like our place, L?"

Leila surveyed the shit walls, the chipped paint. "It's your place. And it looks a little cheap."

"Money isn't endless, I have lawyers to pay. Then you're another expense, swiping my credit card, asking for envelopes. It can't all be glamorous."

"You're so sensitive. I never said it had to be."

"You don't appreciate anything I do."

"I do appreciate it, I do."

"I try to pretend otherwise, but it's true. You just want money."

That was true. "That's not true," Leila said. She kissed the dead weight of his palm. They made amends and retreated to the kitchen. Matthew took his medication and poured Leila a glass of white cooking wine.

"A housewarming," he said. "It's a good thing you hold it better than your mom. I'll never forget that Christmas dinner with your dad, how ashamed he was."

Leila sipped. "You brought the alcohol, you wanted her to drink."

"Can't force a horse. She looks like one, too."

"But you kept looking at her."

"Who would look at her?" Matthew brushed aside the stray hairs on Leila's neck. "Stay here whenever you'd like."

"I probably won't want to. I have a home already, and a lot to study. I'm busy."

"Study, study, study. These days it's nothing else with you, she puts so much pressure on you, controls you."

"It's my own volition."

"Nonsense." He kissed her cheek. "After high school, you can live here permanently."

"No, after high school I'm going to college."

"You don't have to; I'll take care of you. That pressure is off."

"I'm thinking about Princeton."

She wiped her cheek. He topped off her cooking wine. "This isn't far from there. You can live here and go."

"I'll be staying in a dorm."

"You say that now, but you'll change your mind. Think how nice it'll be to come home to me after classes."

"Won't you be dead? I thought your heart wasn't in good shape, that you have three months."

"My doctor put me on a good medication, I have more time. Anyway, think. You'll go to classes, and I'll cook dinner—"

"I'll want to stay skinny."

"Skinny, stupid. I hate your new figure. You've lost so much weight."

"Who cares if you hate it? It's not for you."

Matthew's grip tightened against the neck of the bottle. "I don't think you'll make it at Princeton, I'm not sure you even want to go to college. It's always been your mother through your mouth. I've argued with her, told her, this girl wants to be onscreen."

"I was never a good actress. Even my advertisement is pretty shit."

"Forget actress. You could be a supermarket florist, decorate sheet cakes. I'd support you."

"Maybe I'll be a doctor, an engineer, the full stereotype."

"No. *She* wants that. She wants you to be what she couldn't be."

"But she is an engineer. You just sell drugs."

He opened and closed his mouth, at a loss for a rebuttal. He fished for pity in its place: for so long he'd wanted to give someone a home. Louise had even kept the cats.

He began to cry. It was a wretched sound.

"This place is so nice," Leila lied, to make it end.

Mini-Me

After Leila took the PSAT exam she continued her tutoring sessions with Adrian.

"Told her mother she was taking classes for the real SAT," said Devika Gill, clicking her tongue.

With each fake session Leila's crush intensified. She spent hours making changes to her old man screenplay in preparation to share. For instance she made the young girl more selfless and less materialistic, in case Adrian assumed she was drawing from her own defective character.

"This got honorable mention," she said, and handed Arian the stapled booklet of pages.

They sat in a blush-colored study room and pretended to be strangers sharing neighboring seats. Adrian had signed the tutoring company's *friendly but not friends* policy with minors. He wore a backwards baseball cap to appear surreptitious. "I'll read it soon," he said. He handed Leila pages of his own, a short story.

The next session he still hadn't read her script. He insisted he was too busy with classes and handed her another story. This frustrated Leila, who didn't care about his work. But she was enthralled by the scent of him, by the way his fingers strayed along her fingers and calves as she read his little fictions, so she put the frustration aside. Adrian often read over her shoulder. Occasionally he'd be impressed by a bland turn of his own phrase—*Every paper is a palimpsest*—and pause to tweet it to his twenty-four followers. In his first story a young protagonist sipped whiskey at an eating club and discussed *Powers of Horror* with several other young whiskey-drinking men

("You probably won't get this one," he reasoned). In another, a fourteen-year-old boy discovers his older sister's used tampons in their shared bathroom wastebasket and investigates the blood clumps.

Adrian wanted to know if he got the details right. "Does this seem real to you?" he asked, twisting the collar of Leila's lace shirt. "Is this what it's like for a girl?"

"That's exactly what it's like," Leila nodded, though it wasn't at all. She ran her foot up Adrian's hairy shin. He stroked her wrist.

"You're very good," she continued, though she found his stories boring. "Maybe if you made this change..."

Suggestions annoyed him. "That's amateur hour," he said, and retracted his fingers from her wrist. Leila reverted to praise, so that he would touch her again.

Anita
How's tuition? I am so proud of u for getting some sense. Good time to start on the SATs ✓✓
Matthew is at Karina's house again. Can you believe ✓✓

At lunch Leila followed Adrian to the café downstairs.

"When will you read my play?"

"What's my reward if I do?"

"I'll make a Twitter and retweet your lines. Anonymous tutor."

Adrian laughed but stiffened. "You won't do that. I'll read it, I swear."

Leila wrote the starts of new scenes, to have more material to share with him. She wrote about women in the neighborhood stabbing one another in the back, gossiping and drinking tea. The women rolled in the filth of their sad marriages, which they stayed in so their children could have happiness, as if they both could not have happiness at the same time, and one joy canceled the other.

("The problem was she thought she was better than all of us," said Hema Rao. "I found a draft of one of her stupid melodramas in the market, behind the rambutans. She must have dropped it. And she writes like we are some stupid women holed up in suburban houses, trapped in domestic dramas. That we only know small things. How to pick ripe fruit from the bin, how to launder fabrics so they won't wrinkle, how to follow along in the language the priests chant in. I mean, I make six figures, you know? The dogs eat fresh foods.")

Adrian still didn't have time for her lengthier script, but he read the short impromptu scenes. "Nice effort," he said, chewing an oat bar. "You remind me of me, when I was younger."

Leila was astounded by his ego, even larger than hers. She disliked the sight of him chewing the oat bar with his mouth open, but his presence continued to turn on a slow faucet between her legs. "Thank you, I'm so flattered."

He handed her five stapled pages. "I have another story for you. It's kind of explicit, though." This time he didn't read over her shoulder but eyed her closely as she read the piece, in which his thinly veiled alias had a threesome in a diner bathroom.

"I'm not trying to, you know, creep you out," he said. "I'm just curious what you think."

"How do they all fit into the stall?"

He took the pages back. "No one would ask that question," he sniffed. "Sex is hard to write, you wouldn't know."

"It's in my script, though, the one you never read."

"I did read it. I didn't want to tell you, but no offense, the intimate details aren't so convincing. And they were so bleak, it was hard to get through."

"But they're real."

"That's not the same as good," Arian said, but a private understanding fell over his features. "Want to go somewhere more private?"

She followed him to his dorm room in an old brick building with no AC. The wood of his twin bed was tacky with a jam-like substance.

"Sorry, that's actually jam," Adrian said.

Leila sat on his navy comforter and felt a lump underneath her. It was a Wonder Bread loaf.

Adrian set the bread on his desk and undressed Leila. He guided her head down his stout torso. *Beg me for it*, he said. Leila did, unsure if she really wanted the thing she begged for. Halfway down his navel she paused and considered asking him to shower.

After she finished, he dragged a hand up her thigh. Leila clamped her knees shut.

"I'll be gentle," Adrian said. Even gentle didn't work. He offered her a shot of Popov from his desk. The bottle sat half empty, next to the jam and bread. After Leila's third failed attempt to relax she got up and dressed quietly. Adrian zipped his pants.

"I'm sorry," Leila said. "Can I see you again?"

Adrian scratched his scalp. "Maybe we shouldn't have done this." They needed to maintain distance, boundaries, he said. They'd both get in trouble if anyone found out. And he had a girlfriend who lived out of state. He made mistakes like this sometimes because he missed her so much. "Want to see a photograph?"

"No." Despite the insult Leila still wanted him. She craved the strange sensations only he had inspired in her and wanted to see them to fruition. "What about in the library, can I still see you there? You could help me fix my script."

"I don't think it's very good," he said. "I don't want to be the old man in it."

"It got honorable mention. And you're twenty-one, you're not the man."

And the same way she had confessed to Riya she confessed to him who the man was.

"But don't tell anyone," Leila said. "He'll be ruined."

He promised. Leila let herself out into the courtyard.

Leila
Why did you take advantage of me if you had a girlfriend ✓✓

Adrian
Take advantage? scary that you'd make an accusation like that. ✓✓
Are you telling someone? Do you know how much I'd lose if you do? ✓✓

Leila
Wow one power I have here ✓✓

Adrian
Wow. It's not about power, Leila. Not all men are abusive. I've never tried to dominate you. In fact, you're being abusive right now, manipulating me ✓✓
I'd have to tell what you told me. Besides, don't you want to do it again? ✓✓

Nothing More, Nothing Else

Leila
I have a secret ✓✓
I had sex ✓✓

EmmaXXX
What. with who ✓✓
I'm so hurt, so disappointed. ✓✓

"The more she met that godawful boy, the less patience she had for Matthew," said Aparna Naik. "Matthew knew something was wrong. She turned down all his auditions and invites. He came by the house, smoked a blunt with Papa, cried, and ate our whole bag of hot mix." She snapped her fingers. "Like that."

Matthew tried to visit Leila spontaneously so that she could not decline or cancel. He flew to Croatia and back on a work trip. From the airport he drove straight to the Sharmas'.

Anita was sweeping the staircase with an old shirt, headphones in her ears. Leila pushed aside the foyer curtains. Outside Matthew was slamming his car door.

"Tell him I'm not here."

Anita narrowed her eyes and paused her music. "Why?"

"I have to study, he'll bother me."

"I'm not your servant; you can speak for yourself."

"Just tell him."

Leila went upstairs and shut herself in the upstairs study. For Adrian she had felt real desire and happily debased herself for it. She could no longer fake it for Matthew. She heard the front door opening. He chatted with Anita about his flight and his time in Zagreb. He wanted to see Leila. *She has no time, she's been busy studying and wants no disturbances*, Anita told him.

Nonetheless Leila heard Matthew's footsteps on the wooden staircase. He knocked on her bedroom door, then opened the door to the study and set a wrapped gift on the desk where Leila worked.

Leila tore the wrapping open. Inside was a powder-pink sweater. "It's not cashmere."

"I came straight from the airport, you're too busy to say hello?"

"I'm studying."

"For? Your test is over."

"I'm revising my screenplay. My tutor had some ideas for it."

"Is this the tutor you had sex with?"

"No, not him."

"Then who?"

"It's not your business."

"And the play. Why haven't you ever shared it with me?"

"Because it's about you."

Matthew perked up. "Me?"

"About your perversions. In it, I gave you an ugly, skinny cock. Like a throat swab."

"You must be joking."

"I am definitely not. Can you get me the same color in a hundred percent cashmere?"

"You submitted that." He paced around the room, mussing his hair. "Never mind, there's so many stories like that, done to death, and yours isn't true."

"It is true," Leila said. "I'll sell it and make a lot of money off it. It'll be hard for the studio to find a man as ugly as you for the adaptation."

"God. You are your mother's child. Come home now, we need to talk."

"I am home."

"Our home."

"I would rather die."

"Stop."

"I'd rather drink myself to death with your cheap cooking wine."

"Stop it. You've never gotten drunk."

"You've given me wine."
"I said stop. You're a child. You have to listen. You're a child."
He raised a hand, dropped it, then walked out the door.
"Please shut it behind you," Leila called after him.

Depression This, Depression That!

IN PALMER SQUARE, where Leila went after seeing Adrian, she bought peppermint tea and leafed through pulp books at a campus store. She sipped the rest of the tea on the bus ride home. Through her greasy window, she spied Manu Gill and his boys throwing water balloons at the beige panels of Tejas Kaushal's house.

Leila opened the garage door. She found Anita in the kitchen, peeling cucumbers on the kitchen floor. The peels caught on a blue blanket.

"You're late." Anita could see without looking how high Leila's hemline rode. How sticky and dirty-sneakered from the bus. "Where were you, looking like that?"

"Tutoring. Then a bookstore."

"Sure. What book did you buy?"

"Just browsing." Leila squatted on the blanket. "Nothing good."

"Sure."

Anita tossed Leila a knife.

"Don't bloody sit like that," Anita said. "Legs open like that."

"We're at home."

"So what, who wants to see you?"

Leila's chest pounded. "Why are you so mad?"

"You're seeing that tutor. You lied, there's no SAT class."

"Yes, I'm getting tutored."

"You took your test. You don't give him the checks. I looked."

"He doesn't want to be paid, he's volunteering."

"And you're a charity case? I got off early and drove to town to pick you up today, and there you were, leaving the dorms."

"That wasn't me."

"Don't lie. You left a chat open with EmmaXXX and told her you had sex. Which bitch is that?"

"Riya," Leila lied.

"I threw away your damn Sephora makeup. See who will have sex with you now."

"I'm still cute!" Leila shrieked, but her breath grew frenzied. "It's fine if you threw it all out."

"That's what you think."

"I paid for that, Mummy."

"With what money?"

"Money that I earned."

"From what? You don't even wipe your sink."

Leila grew faint, as if her head was in a room separate from her body. She thought of Matthew's quaint apartment with the first shred of longing she ever had for that place. "I miss Matthew. I'm stuck with you."

Anita flung her knife in the air. Cucumbers flew like missiles. "Want to know what I think? I think it is me stuck here with *you*. Maybe your uncle was right, and I am abusive. I am unfit—whatever else you tell him, whatever you two call me. You are afraid of tampons. How are you doing all of this?"

"I'm not having sex," Leila protested. It was true. The act was too painful to finish. "I lied to EmmaXXX."

"Why lie about that?"

"To seem intriguing."

"You think it's intriguing to be a loose woman?"

"Yes."

Anita scooped her green skins into a pile. "I'm not built for this," she muttered. "If I had freedoms like you, I wouldn't have wasted them lying and slutting around. I would have been a CEO of a Fortune 500 company."

Anita slid her knife across the blanket.

"Take it. Kill me off."

"Mummy," Leila said. "Mummy, this is a butter knife."

"Call your uncle, then, go to him. Why are you crying?"

"I can't say."

"Tell me."

"Depression."

"Good god," Anita said. "Your depression this. Your depression that! How should I feel? In everything I indulge you. Meanwhile I just endure. What is the problem?"

And Leila could not answer the question without ruining two men's lives. "Self-regard."

"What the fuck is that? There's nothing more I can do for you. This is more than anyone has ever done for me. Tomorrow I'll go to India. To my mother's house, only there's no mother's house for me anymore."

All evening Leila tried getting back into Anita's good graces. She cleaned egg curds out of Teflon pans, hand-washed the delicates in the kitchen sink, Windexed the kitchen windows so thoroughly that a robin mistook the glass for air. Leila heard the thump of death before she saw the plume of dark feathers. The body fell into the potted rose plant Ashok used for prayers. The roses were mostly dead, despite Anita and Leila's best efforts. Every now and again a bud appeared, and a flower bloomed. Leila gave up and left the bird's body in the pot. Anita would clean it. She loved birds.

Tuition

Because anita no longer trusted Leila to go into town alone, she sent Adrian emails of frantic scenes and texts, desperate attempts to maintain his interest.

Leila
What are you reading these days ✓✓

Adrian
The powers of horror ✓✓
Doing a paper on abjection ✓✓

Leila
Can I read ur paper ✓✓

Arian said no, the paper was raw, but he enjoyed explaining abjection to her.

Adrian
Like the revulsion you feel when you heat a glass of milk and it forms that skin on top ✓✓

Leila
I'm not easily revulsed, I drink the skin. ✓✓

Leila did not drink the skin. To impress him she sent him an old news link about a woman who raised a primate. *Is this abject?* Against advisement the woman kept the primate past his docile youth, into his wild adulthood. She could not handle the grown primate, who had no apparent recollection of his years of domesticity. One evening, during a fit, the woman fed him a Xanax and called a friend to come help her. The friend had babysat the primate as a chimp. She arrived at the house with a toy he loved then. *He flipped, he tried to kill and eat the babysitter*, Leila told Adrian. *The woman who raised the chimp got a knife. She stabbed him in the back. He looked at her with confusion; in an interview she said it was like stabbing herself.* The babysitter survived and debuted her ruined face on *Oprah*.

Adrian's responses grew terse. *I don't think you understand what abjection is*, he said.

Leila
Can I come over ✓✓

Adrian
Gf in town, maybe next time ✓✓

Sometimes he would be alone with an hour to spare. Those times Leila enlisted Matthew to chauffeur her around to avoid Anita's suspicions.

But Matthew had his own. In his rearview mirror he watched Leila hunched over her phone.

"How is it going, L?"

"So good."

"What were you up to in town?"

"Hm?"

"What were you up to, who are you texting?"

"The bookstore. And I'm not texting."

("That was true," said Jyoti Kaushal. "She was posting on a Reddit forum—I found the post.")

Guy I am seeing (M21) intimately is now ignoring me (15F) I feel sick is there hope

Matthew drove past Kwality and the Cash & Carry. The lot was flooded with cars. Aparna and the bag boys stood outside on ladders and hung string lights for Diwali.

"If you're not texting, why is your phone going off?"

Leila unlocked her screen. Replies flooded her Reddit post:

Skinnydippedx0x0
you are underage ... so much to despair of in this post, I'm not sure where to begin.

VainLicorice
oh, honey that's statutory rape

YourMommmmm
maybe if u weren't such a whore, he would talk to u

Matthew turned onto Willow Road. Leila unfastened her seat belt. The door was child-locked.

Matthew stared firmly ahead at the garage door. "I know you're talking to that boy. It's fine, really. Just tell me what his name is."

"There's no boy."

"Show me your phone."

After a quick and futile struggle he reached back and pried it from her lap. The screen was unlocked. Matthew read for a while and put his face in his hands. Twenty-one? Such a breach of power.

"But I love him," Leila said.

Love him. He could be fired, did Leila know that? She could be ruining his life, this man she claimed to love. And what kind of pathetic man bothered with a high school girl. A bad sign, a red flag, Leila should have the sense to see it herself. Only a man discarded by women his own age would do a thing like that. If she accepted treatment like this, she would grow up to accept anything.

"He has a girlfriend around his age," Leila said.

"And her, you don't care about her? My god, L, I feel sick when I think of the woman you're becoming."

She wasn't to see this boy anymore, he ordered. If she did, he would have no choice but to tell Anita about it.

"She knows about him," Leila said. "She saw my message to you, to EmmaXXX."

"She knows it's still going on?"

"I won't see him again. Please unlock the door."

He turned off the child lock. Leila slammed the door shut.

Matthew
I'm glad I found out, L. He's taking advantage of you. You don't see it, you're letting it happen ✓✓

Leila
Then what about you ✓✓

Matthew
Don't mischaracterize. I never hurt you, I never take advantage. I teach you ✓✓

Leila
That's what you're doing? Lol ✓✓
Also, can you pls transfer me $200 I want to get my hair done pls ✓✓

~

ADRIAN THUMBED THROUGH Leila's new auburn highlights. The ceiling fan whirred above them in his dorm room.

"How do you sneak away to see me this much?" Adrian asked.

Leila stood up and slipped her dress on. She tied her sneakers in the dim light of his working lamp. "I have a cover."

"Your mother believes it?"

"If she ever suspected anything, I'd say I was studying at school."

"She's fine with that?"

"She really wants me to go to Princeton."

He grimaced.

"What? Don't you think I could get in here?"

He didn't answer. Leila gave him oral. It trimmed the silence. Adrian walked to the window and lit a cigarette through the panes.

"God," he said, on the first smoke, "I hope not."

∽

"YOU CALL ME ONLY when you want to see him," Matthew accused. He'd waited for Leila in the parking lot of the public library for half an hour. He gripped the steering wheel tight, with white knuckles.

Leila popped a raspberry into her mouth from the plastic container he'd kept on the dashboard. She put her feet up. "I do want to see you."

"I can't lie to your mother like this anymore. I told you to stop, you said it wasn't going on anymore. I'm concerned."

"You're not concerned, you're jealous. I like it with him and not with you."

"I'm not. He's not a nice man and look at you," he said, surveying her short gingham dress. "The women talk to me, you know. Karina was driving through town and saw you with him. She asked me who he was. Even she thinks you're dressing like a whore."

"You got me this dress. Now you're slut-shaming me."

"I'm done enabling you."

Leila ate another raspberry. "If you tell mom about this, I'll tell her about you. And all the women."

Matthew reached into his glove compartment and unscrewed his pill canister and popped one. "You do make me sick."

"You're on the good medications now, right?"

"Because of you they're not working. You're remorseless, L. You need professional help. Stop calling me for this. I won't pick up anymore. Stop asking me to lie. I love you. Do you expect me to let somebody rape you?"

"It's not rape, I want it."

"You're fifteen. It's statutory rape."

"What about you? Your lewd acts with a child."

The car turned onto Willow Road. Tejas Kaushal jogged past in his visor.

"I have never," Matthew wheezed. "I have never."

"What about you coming to my room when Dad died? You rubbing all that eczema lotion on me—"

"I told you—I'm teaching you."

"Teaching me what?"

"For when you love a man who respects you. It's disgusting you'd mischaracterize."

"You keep saying that word. I'm not mischaracterizing. If I'm remorseless, it's because you made me this way."

"It's childish not to take accountability for yourself," Matthew said. "A victim mentality will get you nowhere." He became taciturn. "When I got married, I wanted so badly to be a father. Louise said she wanted to be free. She feared she'd love our child too little; that I'd love too much. When I met you, I knew what she meant. I thought I did."

"I'm sick of this old sob story, it's good you never had one."

She dialed a number on her cell phone.

"L, who are you calling?"

"The cops. I want to tell them about your lewd acts."

The car screeched to a halt.

"Call them, go ahead," Matthew said, white spit in the corner of his lips. "Tell them how I pay for your life. Hand you checks. Get your hair done. Pay for your mother's dresses, your shoes, your shows. Tell them about your college friend, how you manipulated him too. Who's the common denominator, what will they think?"

He slammed his fist on the dashboard. Leila whimpered. Whether her fear was real or an act, it moved Matthew. He lowered his voice and drove to her to Hema's Dunkin' drive-thru to placate her.

"Hema, so well you look," Matthew said, into the window.

Hema beamed. "You won't get anything free here, bhai."

"One coffee, seven Splendas." He turned to the back seat. "A doughnut for you, L, and what for your mom? Let's get her something too."

"She hates fat. She hates you."

"Bad day, bratty day," Matthew told Hema. "One Boston Kreme."

Concerned Citizen Mr. Pillai

"In the end Matthew reported Leila's college boy," Jyoti Kaushal said. "Said that it was his duty. That somebody in that house had to be responsible."

"And why would he approach a police officer, if he too was also a bloody pervert?" Hema Rao said. "Don't judge us for what we didn't know."

The women hummed in assent. They remembered the day Matthew made the report. A police car showed up at the Sharmas'. Leila sat in the back seat of a cop car and pleaded her case to two policemen—one average, the other ugly; the very same pair that had plagued the neighborhood in the days after Matthew's death. The officers read Leila the statutes and the Romeo and Juliet rules. They asked her what went in and where.

Leila sobbed.

The ugly officer rolled his eyes. "If you could do this, you can speak about it."

"It's my fault," Leila said. "I wanted it all. I'm almost sixteen, it's almost not a problem."

"But you're not sixteen."

"Worse things have happened to me. And I love him."

"If you even cared about him," the ugly officer said, "you wouldn't put him in this position."

The average-looking policeman chewed his pen. He had been thinking, he said. In his time, he had encountered girls from families like Leila's, girls who would grow up to have marriages they didn't want and soiled the goods to shirk the expectation. *A damaged goods situation. So there's no more arrangement possible.*

So, he concluded. *My theory is you did the same.*

Leila stared at the three lines along his forehead.

"Sorry," Leila said. "But no. I appreciate you thinking so hard about this."

Matthew
mall tomorrow, baby? I'm so sorry but it had to be done ✓✓

Leila
I never want to talk to you again ✓✓

Matthew
That boy was bad news ✓✓
I'll buy you anything. ✓✓
Come on baby. ✓✓
I'll have to find a new girl, if you treat me like this. ✓✓
My heart's failing. I have two months left. The doctors say it's final this time ✓✓

~

THE OFFICERS RELENTED to Leila's hysterics and pressed no charges against Adrian, let alone contact him. Leila was soothed. She'd warned him in advance that they could come for him. Now she'd saved a young man with more potential than her, who would go on tutoring girls about abjection.

Adrian
Just wanted to say you saved me ✓✓
It was going to be ruined. I wouldn't graduate ✓✓
Go to med school or tutor ✓✓
Thank you. I love you ✓✓

Leila
Nbd it's just my life that's ruined. ✓✓

Leila ate a sleeve of saltines, made an Adrian on Sims, and trapped him in a basement. She was unsure what to do with her prisoner; the fact she'd made him a prisoner unnerved her. Perhaps Matthew was right, she'd become remorseless, a monster. Leila released Sim-Adrian. He returned to Simville unbothered and chatted up Leila's avatar, a Sasha 2.0, at a café. Leila made Sasha invite him back to her house. The Sims went for a swim in the pool. Leila ordered Sasha to leave the pool, paused the game, and deleted the ladder. Sim-Adrian drowned and returned as a ghost.

~

THE SPECTACLE OF THE whole affair, from Matthew's police report to the cop car in the driveway, embarrassed Anita. She began applying for software engineering jobs in in California, thousands of miles away from the women. She was endlessly relieved that the officers had done nothing. There would be no courtroom, no lawyers, no cross-examination of her daughter's sluthood.

"That's why I didn't make the report myself," Anita told Leila. The two perused the Cash & Carry for aloe. "The cops are useless here, corrupt. That boy was always going to go free. And now, look at you, you're left with bad skin. Is that your phone?"

Adrian
Don't be so dramatic ✓✓

Leila tossed a sleeve of Parle-G biscuits into the cart. A voice sounded off in the next aisle over, the Goya beans.

It was Nasreen Farouk's: "That girl, what a shame."

Anita pressed an ear to a bag of rice.

"Mom, let's go."

"Shut up. They're talking about you, Leila. Let's hear them, shameless fucks. At the end of the day, you're still getting A's, no matter what other bullshit you do."

But the women were speaking about Riya. She'd put on more weight around the face and flunked out of another handful of classes. Not even Matthew could sweet-talk the dean, and anyway Riya didn't want to return to school. The Dixits couldn't convince or coerce her to go to class.

"Her mother was telling, it has been so hard," Devika Gill said. "Made her so— promise you won't tell?"

"Of course," said Nasreen.

"*Depressed.*"

"O-ho. Big deal. These girls act as if depression is bone cancer. Will she ever go back?"

"I don't know. Karina paid for her to go on a spring break trip with her friends; in exchange she'll reconsider. Me, I would have cut the ticket itself in half."

"So sad for the Dixits. They did everything right."

"They've tried everything, came to her dorm room itself. She wouldn't open the door. They sent Matthew. God knows he has enough on his plate. He took her to a doctor. Prescribed her medication. It's made her gain more weight, poor thing."

"O-ho! How much weight?"

"Twenty, thirty, forty pounds? Shame—such a pretty girl. What does she have to be so miserable about? Tell me, if *she* is sad, how should *I* feel?"

∼

BACK HOME, ANITA SET CAULIFLOWER florets in a pan and opened her computer. One of the companies she applied to had advanced her to the second round of interviews. She had a weekend to complete and submit a work sample.

"Leila, I'm busy, watch the pan," Anita said. "So. Karina's daughter is depressed. Did Matthew tell you he went to her school?"

Leila got up from the sofa, where she'd sat opening and closing Riya's contact on her phone. "He told me nothing."

"*Con-stant-ly* Karina talks shit. She has a rich husband and they hardly have school fees. Karina stews in temple or sits on her ass until her ass drips into the couch cushions. I too can order a print of *Bride's Toilet* and act as if I'm a curator."

"I like her art."

Anita slammed her laptop shut. "Okay, like it." She shooed Leila from the cauliflower pan. "It's burning, you cannot so much as watch a pan. Everything is better at other people's houses. Other people are perfect." Anita flipped the florets. "Karina had so much to say when Matthew helped us. Now look. Even that coddled girl can't manage a simple degree, no?"

Leila felt a stinging between her legs. "I'm going to the bathroom."

∼

ON THE TOILET BOWL, the stinging turned to burning. Leila opened Facebook. She searched for Riya's account, which she'd muted, tired of seeing the happy sorority house posts, warmly lit at a New Brunswick pub. Why should she be happy and not Leila? Why should life not stick its fingers inside her too? Now she wished for a happy post, some stupid photo of Riya drinking bubble tea. *User not found*, the search returned.

Leila washed her hands and returned to the kitchen. "I think Riya blocked me. Can I check her account on your phone?"

"Why should she block you? Why check on her at all? Does she care about you?" Anita ripped the purple skins from two onions. "I'll never forget how she blamed you as children. Who cares what she thinks? Would I get anywhere if I cared what these small-small women thought of me? None of them work as hard as me. None of them did engineering. None of them are single—"

"Some are."

"Whatever. It is stupid to fret over people who don't care."

Leila
did you block me? ✓✓

Riya
just deactivated ✓✓

Leila
Are you okay? I heard Matthew visited. ✓✓

Riya
Yes, he did ✓✓

Leila
Did he do anything weird✓✓

Riya
What no? ✓✓

Leila
Did he do anything to you? Anything perverted. I told you he's a pervert ✓✓

Riya
No ew omg. ✓✓

So Leila had worried for nothing. So Riya was too valuable for violation after all. Why care? She'd done nothing when Leila confided in her. Leila retired to the couch and napped as the cauliflower cooked. She woke to one new message:

Riya
Actually do you have a second ✓✓

                                                Leila
                                             what is it ✓✓

The checks turned blue. Riya didn't write back. The discomfort Leila felt in the supermarket returned. Leila went to the bathroom again and tried to urinate. The burning was unbearable.

Leila walked back to the kitchen, crossing her legs. She dispensed water and ice into a steel cup.

"Set the table, Leila," Anita said. "I said, set the table, you're in some daze? Like a servant I cook, the work sample is due, and you nap. Why do you look so ill?"

"Cauliflower smells like gas."

Anita wrinkled her nose and shut the flame off. "Why do you say such things? Now that's all I can think about."

The two packed the cauliflower for another evening and drove to Kwality Meats. Leila ordered two chapli kebabs. She and Anita ate them in the car.

"Don't make a mess on these seats, Leila."

"You're the one spilling the tamarind." She crossed her legs. "I need to go to a gynecologist."

"For what?"

"I can't say."

"For what? My god. For what?"

"A little burning, nothing nefarious."

"My god. You've done it now. My god. When I was your age, I wasn't opening my legs. I studied hard. I liked no one. I worked in my uncle's shop, unspooling fabric."

"Yes, I know. You always tell the same stories, Mother."

"Sorry! It is no variety show. I have always lived the same sorry life."

The uncle was infirm now, Anita continued, senile and shuffling in a daughter's attic. He'd written Anita for money a handful of times. He'd lost his shop and house.

The envelopes were large and yellow, with Queen Elizabeth stamps on the corner. Anita had read them and burned them on the stove. *Bury and move on*, she said.

Leila
My body is ruined thanks a lot ✓✓
It's burning there ✓✓

Matthew
It's probably just a UTI, L, my god, calm down, I'll take you to a doctor✓✓

Leila
No that's ok mom will ✓✓

~

ANITA SET THE appointment. Matthew called her directly.

"I can take her to a real expert, whatever the problem is," Matthew said, over the phone. "Your doctor must be garbage, like your insurance."

"I don't want to discuss this with you."

"Why won't you tell me what the problem is, so I can find the right specialist? You've got to be less of an Indian about these things, Anita."

"You're a bloody Indian," Anita replied. "I'm a bloody Indian. Sometimes I wish I'd just stayed there. This country here is the worst of all. Capitalist and cruel."

"I'm British, Didi."

"Even her father wouldn't have pushed to take her. Why are *you* pushing?" Anita tilted her head to the side and coughed up smoke-phlegm. "Also, do not call me Didi. Because my husband was an older man, because you think you know so much more than me, you pretend as if I'm older than you. Man, you are *ten-plus* years older than me. I am not your Didi, okay? I am not even your sister. Leila doesn't need you to take her to any bloody doctor."

Matthew wheezed. "I'm unwell, Anita. My cardiovascular disease is kicking in. The doctor upped my aspirin. I told Leila I have months left, didn't she tell you? You take advantage of me when you need to and talk to me with disrespect. Volatile, you are. You both are."

"Yes, I am volatile, she is volatile. Anything else?"

"I want to make sure Leila has a good home when the sickness takes me totally."

"Leila has the right home."

"Maybe she has a disease, for all you know. Who knows what she did with that boy, right under your nose? I'm worried she'll go to the dogs."

"Shut up. She'll be fine."

"This fault starts at the mother's level. She knew nothing about sex, because of you. I reported that boy, you knew and did nothing—"

"Disgusting. She has taken a fucking biology class. She is not like me. You cannot imagine how innocent I was. I thought babies came out of your stomach."

"I know her. She won't go to college. That's what you want, and you act like she is an arm, an extension of you. Do you think a girl in her situation will go to Princeton? Girls like her, I've known them; they're lost causes. They need people who can steer them on the right path."

"Thanks for your fucking feedback." Anita hung up.

Matthew
Your mother L. My god. Out-of-control. ✓✓
Come stay in our apartment. ✓✓
I'm concerned about you; I'll take you to a better doctor ✓✓

Leila
You think I'm a lost cause? ✓✓

Matthew
Why is she telling you that?

Leila
I was listening in ✓✓

Matthew
Being with your mother is terrible for your mental health.
Now your physical health is impacted too. I will escalate
this, legally. ✓✓

Leila
don't contact me anymore. No texts, no email. Only money ✓✓

Matthew
I'm running out ✓✓
My treatments, they're expensive. ✓✓
Doctor says we'll up the heart pill dosage ✓✓

∼

AT THE CLINIC where Anita brought her, a doctor with purple eyeliner instructed Leila to relax in metal stirrups. She couldn't keep her legs open.

"I'm out of commission," Leila said.

Was she sexually active, did she have trauma? No and no. The doctor prescribed her a full course of antibiotics to pick up from the pharmacy. Leila thanked her and returned to the waiting room. Anita hunched over her phone.

"Mummy, what is it?"

"See what your uncle is telling people."

Jyoti
Matthew said Leila has some sexual sickness, Anita. ✓✓
And you're not taking her to a doctor? Does it spread? ✓✓

A Disappearance
(The Unhappy Kind)

Leila went to the market to clear Anita's name and her own. Aparna Naik pored through a crate of okra. A new bazaar had opened up across the street. The owners spread a rumor that a garter snake was discovered in a crate of Cash & Carry okra. Aparna inspected the boxes for life inside, ruining her fresh nails for her tenth date with a matrimonial site bachelor.

"A hoax is enough to kill business," Aparna said. "You came alone? No Mom? No Matthew? Papa misses him."

"Matthew is a pervert," Leila said. "What he said about me isn't true."

"A pervert how?"

"Hasn't he ever looked at you?"

Aparna squatted and opened an unexamined okra crate. "All men look, I just pull my skirt down. Otherwise, it looks like you want them to see. I've been worried about you, the way you dress," she said. "It's not what *I* think. I am just telling you what these women once told me."

~

When taking out the trash, Leila caught Jyoti Kaushal retching into the Sharmas' backyard. Jyoti wiped her mouth with the collar of her green nightgown.

"Sorry. Tejas is particular about his shrubs."

"We're particular about the lawn."

"Your lawn is dead. Where it's not dead, it's crabgrass. And I'm pregnant."

"Okay, sorry, vomit. Vomit. Can I come in for tea?"

The request surprised Jyoti, but she acquiesced. The Kaushals' house stank of mildew. A Krishna quilt hung blue from the doorway along with streamers of fake flowers. The living room ottoman was obscured by stacks of blouses and jeans. Jyoti shoved them aside. QVC ran on the television, an infomercial about a neck-tightening cream.

Jyoti selected her most chipped mug from the cabinet. She handed Leila a watery tea.

"Thank you," Leila said. "And congratulations."

"It's a girl."

"Don't let her around Matthew. He's a pedophile. He pulls me out of school, gets sick notes from Tejas, and does whatever he wants with me."

"Tejas is a good doctor. He would never give a fake note."

Leila spotted a cut on Jyoti's cheek, masked with foundation.

"How'd you get that?"

Jyoti covered the mark with her hair.

"I fell on a plant."

"You can get help. There's a hotline."

"I said, I fell on a plant. That means I fell on a plant. Do you think I don't know how to dial a hotline?" Jyoti pressed a hand to her belly. "I'm not part of some trauma porn. This is what I fear, having children here. They'll think I cannot speak. That they must do it for me. Botched translators. As if they know what I have to say. In the end they're the ones with nothing to say."

Leila thanked Jyoti for the diluted tea and walked home. Hattie and Baloo howled from behind the glass of Hema's doorway. A cop car circled into the block. The women drew their blinds open. Had Leila slept with a new college boy? Had someone reported Tejas for wife beating? Leila peeked out her window with excitement—had the women she confided in made a report?

But the police car parked in front of the Dixits' house.

"A change of pace," Devika Gill said, cheerfully.

Phones around the block dinged with a shared WhatsApp link from the local paper.

Rutgers Student Gone Missing on Spring Break Trip to Panama City, Florida

The woman, Riya Dixit, 19, is a freshman at Rutgers from Central Jersey.

"She'd been depressed but seemed excited to go on this trip," one witness said. "We went out to a nightclub and drank. She went overboard. We wanted to leave, she wanted to stay, alone."

The woman was last sighted leaving the nightclub at 2:29 a.m.

"I think she was tripping hard on something," another witness said. "Or she left with a few guys."

The woman's clothes and cellphone, waterlogged, were discovered in a public trash can on the boardwalk. Anyone with information should call the local precinct.

Leila read the page twenty-one times.

Downstairs Anita had the local ABC news on. *Florida police are saying what was a rescue mission is now a recovery mission, a search for a body*, said the anchor in a bandage dress. The segment cut to Karina, who had dressed in her best crepe saree, sitting at her kitchen table. Beside her Rajesh, in business casual, folded his hands in his lap, stone-faced. *Bride's Toilet* loomed blurrily behind them.

Karina looked squarely into the camera. Kohl smudged her heavy-lidded eyes.

"Please come home, Riya," she said. "We pushed this channel to do a ninety-second segment on you, they would only agree to forty-five."

Rajesh cried. "If you are watching this, please come home."

∽

AFTER THE NEWS a heat wave percolated in the township, viscous as egg yolk.

Leila
I need to meet with you ✓✓

Matthew
I'll come now. Madeleine's? ✓✓

Leila
Kwality Meats ✓✓

Matthew
That shithole? ✓✓

∽

THE LUNCH CROWD had already trickled out at Kwality. Only the dregs of cold mutton and matar paneer with the paneer fished out remained on the buffet table. The restaurant sweltered. The fan was broken. Nasreen fanned herself with a stack of bills, glued to the local ABC news on the corner television.

Matthew and Leila sat at a table near the window. Leila swallowed an antibiotic from the container in her purse.

"What's that?" Matthew asked her.

"For my problem. The doctor told me to take them with food."

"I'm so happy you called me, L. Things have gotten so bad lately between us, I know you didn't mean it, but they'll be better soon. And I could have taken you someplace better than this."

Leila dragged a knife across the table. "Better."

Nasreen came around with a pad for orders. "Ready?"

"Tea, eight Splendas. No real sugar."

"Everyone knows about your diabetes, sir," Nasreen said.

"Now it's hypertension too. Cardiovascular disease."

"O-ho. I've had hypertension forever."

Leila ordered a seekh kebab, a chicken samosa, and a paper bowl of bhel puri. She cut lines into her green paper placemat with the table knife.

"L," Matthew said softly. "I have some news. Louise moved out. Sent me the divorce papers. Left the cats. It's official."

"Sorry to hear that. Did you hear—"

"I was thinking. We can break the apartment lease here. You can come stay at the house upstate."

"What?"

"I have a note from the old therapist, she's spoken to your mom before, she agrees with me too. It's in your best interest to stay with me, your mother's not fit. I'll come for you on your birthday. I bought bedding, clothes, books. You won't need anything. So?"

"I don't even go to that therapist anymore."

"Don't you want to come?"

"I want to stay with Mom. She and I want nothing to do with you. By your own math you should be dead by now."

Beads of sweat dripped down Matthew's forehead. "Each extra day is a gift. I don't want to waste any more of ours fighting."

"Did you hear about Riya?"

"Dixit?"

"Yes, the girl in the block who you never stopped ogling."

"Yes, I heard. She was depressed, L. I helped her as much as I could, but she'd really gone south, L. I swear I had nothing to do with any of that. That's your mother getting to you."

He dabbed his sweat with his kerchief. "Between you and me, your mother's been *looking* at me. She must be missing a man around, I understand. But I don't think of her that way, kiddo. I'm not attracted to her. A temper like hers. How could any man be?"

Nasreen dropped off a plate of onions.

"Anything else I can get you? Another tea, coffee?"

"One coffee, nine Splendas," Matthew said.

Leila cut into her meat. "I know you visited Riya at school. I asked if you did anything to her. She said no. She seemed disgusted by the idea. But I'm not so sure."

Matthew unbuttoned the top button of his shirt.

"I feel sick," he said, quietly. "My sugar. My heart. Please."

He did look sick. Foam trickled from the edges of his mouth. Leila eyed the Choking Victim poster hung on the back wall. If he stopped breathing in front of her, she and Nasreen might consult the poster for instructions, press his stubbled face into the green carpet and its permanent flecks of goat curry stains. EMTs would squeeze through the little door, past the notice with the C− health rating.

"Riya asked to talk to me once. Then she stopped responding. Did you do to her what you did to me?"

"Please—" Matthew wheezed. "What have I done to you except care for you?"

A waiter came around with a coffee and a pitcher of water.

Matthew popped his collar. The kerchief soiled, he blotted his face with a napkin. The waiter looked at Leila and back at Matthew, who was now sinking into the table.

"Should I call the ambulance for your father?"

"He's fine. Just the check, please."

In case Matthew was really dying, Leila poured water into his plastic cup. Matthew downed it. Liquid ran down his jowls. Nasreen tacked a paper check onto the table and squeezed Matthew's shoulder.

"Dear, you look awful," Nasreen said. "You need a doctor, man? Need a menu?"

Matthew unzipped his fanny pack for his pill canister. He swallowed one dry and squared the bill. He gave Leila the silent treatment in the car, sitting her in the back seat where she couldn't control the radio. "Black Velvet" played.

"This shit is so old and so boring," Leila said.

"I was dying back there, L, and you didn't care."

Leila kicked the back of his seat.

"Please, I gave you water. And my mom would never fucking like you. Wanna know why?"

The signal turned green. Matthew passed a Wawa.

"Wait—can we stop for a smoothie?"

"No."

Leila kicked harder.

"Well, it's because you're ugly. An old, ugly fuck. That's what you are. A monster. You used to show us those Polaroids of you when you were young, how handsome you were. Mom and I laughed about it together." Leila looped her fingers into his headrest and tugged Matthew's silver neck hairs. "I wouldn't have wanted you then. I don't want you now. Motherfucker. You told me the doctor said you were dying, and I've been patient. You *should* die."

"Please stop."

"Pull over. I'll kill you myself. I'll strangle you, pull over."

On the street, grandpapas walked with canes and orthopedic shoes. A young father pushed a stroller down the bike path. The signal turned red. Cars lined up behind the beemer and honked: Aparna Naik's Jeep, Devika Gill's Civic, a cop car with dormant red-blue lights. Matthew pulled over to the shoulder.

"I'm dying, I'm dying!" he cried. "I'll die right now, I swear."

Leila kicked the seat. "I would rather anyone but you."

A cop car with the two officers, one ugly, one average, overtook the beemer. One officer threw his clementine peels out the window as the other sped off behind Aparna's over-the-limit Jeep.

Matthew's breath steadied. "I'm sorry about Riya. But I swear to you, I had nothing to do with it. Girls like her—it's only a matter of time."

He turned the radio on high and merged back onto the lane. Leila kicked his seat again. Her foot caught in a strap. She reached down. It was his fanny pack of medications, fallen onto the back seat floor.

"Actually turn the music up, I like it," Leila said.

Covered by sound, Leila unzipped the pouch. There were Matthew's heart pills, his insulin jabs. Quietly Leila reached into her own purse and poured her UTI antibiotics into her palm. They were small and white and round, nearly identical to Matthew's pills.

"What are you doing back there?"

Leila tossed the fanny pack to the passenger seat. "Nothing, you dropped this."

～

AN OUTPOURING OF GRIEF for Riya overtook Willow Road. The Kaushals organized a tiny vigil at the temple's small hall. Nasreen Farouk put up Missing posters at Kwality and sat at the countertop with her head in her hands, a pink glass of falooda melting beside her. Missing posters went up at the Cash & Carry and at Hema's Dunkin' Donuts, next to a promotional sign for caffeinated lemonades. Men in pursuit of good karma made promises to Rajesh Dixit about journeying down to Florida and forming a search party of their own. The women made no such promises, knowing there was nothing to be done except grieve. They fried their grief in oil and watched the edges bubble and hiss. They warmed it on thavas and pressed their hands to their faces to see if it was hot enough; they pressed their own children closer and tightened their curfews, as though they might disappear too.

"It probably happened because Riya was so beautiful, the most beautiful girl in the block," Jyoti Kaushal speculated, as she purchased baby onesies at Target. "It's good, then, if my child comes out looking like Tejas."

Behind her, Devika Gill let Manu dump two varieties of ice cream into their cart, so grateful she was to have him safe with her.

"The horoscopes were bad," Devika moaned. "Everyone's. I was telling Karina."

～

KARINA DIXIT PAID for photos of Riya to appear in various local papers. She sent sizable checks to gurus who promised to help and holed herself up at temple until the priests nudged her to go home and shower. Night after night the neighborhood woke to the sound of her wailing and smashing jars onto the granite.

"I thought it was an animal," said Tejas. "I nearly called Animal Control."

"Of course you did," Hema Rao said.

The news rattled Anita. "How nasty I'd always been to her," Anita told Leila over breakfast oatmeal, a Missing poster spread out on the table between them. "Such a beautiful girl, even after she got fat."

She eyed Leila pointedly. "That's why you must be careful with these outside boys, Leila. They are here only to use us. Dump our bodies in bins and go marry white girls."

"Why are you always talking like we're one? *Ours, us.* Who's *we*? You hardly cared about her before."

"Before was before. Who knows what diseases these boys carry?" Anita said. "Her poor mother. When I was pregnant with you, I would see them walking together. The time and money and loneliness and blood it takes to raise even one child. And now it's a waste. All because Riya had to go—"

"What?"

"It's too dirty, I can't say it. Careless."

"You are kind of saying it."

"Her poor mother. I should call her."

"You hate her mother."

"I never said I hate her."

"Then it's implicit. You don't have to say it."

"I know what implicit bloody means! You girls go to fancy schools and forget I've gone to school too. I can talk with a big mouth, just like you, if I wanted. If I hated anyone, I hated them for you."

"No one even knows what happened. How do you know she wasn't being careful?"

"Don't twist my words, hero. I am just saying, girls should be careful."

"You're talking about me."

"Not everything has to be about you."

"Men should be careful."

"This country should be socialist. We can want and want. Certain things won't happen. It's a waste of time to hope differently. And I can't control men. I can only control you. Thank god it wasn't you. This is what happens if you keep acting the way you've been acting. From now on, no more studying in town. Or whatever it is you keep doing there. Come straight home after school. Don't think of asking Matthew behind my back."

"I don't ask him."

"Don't lie to me. Don't ever see that stinking boy again."

"But he made me happy."

"That's happiness to you? He doesn't give a tendril of a shit about you."

"Sometimes it felt like he did. Hasn't anybody made you happy like that before?"

Anita's mouth thinned. "Foolish, to put your happiness in one idiot."

"Did Matthew tell you that I asked him to take me to town?"

"He didn't need to. As a mother I know."

"You know nothing."

"Fine! I know nothing. You know everything. Useful girl. American girl. Educated girl. I am nothing. I should be the one to disappear. Do not put my face in the paper when I'm gone."

With this Anita went silent, and smiled a little, pleased to have the grand finale of the argument.

Leila also wanted the final say. "Matthew must have touched her. Those times he went to visit her."

The remaining color pooled out of Anita's face. She resembled the "after" in a Ponds Whitening Cream advertisement.

"She told you that?"

"She didn't have to. I know, he's done it to me for years."

Anita's crying face was gnarled and lined, like a tightly wound fist. Her shoulders shook.

She reached for Leila's hand.

Leila withdrew hers. "How can you be surprised? You knew it. He did it inside this house. You didn't hear him? In my room, in the study. While you swept downstairs he shut the door. Didn't you hear it? His wife never came to the hotels with us. Remember when she came over and we went to a Broadway show? She left at intermission. He says they're divorced now. Maybe they have been for years. He got a place in Princeton. For himself and me. If you Google me, I'm listed under that address. That's why he could always pick me up so quickly after school. It was easy for him. You let him."

Anita swayed in her seat, as if she might faint into her oatmeal. "I can't hear this," she said. "I can't hear this. I didn't know. You never told me. You told me she was there. Don't you have a mouth to speak? Haven't I always said to use it?"

"You once told me I belong in house."

"You always said you wanted to go. When he was gone you missed him."

"I didn't want anything. And now he wants me to leave you and live with him. He told that stupid therapist you're abusive. She wrote a note. He told my school. They all believe him."

Cheeks glazed over with damp streaks, Anita wouldn't look at Leila. "People will believe anything in a British accent."

"You sent me with him, of course you knew."

Anita pressed her hands together in supplication. "I didn't. How can you say I would have known? Do you think I wanted this for my child? This wasn't supposed to happen to you, no no." She wiped her face with the collar of her dressing gown. "I even asked you—Leila, is something off? Is he a bad man? And you said no. You always chose him. I didn't blame you. I am not any mother. I tried to keep you here. I told you, don't take his gifts. Don't live beyond your means. Still you chose him."

"I'm a child. I don't have choices."

"You're almost sixteen. When I was your age, I was no child. Are you so helpless?"

"I felt sorry for him. He told me he was dying. He told me the diabetes was getting to him, then his heart."

"So let him die! Every cell of his should burst. Someone should pull him apart string by string, like a—" Anita searched for the winning simile. "Like a string cheese. Why are you handing me the phone?

Leila dangled the landline between them.

"Call the police, Mother."

"You want to call the cops on me? Go ahead. I deserve it. According to you, I knew."

"Call on Matthew."

Anita took the phone. Her hands trembled.

"Leila, did you hear what happened with Devika's car accident? The cops didn't believe her over that white woman, and now her car insurance is through the roof."

Anita set the phone down. "There's no point dragging this nightmare on. What will the cops think of you, reporting not one, but two men? I heard you crying in the car over that idiot boy. They'll think, *How can it be true that this girl is twice a victim?* They didn't do anything the first time, not a single charge. What will they do now? You'll look like a liar. Let's bury and move on."

"Please call."

"Please think. You'll go to court. You'll stand on a stand and tell a stupid testimony. They will ask you about your stinking college boy; Matthew knows all about him. A lawyer will cross-examine you. Cops, lawyers, judges will pick you apart, call you a slut. A government worker will take you away from me. You still want me to call?"

"You're the one who thinks I'm a slut."

"Enough," Anita said, shaking a hand in the air. "I've had enough. I'm getting away. I'm leaving. I will die. I will leave."

Anita got her keys out of the medicine cabinet, threw the paper with Riya's black-and-white face on it into the trash can, and stormed into the garage. She slammed the door behind her. Leila dipped a spoon into her oatmeal and listened to the low rumble of Anita's engine revving, the garage door opening. Once she was gone Leila retrieved the Missing poster from the bin and smoothed it out. She opened WhatsApp. *Last seen two weeks ago*, Riya's status read.

Leila
Hey are you there? ✓
Are you? ✓
I hope you're ok ✓
hope this is just melodrama on your part ✓
I told you about him ✓
did he do something to you? ✓
?? ✓
Do you have self-regard ✓
are you ok ✓
just answer ✓

Blue checks never appeared. Leila called Anita, who had been gone for some time now. Her mother's phone vibrated on the table. Leila felt a familiar paranoia. What if this time Anita had gone to disappear in earnest at last? Maybe she had driven to the Home Depot and swallowed pesticides in the parking lot, or to the canal in Princeton to drown herself, the final figurine in her nesting dolls of death threats.

The garage door rumbled, and Leila's panic dissipated. Anita stormed inside with a Cash & Carry grocery bag. She set it on the countertop and fished under the medicine cabinet for a notebook and a pen. It was the same notebook, Leila realized, panic rising in her throat again, that she'd used to write notes for her screenplay, about the old man and the girl.

"Where were you?" Leila asked. "What are you writing?"

"We had no milk. I'm writing nothing." She flipped past Leila's scribbles and squinted at them. "And what are these?"

"Notes from my play, you remember, honorable mention."

Anita read them. "This is what you submitted? In public?"

"Yes, and we went to dinner to celebrate."

"I didn't read it then. You want to parade this for specks of fame? Be careful, Leila, or it is the only lens out of which people will ever see you."

Anita scribbled something onto a fresh sheet. She tore it out and pocketed it.

"So you had the time to write all this, but you could not tell me, like some poor girl with no options. I had no options to tell. You believed him, Leila, really, when he told you he was dying? Idiot. Someone should kill him, really."

"Or someone could report it."

"I told you, that would ruin you forever, and for what, this temporary damage? Those bloody officers, the questions they asked you; they think we're backward. They too will think I knew; that I allowed it. My own daughter thinks I allowed it. It will show up on a Google search for you, forever. When you apply to college, to a job, there our name will be, forever."

Anita retired to the table and slumped over the placemat. After a few dry sobs she wiped her eyes and lit a cigarette.

"Those will kill you one day, Mother," Leila said.

Smoke poured out from Anita's nostrils. "Good. Kill me off."

"Kill him off."

Anita put her ash out onto the placemat. "Sure, sure. Someone should. Bury him and move on."

～

OUTSIDE THE WOMEN FANNED themselves on front porches, whispering condolences. Their grief had mellowed into gossipy theories about Riya's disappearance. How she might have run off with a dangerous boy to do a filthy thing or taken mushrooms and walked into the water.

"Everyone knows you have to microdose," said Aparna Naik.

"Then again, Riya was a fast girl," said Devika Gill. "Had a boy around so early."

"I wondered, too, if she simply went off the grid, assumed a new identity," Jyoti said.

As they gossiped Leila walked around the block eating a bruised peach. One bite and the skin peeled like fabric. That, she thought, must be her appeal to Matthew. Not her specialness, just her ease.

"Matthew violated her, Auntie," Leila told Devika. "She more or less told me. He did it to me too." She waved at Aparna and Jyoti. "I told you. And I told you."

Devika shrugged. "Who has not been violated? Is this your star moment? You don't see me disappearing, throwing my mother's heart in the waste bin."

～

THE REVELATION OF VIOLATION had legs. Devika told Nasreen; Nasreen told Shayma Matthews, who told Karina Dixit: *Leila Sharma confirmed it. Poor thing, Riya, adrift in a Florida ocean, remember her in her purple clips and frocks, how sweet her voice in the school choir, not so smart but so very fair. What pain, what shame, no wonder she took a drug, no wonder she wandered off.*

~

LEILA AND ANITA woke to a banging on the door in the middle of the night. The two rushed downstairs. Through the peephole Leila saw Karina Dixit standing on the front porch. Leila opened the latch. Karina barreled past in a nightgown and one sock, her droopy breasts swinging ridiculously as she wagged a finger in Anita's face.

"How could you bring him into my neighborhood?" she shrieked. "How could you when I have done so much for you? When you had no one, I took your daughter in. When you left her in my lawn, in my house. This is how you repay me?"

"Calm down, woman," Anita replied, coolly. "You think I would knowingly bring a monster into my house? Think he has not touched my child too? He touched her more."

"Her face is flat! How could he touch her more? And your child is another, my god. I've seen her with him. Little wife, she acts like. Bleeding his wallet dry."

"She's a child."

"I will report him," Karina said. "I will report you." She jingle-jangled her keys in the air. "I will drive to the police station right now."

Anita wrinkled her nose at Karina's nightgown. "Wearing that?"

"My child is gone," Karina spat. "Yours is here. Even if she leads a shit life, she gets a life."

Anita opened her mouth to fight, then closed it and embraced her.

THAT SUNDAY IN QUESTION

Super Sweet Sixteen

Anita threw a party for Leila's sixteenth birthday and invited the women of Willow Road. It was a belated attempt to spread goodwill in the neighborhood. Also to dispel the whispers that she'd introduced a monster into the concrete loop.

"Besides," Anita told Leila, puffing air into a red balloon, "I got the job in California. Soon we can get out of here, away from these women."

Leila released her own balloon and watched it descend to the carpet.. The thought of seeing those women, who probably wished it was her gone and not Riya, made her anxious. Since Riya's disappearance Leila slept poorly at night. She woke at odd hours with stomach cramps. Loose hairs collected on her pillowcase. Leila made knots out of them. The knots got larger and larger. She stored them in an earring tin.

Two hours before the party Leila slid a bobby pin into her thinning hair and combed it. She chewed a warm peach ring from the bag she'd nicked from the neighborhood boys earlier that day and set the package next to the jewelry tin and a cardboard box the FedEx man handed her that morning, from Matthew. He hadn't spoken to her since that lunch at Kwality Meats but he'd sent her a birthday gift. Diamond stud earrings, solitaire cut. Leila knew she shouldn't accept them, but they were a full carat. An authenticating note said so, even if Arvind Gohel called them fake. She considered her reflection in the bedroom mirror. If she kept her hair down, who'd notice? She was fastening the studs when Anita knocked and opened the door with a plate of cut mangoes and melon arranged into a heart shape.

"Happy birthday," Anita said. "My god. Your hair is so thin, you are looking so dead—I cannot see you looking so dead. Drink some aloe vera."

She set the fruit plate on Leila's blue duvet, next to the two plush Dalmatians.

"The women are coming soon, come, I have a surprise."

Leila followed her mother downstairs. On the kitchen table sat a six-inch eggless cake from Hot Breads. The sponge was slathered in pink cream topped with damp strawberries. Pink sugar flowers trimmed the edges. HAPPY SIXTEENTH, LEILA! Anita had piped on the center, in red.

Leila hugged her. "Thank you."

～

FOR A FEW HOURS the Sharmas' house filled with chatter and a mild current of laughter.

Leila hovered in the kitchen corner, clutching a cherry soda and enjoying the brief absence of bad blood. A huddle of older women surrounded Aparna, who'd soured on her matrimonial site bachelor after their eleventh date.

"He'd been inhaling bath salts, he asked me if I'd let him bite me after dinner. I went to the bathroom, told him I had IBS, and took a taxi to Penn Station."

"That's why I'm veg," said Jyoti Kaushal, sitting on the sofa with a soggy plate of bhel puri. "Too many dormant cannibals out there."

Jyoti patted the plastic on the couch cushions. "Anita, has it not been years? When will you remove these?"

"When I'm happy," Anita replied. "Anyway, we're moving to California, you know. I got a new job there."

("Even now, bragging about herself," Hema Rao whispered to Nasreen Farouk.)

Anita raised a glass of white wine to her lips. Droplets splattered down the front of her dress. Leila followed her to the kitchen and was intercepted by Devika:

"Leila, were you selling drugs to Manu this morning?"

"They were Wawa peach rings, Auntie, excuse me."

Anita stood at the sink and poured out her glass, hands shaking. "I should not drink," she said, then punctuated this declaration with a few last sips. "I should not have invited these people."

"It's nice," Leila said. "It feels like we're the Happy Kind."

"I thought, only for today. For one day I wanted to show them you are good, that we are good, that we are fine. Now they can stop pressing their noses up against my ugly life." Anita got herself a glass of water. "We will do something nice on our own for your birthday, too. After they leave, I'll take you to the city. You can pick a restaurant."

"Sure," Leila said, though she knew it would never happen. Her mother hated the city and public transit. She never felt comfortable driving to New York, where one could so easily run over a jaywalker.

"Good thing I only put the cheap wine out for these neighbors," Anita said. "Has anyone even come with a gift?"

"Aparna got me earrings. Shaped like ice cream."

"I saw. They're fake." Anita squinted. "Are you wearing diamonds?"

"These are also fake." Leila fanned herself. "I ordered them online. Maybe we should turn on the AC."

"The bill is skyrocketing."

The women gathered around the dining table for cake, their perfume and sweat amplified by humidity. Leila portioned out large squares. Each woman fed her a bite off a plastic fork, for good luck. Karina, who grudgingly accepted a last-minute invitation at the insistence of the women ("We told her, it will be good for you, to get out, to bury the muck with Anita and move on," Devika explained), waved her hands in her face when someone passed her a slice.

"I can't possibly," she told Nasreen. "The search parties are still looking. They think Riya cannot have gotten far. By this point a body would float in water."

The women quieted. Karina took her slice and separated the sponge from the cream with her fork. "Everyone is tired of hearing me talk about this, I can see it in your faces. I know it is not the time and place."

"The bodies I have seen, in my lifetime," Nasreen chimed in. "It's never the time and place. Whose phone keeps going off?"

"It's my Facebook notifications, Auntie," Leila lied. "Birthday wishes."

Matthew
L, did you like the earrings ✓✓
Haven't heard from you ✓✓
I'm coming over, I'm on the way ✓✓
Pack your things. ✓✓

Leila
If you come here, I'm calling the police ✓✓
Yeah the earrings are nice ✓✓

Forty minutes later the doorbell rang.

"Who is it, Anita?" Devika said. "Everyone is here, only."

"A delivery, most likely," Anita said. "Or a Jehovah's Witness. Or one of Tejas's Hare Krishnas."

The bell rang again and again. Then the landline. Then the women's cellphones.

Leila pushed the window curtains aside. "It's Matthew."

"Ignore," Anita said, and patted her on the back, as if she was an infant to burp. "Just ignore."

The calls dropped off; the women tensed. The garage door opened of its own accord, and Matthew, his stubble in disarray, his Hermès pants unironed, entered with his Whole Foods tote.

"I have the code, sorry, Anita," Matthew said. "You didn't hear your bell. Or your phone."

Anita grabbed the cake knife off the table. "Get out."

Matthew stood still. He raised his hands in front of his chest and laughed. "What soap opera have I walked into?"

"Get out of my house. What are you doing here? Didn't you get my letter?"

Leila remembered her mother scribbling in her notebook.

"Your penmanship's illegible." Matthew turned to Leila, his eyes small and pleading behind his tinted lenses.

"Happy birthday, L. The diamonds look so good on you."

"Anita, what is he doing here?" Devika whisper-scolded. "Karina is so upset, she's gone upstairs to rest, and your beds don't even have sheets."

"They're in the wash, my god," Anita replied.

Nasreen gave Matthew the finger. "Out, man."

Matthew looked squarely at Devika. "I've been raising her child, that's what I've been doing here. Leila? Are you ready now? Your room is ready. Everything is ready. You didn't like the old apartment, I know. This one's in Manhattan. I've spent an arm and a leg for it. I found a new school for you, a girls' school, such good girls there. It's uptown. I don't trust the subway—I'll drive you there. Leila?" He trembled. His hand wandered to his belt. Would he jack off in front of the birthday party, Leila wondered, but no, he was merely shaking his pill bottle.

"I'm already dying," he wheezed. "If you don't come, I might as well take all of this and die."

"Not this again," Leila said, rolling her eyes. "Please get out."

Anita shoved him. "Take the bloody pills, then. Die."

She brandished the cake knife at him and spat in his face.

A trail of saliva dripped down Matthew's chin. He wiped it off, sauntered toward the table with the cake, and broke off a piece with his hand, as if he were any houseguest.

"Sir," Aparna said. "Your diabetes."

He licked the icing off his finger. "This cake is shit, Leila. I could have gotten you a better cake."

"Get out of here, you sick man. Greedy man," Anita said, and shoved him again. "I don't need you for anything. We don't need you for anything. I thought I was doing some charity for you. I thought, this man is lonely, he has no children, even his wife does not want to reproduce with him. I thought, he was like my pathetic brother. So I let you into my home."

"This is abuse, Anita. Get your hands off me. Someone should call the police."

"If someone hit you, if someone stabbed you, it would be too easy, not enough. You deserve to be pulled apart, like string cheese."

Aparna nodded. "Nice simile."

"You think you're some powerful woman, some excellent mother," Matthew said to Anita. "You're no more than a leech. These women talk about it. They think your daughter would be better off with me. Everyone agrees."

Anita blinked. "I'll call the police."

"I'll call DYFS," he countered. "They will take her. I have a good lawyer."

He turned to Leila. "Please, L. Clothes, bedding, bras, it's all in the back. Come with me. Leave here."

"Get out of my house," Anita repeated. "Out of my house, my house, *my* house. *I'll* call the police."

Leila turned to Anita, who looked so tired and frail, one hand still shaking on the handle of the cake knife. She had never loved someone so much and so little.

"I'll go with him," Leila announced. "Let me pack."

The room stared at Matthew.

"She wants to go, see?" he sputtered. "This is an abusive home, and I'm taking her out of it. Nothing to twist your knickers about here. I'll wait in the car, Leila."

He left through the open garage door. The women started up: "*Is she going?*"

"*They have an apartment?*"

" '*Twist your knickers,' what the fuck is that language?*"

"*Let him rot. Don't let her go.*"

"*How much is the rent?*"

"What of the wife? Open relationship my ass."

Leila tugged on Anita's sleeve. "I don't want to go, I just wanted him to get out."

"We'll think of something," Anita replied. "In the meantime, you pack as if you are going."

"You could call the police."

"Those stupid officers, I don't know, Leila. Who knows how good Matthew's lawyer is, what all money can buy. How can *I* be abusive, Leila? How dare he? I'll trail the car, I'll get you. Don't worry."

Leila went upstairs to pack a bag, tiptoeing past the room where Karina lay with a damp cloth over her face. When she came downstairs, Anita was holding a fanny pack Matthew had dropped near the garage door threshold.

"He left his meds," she said. She unzipped the pouch and took out an insulin pen. "Someone should drain these."

The women were quiet.

"The crazy person who does that will be arrested for murder, and already I have so much ticket drama with the cops," said Devika. But she took one needle and injected it into her own abdomen. "I have insulin resistance," she explained.

"Already I have a speeding ticket," said Aparna, who pocketed one before heading out for her evening Cash & Carry shift.

"I have used up my Visa," said another woman, with another syringe. "I cannot run this risk for *you*—"

"It's not our problem, Anita. You're the mother. It was your responsibility. How can you ask this?"

So on and so on the women argued.

"At least someone should just call the cops," Anita said. "It can't be me, after the year we've had, whatever lawyer Matthew has."

The women packed the empty vials back in the fanny pack. No one was willing to do that.

Matthew honked his car horn. Anita and Leila left the house together. The evening was crisp and boys in the block screamed joyously, turning their lawns into cricket fields and striking the turf with bats.

"For now, you go," Anita whispered. "Anyway, didn't you always say I let you go with him? I'll follow. He won't do another thing to us."

"To me," Leila said.

"To you."

Matthew rolled the window down. Leila handed him the fanny pack.

"You forgot this," she said.

Anita burst into hysterics. "Take her!" she said, stamping her foot in the damp grass. "Take her, she doesn't want to be with me! She never has!"

Anita went back inside. Leila strapped herself into the back seat.

"My god, all that drama, those women," Matthew said. "Did you put your seat belt on? Are you excited? The earrings look lovely on you."

Leila looked at her hands. Her fingers shook. "Sure, yes."

"This is what you wanted, you know? You are the one who said you wanted to get out of here one day. It was your choice. You're not a child."

"Yes," Leila said. "I wanted this."

He careened out of the block and sped down the highway. Leila wiped her palms on her birthday dress. Maybe Anita wouldn't come after all. Child-free, she could move to California alone, find a new husband, have a better daughter and a lemon tree. Life in New York with Matthew would not be much worse than life was now. People would assume they were father and daughter, a configuration of care she would never otherwise find herself in. There would be fine dinners, with complimentary soft breads, no mother eating Persian cucumbers and harping on about body fat. There would be diamond earrings. For such luxuries, her body was a nominal price to pay. She looked out the window at the Cash & Carry. Maybe this was the last time she'd see it. Suddenly the price seemed exorbitant.

"Hey." Leila looped her fingers around the headrest. "Can you at least get me some laddus?"

"There's no time."

"Just having a craving. Besides, when will we ever be here again?"

He sighed and turned in to the familiar strip. Leila remained in the child-locked car while he shopped. Matthew returned, breathing heavily. He handed Leila the THANK YOU FOR SHOPPING bag. It weighed four ounces, maximum.

"Aparna was at the register, I could have crawled out of my skin," he murmured.

"Sorry," said Leila. She bit into one of the sweets and held one out to the driver's seat. "Want one?"

"I had that cake already," said Matthew, but took it. "It's fine, I'll take my meds."

Leila heard him unzip his fanny pack. Her pulse quickened, but he didn't notice the syringes were empty when he jabbed himself.

"I shouldn't have anything more," he said. "My sugar, my heart."

"Have another," Leila said. "I love you. And it's my birthday after all."

Despite himself he popped back another sweet. They drove past the mall, the twinkling red lights of the Cheesecake Factory, where teenagers dressed to the nines crowded outside and waited for their buzzers to ring.

A few miles before the tunnel Matthew stopped at a rest stop for McDonald's. He ordered a Big Mac through the drive-thru and sweated profusely. He wiped his face with his soggy pocket kerchief.

"All this sugar, no real food," he said. He at the meat patties and left behind the buns and cheese. "I'm going keto," he told Leila.

Food didn't improve his condition. The sweat soaked through his shirt, his good pants. He popped a pill and switched lanes, onto a highway that would take him to upstate New York. He wasn't feeling well, he said, his heart was slowing; he'd stop at his old house to rest before they carried on to the city. It would be empty inside; Louise was off with her new man. Leila fixed her gaze out the window. Another billboard, of a blonde girl with chocolate-stained teeth, loomed brightly in the distance. TURN BACK FOR CHOCOLATE CO.

"Sweet girl," Matthew said, faintly. "A sweet girl in that chocolate ad. We'll get you in another ad, Leila, with wider circulation this time."

Anita
Leila why has he switched lanes ✓✓
Horrible driver ✓✓

He turned on the radio to the soft jazz station. The air in the car was like chloroform.

Leila opened the sunroof: "It's sweaty in here," she said, and grazed the air with her fingertips, for Anita to see.

"What are you doing?" Matthew said. "Get down. I feel faint. Get down."

He pulled over. Leila spotted the blue speck of Anita's Chevrolet in the distance.

"Maybe you need more of your heart medicine," Leila suggested. "You don't look well."

"Yes," he agreed. "Yes. I'm very sick."

He swallowed one pill, then another. He wiped his mouth and turned onto a quiet back road with broken streetlamps.

"I don't feel any better," he said. "Come here, help me. Call 911."

"I'm coming," Leila lied. "Have a few more pills. A little more of your insulin, maybe."

He took both. Leila saw Anita's car creeping closer in the rearview mirror. The air in the beemer grew hazier and fruitier. Matthew groaned. He slumped over the steering wheel.

Anita pulled up behind him, a canister of disinfectant wipes in her cup holder.

"Take these," she said, handing Leila the wipes. "No, you're missing the spots, your own prints."

The Sharmas wiped themselves away. Leila slid into the back seat of Anita's Chevrolet. Anita drove into the city, into Queens; they slept in the car off a curb in Jackson Heights and awoke midafternoon. They walked half an hour at Anita's request; Anita kept checking her maps, frequently losing her way.

"Everything is different," she observed, but finally found what she had been looking for, a lunch buffet at a diner. "Your dad's apartment was nearby. Such a small place."

They got a table and ordered filter coffees.

"I'm a monster!" Leila cried. "I'm going to get in trouble."

Anita poured her filter coffee into a steel basin. "No one will care about him anyway. No one would care for our bodies, either, but the good thing is, his is even less. Come, let's get food."

Leila spooned yogurt onto her plate. Anita pilfered through the lamb and rice.

They sat down with full plates. "I used to smell the meat from here when I was pregnant with you. It made me sick at first," Anita said. "Then it made me hungry. It was thirteen dollars. A waste of money, when we finally went."

"This meat is dry."

"You're a brave girl," Anita said. "At the end of the day that is something. When I was a girl, I could only wish."

SATURDAY EVENING

The Women and the Dogs, After

THE WOMEN WERE WATCHING, cracking open their vermilion shutters to keep eyes on the Sharma house. The DYFS visitor had been parked in the driveway for more than five hours now.

"Her red Nissan," Devika observed, "must be fried in the sun."

The door finally opened at half past five. Anita stood in the doorframe, a dreamy expression across her face. The DYFS woman walked outside and yelped when she gripped the hot handle of her car. She drove off with her windows down and stopped to let an Italian ice truck pass.

"We thought for sure the social worker would take the girl away, that Anita would be arrested, that any minute those stinking officers would come back with handcuffs," said Hema Rao, as she fed her dogs a cherry ice pop. "That they could kiss California goodbye."

"Maybe a separation would have served them both right, mother and daughter," said Jyoti Kaushal. "If only Leila had told about it sooner, thought of someone other than herself."

"She did tell us," Aparna said.

Jyoti shooed her away. "I don't remember that."

~

THE WOMEN FOLDED UP their lawn chairs. Ordinary life resumed. Tejas Kaushal put on his visor and went for a run. Hema left to start her evening Dunkin' shift and left her husband to walk the dogs. But with Parth they pulled. Baloo saw the speck of Tejas in the distance. He snapped the line of his retractable leash and bounded across the development.

Leila was sitting on the front steps with a Wawa turkey hoagie when she saw the dog coming. "Baloo!" she called, and tossed him a piece. "Here!"

He wagged his tail and came, his large pink tongue lolling from the side of his mouth. He ate the turkey and curved his muscled body against Leila's knees. She held on to his frayed leash and fed him another chunk of sandwich.

Anita opened the door. "My god, Leila, you're giving him deli meat? I would cook fresh for him."

Together, they walked the Doberman back to Hema's house. On the broken leash Baloo lurched forward and stopped at random. He was strong and heavyset. Leila struggled to control his weight; after so much pining for a dog she couldn't lead one in the right direction. Baloo lunged after a squirrel and dragged her to a mound of deer shit in the Kaushals' shrubs. He peed on the For Sale sign in front of their house. A priest emerged from the front door.

Anita trailed behind. "Karina had a pooja today, poor thing. Your palm will bleed if you hold him so tight. Don't pull him so hard."

"I'm not."

"Give me the leash. You can't handle him. You don't trust me with a dog? Look now, what he's doing."

Baloo dug into a pile of cut grass and chewed a clump of dirt.

"Leave it. Come—on," Leila grunted. She tugged hard. The dog gagged. Leila slackened her grip on the leash. *I'm so sorry, so sorry so sorry.* She scratched his ears. *I'm so sorry.*

She handed Anita the leash. The dog looked up at Anita with two beads for eyes. He wagged his tail.

Anita scratched his head. Slowly she traced his tan eyebrows with her index finger. "I want a dog's life."

They reached Hema's house. Leila knocked on the door.

"Thank god," Hema cried. "I heard he ran off and came running from work. My baby, my little man. Come, come. I thought he was gone."

Baloo jumped on Hema's thighs. Hema threw her arms around his muscled neck. Hattie ran to the foyer barking. The dogs chased and humped each other until both tired out, then stretched out side by side on the granite floor.

Hema invited the Sharmas inside ("They had never been before, it was the neighborly thing to do," Hema explained) and boiled tea. Anita watched the sleeping

Dobermans breathe, their black sides rising and falling in the soft foyer light. Leila watched them too, their barrel-like chests and half-open eyes, so plainly and marvelously alive.

Hema handed Leila and Anita the teacups. She welcomed more of the women inside, who had come to check on her dog.

"I imagined the worst," Karina Dixit said. "Too often the worst happens."

On the sofa, Hema scratched Hattie behind her pointed ears. "What would she do with him gone?"

"In time she would be fine," Anita said. "In time she would heal."

"A life of healing?" said Hema Rao. "What kind of life is that?"

"That is a sob story, not a life," Devika Gill said.

"Better to bury and move on," Leila said. She clicked her tongue and sipped her tea with the women. Together they hummed in assent.

ACKNOWLEDGMENTS

I have many people to thank for *Men Like Ours*. First and foremost, my agent, Jin Auh. This novel would not have happened without your belief and unwavering support. Thank you also to Abram Scharf, Elizabeth Pratt, and Alexandra Christie, for your help and encouragement along the way. At Bloomsbury, thank you to my editor, Amber Oliver, for shaping this story; also to Sage Gilbert, Callie Garnett, Barbara Darko, and Ragavendra Maripudi. Thank you to my family for nurturing and tolerating my strangest and most ill-advised pursuits. To my friends Sianna Peal, Megan Evershed, Leon Pan, Kate Blandford, Sangeeta Singh-Kurtz, Tara Das, and Isabella Irtifa. To my teachers, for your care and generosity. To Milo. And to Joe Kloc, for the salad days.

A NOTE ON THE AUTHOR

BINDU BANSINATH is a staff writer for *New York* magazine's The Cut. She lives in Jersey City.

A NOTE ON THE TYPE

Garamond refers to a group of old-style serif typefaces named for the sixteenth-century Parisian engraver Claude Garamond. Influenced by the Venetian printer Aldus Manutius and his punchcutter Francesco Griffo's designs, Garamond refined the Renaissance roman letterform in France. With greater contrast between thick and thin strokes, a low x-height, and capitals modeled on Roman square capitals, Garamond has been a celebrated typeface used for book publishing for centuries. Robert Slimbach's 2005 Adobe Garamond Premier Pro is the revival design printed in this book.